W9-BYJ-482

Wonderful

Jill
Barnett

Wonderful

WHEELER
PUBLISHING, INC.
ROCKLAND, MA

★ AN AMERICAN COMPANY ★

Published in Large Print by arrangement with Pocket Books, a division of Simon & Schuster, Inc., in the United States and Canada.

Wheeler Large Print Book Series.

Set in 16 pt Plantin.

Library of Congress Cataloging-in-Publication Data

Barnett , Jill.
   Wonderful / Jill Barnett.
      p. (large print) cm.(Wheeler large print book series)
   ISBN 1-58724-102-1
(hardcover)
   1. Great Britain—History—Medieval period, 1066–1485—Fiction.
2. Knights and knighthood—Fiction. 3. Large type books.
I. Title. II. Series

[PS3552.A6983 W66   2001]
813′.54—dc21

2001045478
CIP

of the ale was linked to the mind of the brewer, to his thoughts or his dreams or his wishes.

No one knew how or why the ale had powers. But it did.

The secret recipe died along with the ancient Picts. But for years and years afterward, many sought to duplicate the brew. Some dug deep into the hills looking for secret coffers that had once belonged to the tattooed dwarves. Others brewed strange green weeds in big black pots and chanted words no one could understand.

Alewives dropped sparkling crystal rocks into their brewing pots. They poured potions and elixirs into their vats of beer and pretended it was the legendary brew. Many were executed for poisoning an innocent aledrinker.

For over eight hundred years no one had ever discovered the recipe. Skeptics said it was all only a wild tale. To them the ale never existed.

But many believed. Some even claimed to have tasted the magic ale on dark nights during a new moon when the little people were said to appear—brownies and fairies, even ghoulies and ghosts. The same kind of magical nights when cider turned into fine wine, when straw could be spun into gold, and when hearts were stolen. Those magical nights when love could be, oh, so wonderful.

For Chris

Song of the Harper

I kiss her
With lips open
And I am drunk
Without a beer.

—from the chapel
of King Inyotef,
ancient Egypt

THE
LEGEND LOST

A long, long time ago, before there was heraldry or chivalry, before there were knights and castles, crusades and jousts, there was an ancient brew, a special ale with strange and potent powers.

It was called *heather ale*.

The creators of the golden ale were wild pagan warriors who lived in the hills of Scotland and painted their naked bodies blue. These Pict warriors drank heather ale before they went to war and became so ferocious in battle that even Julius Caesar claimed he could no subdue them.

The recipe for the ale was a treasured secre the powerful ingredients rumored to be ever thing from forest herbs to moonflowers, fro magic crystals to a certain bloodred heath

Some claimed the magic was not in t recipe, but in the brewers—the dwarves w lived in those wild hills. They said the po

CHAPTER 1

Camrose Castle,
1269

Lady Clio's father claimed her pale silvery hair was her greatest asset...or perhaps his greatest asset, considering he had the duty to see her wed to some poor unsuspecting fool.

To look at Lady Clio of Camrose, one would think she was the image of what every man, knight or king, peasant or merchant, wanted in a wife—someone who was meek in spirit: to make a man feel braver and stronger. A wife who was docile enough to allow a man to be the king of his castle. A woman whose head was as light inside as outside, to assure him that he would be more intelligent and therefore superior.

According to the Church, the color of a woman's hair bespoke her true nature. The men empowered by the Church based this theory on the conclusion that hair grew directly from the brain.

Fiery hair in a woman warned men of a woman's devilish spirit. Since woodland covered two thirds of the English isle, hair the color of tree trunks was considered common and showed the woman had little imagination.

Hair the color of midnight, which everyone knew was the witching hour, crowned the heads of women all too clever and devious. 'Twas even said by those same men of the Church that Eve herself had hair as black as a woman's sin.

But a woman with light hair was perfect.

Unfortunately, those men of the Church did not know Clio. Like a field of golden buttercups that hides a prickly hedgehog, Lady Clio's hair hid her true nature.

She was headstrong and determined, traits admired in men but scoffed at in women. Her father swore she had been born with that stubbornness.

Before Clio's birth, Clio's mother had lost five babes. With Clio, as before, her mother's birthing pains had come before her time. So Clio came into the world two months early. When the priest tried to perform Last Rites over her puny blue body, she kicked his hand and, according to her father, opened her mouth and almost wailed the castle walls down.

To the utter amazement of everyone, Clio lived.

From the first moment of her life she had fought against the impossible. Lady Clio was born fighting to control her own destiny.

Of course, in her mind she wasn't stub-

4

born. Persistent was what she was. Had she given up at birth where would she be?

Dead, that's where.

So Clio believed in being determined. She would not let anyone control her life, for only she held power over her survival.

She believed that with persistence came success. If one of her wonderful plans failed, she could always come up with another.

She was small in stature, but had the heart of a giant. Her mind was sometimes too quick for her own good. Once she got one of her infamous ideas into her head, she seldom thought about the consequences, of which there were usually many.

Yet no one could say she did not learn from her errors. She was not that much of a goose. She seldom made the same mistake twice.

She always made new mistakes.

Which suited her, because she was the one who determined her own future. Even if the path was strewn with the remnants of her failures. At least they were *her* failures.

Clio never allowed something as minor as a lack of skill to daunt her efforts. She firmly believed perfection came with practice. Of course she had no sound reason on which to base this belief. Indeed, history, logic, and her reputation demanded just the opposite.

But she loved a challenge. Embraced it, reveled in it. Those who knew her called her tenacious spirit a mulish exercise in futility. But Clio just didn't believe in giving up. She would just conjure up a new plan—an idea.

Clio thought ideas were wonderful things. Those who had been privy to some of her fiascoes recognized the warning signs. The quiet and sudden stillness of her manner. The small frown line that wrinkled between her brows. The thoughtful chewing of her lower lip or the twisting of her mother's jeweled ring on her finger. Her expression became dovelike. Peaceful.

But whenever Lady Clio got that look and, worse yet, when she claimed aloud that she had one of her "wonderful ideas," those around her immediately lost their sense of peace.

With good reason.

When she had just passed her tenth saint's day, her father paid a large penance to the Gregorian monks for what he referred to as "chanting for help." Months later he'd claimed it was worth eating all those nightly platters of cheap, stringy mutton, since it only took until St. Thomas the Martyr's Day to haul the new catapult out of the moat.

When the tinker's cart had suffered the same fate two years before, it had taken twice as long to recover and had cost him much more.

At age twelve Clio took up a needle and thread to tend a hunting wound of a visiting bishop. After which her father used all the gold in his heavy purse to buy pardons for her from a passing pilgrim.

It seemed that unbeknownst to her father, the lecherous bishop had chased Clio for the entire previous week and had foolishly cornered her on the staircase, where he stole a kiss

and squeezed her small breasts. So when it came time to doctor him, she had smiled sweetly and stitched up his wound in the shape of three sixes, the sign of the devil.

At fifteen, Clio was banished from the queen's court after only two disastrous days, and her father sent the pope a jewel-encrusted golden chalice in the hope of receiving papal prayer on behalf of his daughter and only child.

It had worked, for a week later the betrothal offer arrived from Merrick de Beaucourt, a knight who was then in the Holy Lands making the English king and the Church wealthier under the guise of fighting the infidels.

She asked her father to tell her what Sir Merrick was like. Her father said he was a great warrior.

That was not exactly the answer Clio was looking for.

She wanted to know if he was tall and kind and had a face that was sweet on the eyes. If he could play the lute and sing love poems. If he would hand her his heart on a silver platter.

Her father laughed and claimed Sir Merrick would protect her and that it did not matter whether she liked him or not, because she had no choice. The betrothal was by order of King Henry, his liege lord.

But de Beaucourt was to be gone for four more years and her father caught a chill one exceptionally cold winter day and died a few days later.

Lady Clio became a ward of Henry III.

Queen Eleanor still barred her from court—
once had been quite enough, thank you—and
suggested that the king pawn his new ward
off on one of their enemies, perhaps whoever
was the latest troublesome Welsh prince.

Henry refused. He wasn't ready to start a war.

So until de Beaucourt returned from the Crusade, the king sent Lady Clio to a remote
convent, where her life continued much as it
had before her father's death: one "wonderful
idea" after another.

CHAPTER 2

England,
1275

Merrick de Beaucourt saw his homeland
through eyes older and wiser than those of his
youth. Everything was alive and bright with
color. The trees in Arundel Wood were so thick
and dark they blocked out the sun.

Bluish mist rose from the damp ground like
dwindling smoke from an old campfire. The
dampness on his skin and garments was
welcome because it wasn't his own sweat, but
instead a chilly wetness that was England.

There were no miles of sand. No dry, hot winds. No ever-present cruel sun that could scorch a man as easily as it had scorched the land.

The air smelled of lichen and tasted green. It was wet and cool and felt foreign to him.

Behind him, much in the distance, came the sudden clink of a harness, the soggy thud of hooves on the ground. He cast a quick glance over a shoulder, turned back, and looked down the hillside at the open grassland.

He put his spurs to his horse and took off. He rode hard, leaned low over his mount, urging it on. Air blew his black hair away from his face and his heavy cloak billowed out behind him. He breathed in the cool taste of lush land; it was like finding an oasis in the desert. It had been the simple things, like this, that he had missed the most.

He was used to riding hard, familiar with the powerful ripple of horseflesh beneath him, the sounds of the run where hooves pounded the ground and his heart pounded with excitement.

He could feel the thundering of hooves behind him. The chase.

He listened; it was only one horse.

With the slightest prod of his spur, his horse lurched forward with a burst of speed. They jumped a low stone wall and cut sharply to the left, riding over a grassy hillock and down into a vale.

They splattered through a brook and hammered over a wooden bridge in a few strides, then flew down another hillside as if they were being chased by the desert winds.

9

Speeding toward a copse of trees in the distance, he could feel his pursuer behind him, just as near as before. He cut to the right and rode around the trees.

He looked left, spotted a clearing, turned sharply again, and rode into it.

In one swift motion, he pulled his sword and leapt to the ground, knees bent, hilt gripped in both hands.

Ready.

No sounds came from outside the clearing.

It was as if the rider had not followed.

Merrick remained in stance, still, and alert to sound, taste, smell. The drip of the dew on the leaves. The wet flavor of damp air.

The female scent of perfumed oil.

From behind him came just the barest sound of breath harsh and raspy from the ride.

Merrick straightened and turned. "Show yourself, Roger. You still reek of Elizabeth de Clare's sweet perfume." He stuck his sword in the ground and leaned against it, then crossed one leather boot casually over the other. His spurs clinked together, and he planted his free hand on a cocked hip, waiting.

Roger FitzAlan strolled out from behind a giant elm tree, grinning. "There is much about fair Elizabeth that is sweeter than her scent, my friend."

Merrick straightened and sheathed his sword. "I have yet to meet a woman I thought of as sweet."

"Only because you do not make much time for females."

"Only because there are none left for me after you're through."

"I would share." Roger plucked a speck of imaginary dust from his surcoat. "Besides which, unlike you, I find women more intriguing than war."

"A battleground is no place for a woman."

"I've known you too long, Merrick. You prefer battle on the field. I, on the other hand, prefer my battles in a bed."

Ignoring him, Merrick turned and gave a sharp whistle. His Arab horse left a clump of grass and came to stand near him.

Roger reached out and stroked the Arab's sleek muzzle. " 'Tis hard to believe that from that godforsaken stretch of hell they claim is the Promised Land could come such superb horseflesh."

Merrick knew this was an exceptional horse, the same way he had first known his warhorse, Aries, was exceptional. This smaller, swifter breed was like most Arab mounts—superb— and had been a gift from a Marionite leader. Merrick prized his horses and respected them. He valued them beyond reason.

He glanced up at the sun, then swung up into the saddle. "You're late."

"Elizabeth was pleased to see me." Roger went to his own horse, which was tied behind a tree, and led the mount into the clearing. "I had not thought you were in a hurry."

"I have a betrothal to fulfill and a castle in the Marches that needs its new lord."

"The great Red Lion intends to settle in and

11

become nothing but a fat lord with no one to train but servants. Why does this sound unlikely?"

"Come. Let's be off."

"Ah." Roger nodded knowingly. "Your betrothed awaits."

Merrick ignored him.

"And awaits. And awaits."

"Mount your horse, Roger."

Roger wore a look of a man who had made a fine joke.

Merrick sat in his saddle and waited for Roger to stop grinning at him.

When Roger kept on grinning, Merrick nudged his horse forward. By the time he'd left the clearing, Roger was riding at his side. After a few minutes of silence Merrick said, " 'Tis a woman's due in life. To wait for a man."

Roger snorted, then laughed out loud as if he could not hold it in. " 'Twill be an interesting first meeting between you two. Not even for sweet Elizabeth would I miss it."

Merrick loved Roger like a brother, but there were times when, like a brother, he would have liked to beat that grin off Roger's face. This was one of those times.

Fortunately for Roger's fine, noble nose, Merrick could hear the sounds of his men-at-arms coming down the hillside: the clink of harnesses, the creaking of leather, male laughter, and another bawdy joke. He rode out of the trees and into sight; then, with one arm raised, he signaled to his troops to move west.

Roger and Merrick talked of horses and

past battles while the two of them rode side by side. They had ridden this way for years and each had owed the other his life on more than one occasion. Despite the differences in their manner, they were each other's closest friend.

As he rode beside Merrick, Roger wore the look of a man pleased with himself and his life. There was no doubt the fair Elizabeth de Clare was the person who had given him that look.

At times Merrick envied him. Roger could fit into any situation, meet anyone, even a stranger, with casual ease. It wasn't that simple for Merrick. He was used to taking responsibility. He was a leader and warrior. So, wherever they went, Roger would blend in affably and Merrick would barge in and take over.

They rode in silence for a while; then Merrick admitted, "I've had done with crusades and deserts and the East. Edward wants our home borders protected. And I want some peace in my life."

Roger leaned one arm on his saddle pommel and grinned at him in that irritating way he had when he thought he knew more than Merrick. "You want peace, so you are wedding a woman and fortifying a castle on the Welsh Marches?"

Merrick grunted some response.

Roger gave him a wry look. "Neither one will bring you peace."

"Lady Clio will be meek. I'll most likely have to pull her away from her prayer beads to bed her. She has been in a convent for these past six years."

"Aye, two years longer than promised."

They rode for a few silent minutes.

Roger turned to him. "What have you heard of her? How are her looks?"

"I care nothing for the quality of her looks." Merrick could feel his friend's gaping stare.

"You will if she looks like your horse or if she can fit in your armor." Roger settled back in his saddle. "What if she needs a razor?"

Merrick turned to Roger. "Then I'll teach her to shave."

Roger laughed at that. "Seriously, what have you heard of her? Is she dark or fair?"

He had no idea what his betrothed looked like. He knew only that she had become a ward of Henry, Edward's father. "I never asked. She comes with Camrose and she's a nobleman's daughter. There is nothing else I need to know."

Roger whistled.

Out of the corner of his eye, Merrick could see him shake his head.

After some silence, Roger said, "Elizabeth has black hair. Dark as a starless night...As dark as polished onyx. As dark as the deepest ocean...As—"

"Dark as my anger if you don't cease that witless romantic prattle."

Roger just laughed again, an irritating habit that could annoy Merrick sometimes. Like now.

"You might be surprised at what you'll want from marriage, my friend."

14

"I know what I want. I want peace of mind and a quiet life." Merrick glanced ahead of them at the hillside, where he spotted a clump of bright heather. He turned back to Roger. "Lady's Clio's hair could be purple for all I care."

"Interesting. Purple hair. I wonder what the Church would say of that."

"Why would the Church care about the color of my lady's hair?"

"The latest papal proclamation. I heard of little else when I was in Rome."

"No doubt you heard little else because you spent your days with the ladies."

"The nights only."

"Aye, your few days must have been spent fending off challenges from a line of cuckolded husbands."

"'Few days'?" Roger gave him a mock look. "Surely you have not forgotten how long I was gone?"

"I did not forget. 'Twas quiet, then. No one was pestering me with questions about my future wife."

"Ah, you missed me," Roger said without a pause.

"Continue with this papal proclamation or whatever it was."

"The Church proclaimed a new philosophy regarding a woman's hair."

Merrick was mildly disgusted. The Church and its attempt to control the life of every man was something that had always confounded him. It seemed to him that those men of God could spend their time better praying for man's soul rather than trying to control him. "Have they nothing better to do?"

Roger shrugged. "Probably not."

"So what now? What bit of heavenly knowledge were they now privy to that we poor doomed souls need interpreted?"

"It seems that fair hair is much prized in Italy, as it was in the East. So prized that ladies would spend whole days bleaching their hair in the sun. Some wore crownless hats and rubbed lemons and urine in their hair. The Church proclaimed that such practice damaged the female brain and imperiled their souls."

Merrick could hear the laughter in his friend's voice.

"Lady Clio of the unknown hair color might well have an imperiled soul or, worse yet, a damaged brain from dipping her head in the privy."

Even Merrick had to laugh at that image.

"Don't you wonder who you are wedding, my friend?" Roger said as they rode into a clearing.

Merrick glanced at him. "I'm wedding a woman. I assume she'll behave as such."

But Roger wasn't listening. He was staring off at nothing, lost in thought. "Clio," he murmured slowly, then paused. He spoke her name as if he were tasting it.

Merrick scowled at the horizon. He was not certain he liked it that Roger was thinking so hard about his betrothed.

"I believe, Merrick, that *Clio* sounds like the name of a fair maid, one with pale hair."

Merrick said nothing.

Roger looked at him. "Have you nothing to say?"

"I don't think about her hair."

"You might want to. She could be like the Egyptian Queen, with hair as black as sin. Or..." Roger paused, laughter in his voice "...she might have a beard as black as sin. At night you could take turns using the razor on each other."

"Another jest and I'll show you a new way to use my razor."

"Come now, my friend, I'm only glad to be home. Makes my mood light."

"Your mood is always light."

"Aye. 'Tis a good thing, too. Elsewise we'd be sent packing the moment you began to bark orders at everyone you meet."

"Some of us were born to be leaders."

Roger laughed loud and hard.

"And others," Merrick said pointedly, "were born to annoy and pester and seduce every female who happens to cross his path."

"Not every female, my friend. Only the ones with all their teeth."

"Which eliminates children and grand-mothers."

"*Great*-grandmothers." Roger grinned.

Merrick laughed then. He liked this banter. It made him feel light of heart, too. He prodded his mount forward, down a path that grew steeper and was choked with ferns

17

and gorse and gnarled oak trees. He stopped high atop a sloping hillside above a valley so green it almost hurt his eyes to look at it.

Merrick half stood in his stirrups and looked out at the land before him for so long that the horizon blurred together, until all he could see were the images in his mind.

This was nothing like the last time he'd come home. Years ago. A time when Merrick had been young. Though to him, he had not seemed so young then. Looking back now, he knew he had been a green youth. The years had taught him exactly when it was that youth ended; it ended the moment you stopped yearning to be older.

But he had been young then. It had been early in winter, that part of the season when the trees had no leaves and the twilight turned everything purple.

Ice was on the ground, and thorns were on the path where he had been bothered by a hornet or two. Beneath his horse's hooves the leaves had lain wet and dying under scattered remnants of an early snow, and everything from the sky to the land looked gray and barren.

He'd come back to England after being in France, where he'd won his way through tourney after tourney to earn enough gold and horses to pay his men. And it was there Merrick's life took a different course. He and Prince Edward became friends, a friendship that had lasted through treachery and tourney, through political upheaval and crusade. A friendship that had taken him far from home.

Edward's father, King Henry, had only contempt for the alliance of his heir with a de Beaucourt, a family still tainted with dishonor. There was no love lost between the Plantagenets and the de Beaucourts, mostly due to the fact that over a hundred years before, some greatgrandsire de Beaucourt had stupidly supported the wrong side.

Yet even the king's disdain could not affect the friendship between Edward and Merrick; it was an honorable bond of mutual respect and trust between two strong independent men.

It was that bond that had changed his life. Though it had taken him away for long periods of time, Merrick no longer had to seek means to pay his troops.

He had a good horse beneath him, the weight of his sword at his side, soon he would be married, and like Roger and most of his troops, he, too, was finally home.

It was enough for the moment. He did not know what the future would bring. Yet he knew he would not chew over it today, for today he could do nothing to change it.

He had his horses, his sword, land and a title, and the best of his war prizes—Camrose Castle and all that came with it, a future filled with peace and quiet, and the certain knowledge that a woman, his woman, was waiting.

Summer came to the country,
Red was the heather bell;
But the manner of the brewing
Was none alive to tell.
In graves that were like children's
On many a mountain head,
The Brewsters of the Heather
Lay numbered with the dead.

—by Robert Louis
Stevenson

CHAPTER 3

The Convent of
Our Lady of the Water Springs,
Somerset, England

Clio was on her hands and knees, in the middle of the convent herb garden, her pale blond braids trailing a rippled, snakelike pattern in the dirt as she crawled along burying her nose in the herb plants. She moved slowly, row by row, smelling the fragrant leaves, the flowers, and plump dark berries, searching for the right plant.

A fat orange cat with only one eye sauntered across the cobbled courtyard and plopped down on a pair of thick wooden pattens. He yawned and stretched out his paws so his toes spread wide and his claws showed long and curved; then he pulled back a paw, licked it once, and tucked them both under his furry chest. After a minute he languidly turned his slanted eye away from the misty sun and stared at a gray-and-brown-speckled goshawk perched on the crooked handle of a willow basket.

Neither cat nor bird moved.

"There!" With a sharp snap Clio broke a green sprig from one of the plants and sat back on her bare heels. "This is the one!" She held the herb up to the sunlight.

Dirt still damp with morning dew pressed up between her toes and made cool, wet rings on the rough homespun gown stretched under her sinking knees. She squinted at the herb for a long moment before she muttered, "Perhaps 'tis not the one."

Sitting back on her heels, she frowned for a moment. She should have listened more closely when Sister Amice was explaining her discoveries. The leaves on this plant were not quite heart-shaped and the inside of the stem was not bright green but strawlike and pale. Chewing her lip thoughtfully, she stared at the plants in the garden, twisting the sprig and feeling uncomfortably confused.

None of them had the heart-shaped leaves she needed for her latest ale recipe. After a few quiet seconds she studied the herb twig again, then tossed it into the willow basket and knelt there twisting her mother's ring and thinking.

Clio's tutor at the convent, Sister Amice, had been convinced that if the Greek navigator Pytheas wrote of heather ale in 250 B.C., then it had to have existed, for Pytheas never wrote a lie. However, the good sister died before she could perfect the recipe.

But Clio was determined to make that ale. Whoever was fortunate enough to discover the secret recipe would be wealthy in less time than it took to blink an eye. Discovering the recipe for heather ale was Clio's latest "wonderful idea."

It was also her chance for independence. A woman could brew and sell ale and not lose respectability. In fact the best brewers in the land were women, most of them nuns. For her, the key to her independence, to controlling her own life, lay in Sister Amice's unfinished notes on the lost recipe.

So Clio moved along the rows of herbs, taking some of each plant and tossing it into the basket until it was full. She turned just as the goshawk paced in a rocking gait across the basket handle.

The hawk eyed her for a moment. She tossed the last herb toward him. He swung down like a pendulum, caught it in his beak, and swung back up on his perch.

Clio laughed and shook her head. "Pitt, what will you do with that herb?"

He squawked in answer, flapped his wings, and hopped off the basket with the herb clamped like prey in his beak. Pitt strutted in front of the cat with his breast so puffed out he looked more like a stuffed duck than a fierce bird of prey.

Pitt was more like a duck than a hawk. He did not hunt. As far as Clio knew he had never even flown; he just flapped his wings and hopped and waddled and tried to annoy Cyclops, her one-eyed cat.

The hawk had come to the convent on the shoulder of a traveling acrobat who claimed he'd been sold a worthless bird at the Nottingham fair. Clio happened to hear him negotiating to sell the hawk for mere coppers to the village pieman.

"Turn him into a hot pie! He's not worth a pittance!" the acrobat had claimed. Which was how Pitt, Pittance, came by his name.

"Lady Clio! Lady Clio!" A lad with bright red hair that stuck out from his head like marsh weeds sped across the courtyard, shouting as if God Himself were just around the corner.

The boy leapt over a fishpond and tripped on his big feet.

He crashed into a fountain shaped like a chalice. Water spilled over the fountain lip into the garden, hit the dirt, then sprayed outward.

He skidded right through it. Facedown, and stopped at her knees.

She had mud everywhere. She wiped her eyes,

stood up, and scowled down at him. His name was Thud. No one ever questioned how he came by his name. Within minutes of meeting him, you knew why.

He raised his head and looked up at her. His eyes shone like two full moons through the mud; he looked as if he'd been dipped in it. He spit out a mouthful of dirt, then sneezed a few times.

"Are you hurt?" Clio bent over him.

He shook his head vigorously. Mud clods flipped from his hair.

She stepped back and swiped the mud from her clothes, then moved over to the cat and poked him with her bare toe. "Up, Cyclops."

The cat just lay there.

"Get off my shoes."

He opened his feline eye and gave her a withering look. She wedged a foot under his fat rump and slid into the wooden shoe. He stood with lazy ease, his tail arching back over his head. He turned and gave her an annoyed look, then sauntered over near the basket.

Thud finished wiping off the mud, then stood there and fidgeted, shifting his weight nervously from one foot to the other.

She pinned him with a stare that said, "Hold still."

He froze.

"What are you so excited about?"

"A message arrived." He began to fidget again. "Visitors are coming to the convent."

Clio slid on her other patten and glanced at

24

Thud over her shoulder. "Unless 'tis the king himself, I doubt you need to rush about so."

"But he's finally coming! A rider brought the word. Just now. He was on a horse with shining golden bells on its trappings."

She straightened at that, aware only the king himself or the richest of noblemen had messengers who rode with golden bells. "The king is coming here?"

Thud frowned for a moment. "The king? Him too? No one told me he was coming."

"I meant of the rider with the golden bells. The messenger."

"Oh." Thud scratched his head, frowning. "He was the king's messenger, too? I didn't know that."

Clio stood there for a moment and wondered how long it would take to find out just who was coming.

Thwack, Thud's brother, came lagging along. If Thud was there, Thwack was soon to follow...at his own speed—sometime between now and the end of the world.

For all that Thud was forever in a rush, Thwack never was. He turned to Thud. "The king's messenger was here?" He looked around. "Where?"

Thud shrugged. "I don't know. Lady Clio said the king was coming."

"And I missed it?" Thwack gave a slow disappointed sigh. "Two messengers in one day."

Clio looked from one boy to the other. "I'm so confused."

25

"Aye. Me too," Thud said with great seriousness. "We did not know of the king's visit."

Clio counted to ten, then twenty. At fifty she said, "Tell me about the messenger."

"I didn't see the king's messenger," Thud said, bending back and looking over his shoulder as he wildly slapped at the mud still on his back.

She gave him a moment, then tried again. "Who's coming?"

"The king. You told me so." He stared at the mud on his hands, shrugged and wiped them off on the front of his tunic.

"Thud...

He glanced up at her, then cocked his head. "You look confused, my lady."

"I feel confused."

"Too many messengers," he muttered.

She took a long deep breath, then slipped her arm around the boy's bony shoulders. She leaned toward him and with much patience asked, "What did you come to tell me?"

"About the messenger."

"What about him?"

"He had gold bells on his horse."

"You said that. What else?"

"He wore the badge of the Red Lion."

"The Red Lion?" Clio stopped breathing.

"Aye. Merrick de Beaucourt, the Red Lion."

Her betrothed. After so long she had almost forgotten he really existed. She was certain he had forgotten about her. For four years he was to have been gone.

But four years had turned into six, with nothing

26

but one message over a year ago, and that one insultingly directed to the abbess and not to her, his very own betrothed. She took a deep breath and asked, "What was the message?"

"To prepare for his arrival. He and his men are but a few days away."

Clio didn't speak. She couldn't. Her mind spun from one emotion to another: annoyance and fear, anger and excitement.

Thud and Thwack watched her and exchanged similar looks of surprise, then puzzlement. Thwack tugged on her gown and stared at her from a face too serious to belong to a boy of just ten. "We thought you'd be pleased. Have you nothing to say, my lady?"

"Aye." She turned around and faced the eastern landscape. A long bit of silence surrounded her while she remembered her wistful dreams dying as each day of those years passed her by.

"I have something to say." She stood straighter, stiff, like someone who expected to be hit. She stared at the east wall with a narrow-eyed look, one that did not bode well for her betrothed or for their marriage.

All she said was, " 'Tis about time."

The orderly little convent with its chalk-white walls sat huddled between ripples in the humpbacked English countryside. Founded over a century before and dedicated to the Blessed Virgin, Our Lady of the Water Springs had the words Benedictus locus, "the blessed spot," carved into its foundation stone.

Today, more so than most days, the convent needed all the divine blessings it could get.

"Madame." Merrick de Beaucourt planted his hands on the desk of the abbess, leaned toward her, and pinned her with a black look that did little to hide his anger.

"There must be some mistake. Lady Clio cannot possibly be gone."

The abbess stood her ground. "She left the day after your message arrived."

Merrick paced in front of the desk, glowering at the floor. "She left," he repeated, then stopped in front of the abbess again. "*Left?* She just left? She is a woman. A woman cannot just ride off as she pleases."

"You do not know Lady Clio."

"No, I do not. But I know she was here under the king's protection until I returned."

"She was under his protection. That is true. But he was occupied with the French king and we are a long way from London, my lord."

"God's teeth!" Merrick slammed a fist on the desk.

"Do not curse here, Sir Merrick."

He straightened to his full height. "She is a mere woman!"

Out of the corner of his eye, he saw Roger flinch.

The abbess sat up as straight as the Holy Cross and looked down her long nose at him with an expression almost as haughty as that of the queen herself. "A *mere* woman? As am I." Her voice turned even cooler than his own. "As was the Blessed Virgin *and* as is

28

the queen, *and* I might add, as was your own mother."

At that, Merrick ran a hand through his black hair. He took a moment to seek patience from somewhere and inhaled in a long deep breath. "Back to the subject at hand, madam. That of Lady Clio, who was placed here under your protection and is now gone God knows where."

"I never said I did not know where she was. Only that she was gone."

The woman should have been a queen, Merrick thought, looking at her haughty and imperious stance. Brave knights cowered under his glare. His enemies begged for leniency. Yet this woman spoke to him as if he were a mere annoyance. Very slowly and quietly, he asked, "Where is she?"

"Will you beat her?"

"I have never hit a woman." He paused, then scowled at the abbess. "However, there are moments when I must overcome the urge."

Roger groaned and slapped the heel of his hand against his forehead.

"While I might be a mere woman, my lord, I am a woman of God, and a woman who wields some power. I fight my battles with prayer and am proprietress of the convent and its lands."

"As I have just said. I've never hit a woman and have no intention of doing so in the future, either to you or Lady Clio." He planted his hands on the desk again. "*Now* will you tell me where she is?"

"You won't beat her?" the abbess repeated.

She sighed and tapped a finger against her pursed lips. "I suppose it would do no good if you did."

Merrick and Roger exchanged a bewildered look.

"The Lady Clio has gone to Camrose Castle."

"Finally," Merrick said under his breath, and spun around.

"Wait!" The abbess stood.

One hand on the door, he turned and looked back.

"I did try to discourage her from doing this."

"Apparently you did not try too hard."

The abbess smiled then and gave a wry laugh. "Lady Clio tends to do as she thinks best, my lord."

"Not any longer," Merrick said curtly, and he left.

CHAPTER 4

Camrose Castle,
Glamorgan, the Welsh March

Old Gladdys swore to anyone and everyone who would listen that she was a Druid. This despite the fact that the Druid cult had been extinct for quite a few centuries. The old Welshwoman claimed she was a seer, she had the sight.

When two ravens roosted in the elm tree near the cooper's cottage, Old Gladdys told the cooper's childless widow she would bear twins. Everyone had laughed until the barren widow visited the Michaelmas Fair, and there she wed a blacksmith from Brecon.

Before three harvests had passed, she had four healthy strapping sons, born two at a time. For weeks afterward the village women flocked like doves to Gladdys for her predictions on everything from childbirth to love.

The villagers were a fickle lot, though, and soon Old Gladdys and her prophecies were forgotten. But if someone had asked them who was the homeliest maid in the valley, every last villager would have said 'twas Gerdie the goose girl, who had the great misfortune to look like her geese.

What no one else knew was that Gerdie had visited Old Gladdys during a full moon. Soon the goose girl rose every morning and washed her face with the dew from a tuft of pink valerian growing out of a rock in the river Wye, then broke her fast with turnip soup.

A fortnight later, the most handsome troubadour to ever pass through the village of Clawdd fell passionately in love with Gerdie the goose girl and vowed to use his life and lyre to sing to the world of her rare beauty. The last the villagers had seen of them was the day after they wed, when the singing troubadour and a grinning Gerdie rode off in his cart, her entire flock of geese crammed into the cart bed and honking as the couple disappeared into the horizon.

Afterward, Old Gladdys's prophecies were seldom ignored. If she pointed at six black swans and said it was an omen, all would ask if it was fair or foul. If the wind changed suddenly, women entered their doors backward. If there was an orange moon rising, they would sleep with a sparrow feather beneath their pillows to ward off bad dreams that might come true.

But to Brother Dismas, the monk at Castle Camrose, Old Gladdys was a heretic. And not all there in the head. Should someone mistakenly mention the mad Welshwoman's claim of *the sight*, Brother Dismas crossed himself and said a few Our Fathers, then extended the prayers of Terce by another hour. He tolerated her out of godly condescension for her weak head, his own benevolence and charity...and also because God told him to.

It seemed that God talked to Brother Dismas. Every day.

So that very night, when someone rang at the castle gate after midnight, Old Gladdys sat up in pallet and shrieked, "Trouble! 'Tis trouble! Four bells is trouble!"

No one would answer the call.

Except Brother Dismas. The Lord's deep voice had commanded him to do so.

The gate bell rang and rang, as if someone

32

were beating the metal with a war hammer. Brother Dismas took a fat tallow candle from one of his shrines and lit it from a rush light near the chapel wall. He shuffled across the courtyard and moved toward the inner gatehouse, wondering why God would not let him sleep this night.

Yawning, he stepped over a few sleeping dogs and looked around for the watch guard. He heard a loud snore. Instead of guarding the entrance, the porter was slumped on a stone bench in a dark corner, an empty ale cup in his limp hand.

The bell clattered again, even louder than before. Brother Dismas winced when it rang clear through to his back teeth. He held up his light to the peephole and slid it open with an irritated jerk. He stared outside, blinked, then held the candle higher and took another look.

A moment later he crossed himself and looked up to the heavens. "Merciful Lord, I think you forgot to tell me something."

Clio was in the solar at Camrose Castle, standing in front of a column carved with the likeness of William the Conqueror. The Welsh who had occupied the castle until recently had used the oaken column to hold their daggers. She had pulled four deadly looking two-pronged Welsh skeans from the column the day she first arrived.

She stood back and eyed the likeness for a moment.

William the Conqueror now had dimples.

She turned and paced for a minute or two, the evening warnings of Old Gladdys still fresh in her ears.

"Burn the candles bright this night," Old Gladdys had said. "There were three hawks circling the tower at dawn, the wind this morn was from the east, and the cook found worms in the yeast."

Clio made it a point to ask her what those signs meant, but Old Gladdys only said that was for her to know and for Clio to find out. Cajoling her hadn't worked. Old Gladdys had gone to a nearby hillside, lit a bonfire, then danced around it singing loud chants that sent Brother Dismas off to the chapel in a dither. He spent most of the day on his knees saying the Lord's Prayer.

So with her supper, Clio had passed on the bread, her mind's eye seeing only wormy yeast whenever she looked at a loaf. She ate only a small piece of cheese and some green-pea pottage. Now, her stomach was soured and even fresh milk warmed with honey could not make her sleep.

She paced the room, bored and anxious. As she passed the candle stanchion, her quick steps made the candlelight flicker in odd shapes over the stone walls. She watched for a second, then clutched her gown in her fists and spun around.

On the wall, the outline of a shadow spun and wiggled in a bell shape that looked just like Brother Dismas did when he laughed, his plump belly shaking like eel jelly.

She released her gown and shifted once, her hands crossed high above her head. The shadow appeared to soar up the walls in the shape of a hawk, easy and free. She could remember watching the birds from the window in her small, dull room at the convent and wishing she were a hawk or a falcon or even a lark so she could fly away.

A noblewoman had no freedom. She was born to obey the wishes of men. For the hundredth time she wondered what her life would have been like had she not been born female.

Clio walked over to the narrow castle loophole and opened a heavily studded wood shutter. She stared out at the dark night sky and wondered what it was like to be free like men. What was it like to go crusading, to lie under the stars at the other end of the world, to see places and people and lands that were not home?

She wondered what it would be like to be a knight, and what her betrothed had done for all those years. And she tried to imagine what he looked like.

Would he have a chin like an ax, hands like hams, and scars all over him? Was he called the Red Lion because his hair was bright red like the castle smithy's? She hoped not. The smithy had hair coming out his ears and nose and it stuck out from his head like skimpy tufts of scallions.

So many questions spun through her head that she could not possibly find sleep. No matter how she tried. She had just lain there, fitful, as she had for every night since she had arrived at the castle that had once been her home.

But Camrose was not the same place she remembered from her youth. The castle had been taken by the Welsh shortly after her father's death. She had thought of it as gone forever.

Until she read the message her betrothed had sent to the abbess over a year ago. Camrose had been reclaimed by King Edward, who had been crowned the year before. Now both she and her lands belonged to her future husband by royal command.

The castle did not feel like home. It was a strange place to her, cold and dark even in the light of midday. The walls were higher than before and now made of thicker, heavier stone, walls that made her feel as if she were locked away in a tower.

There were solid shutters on the window openings instead of thinly tanned leather embellished with needlework of falcons twined with ivy and roses and inset into panes of polished horn. Her nurse had told her once that her grandmother had stitched those coverings herself, combining her grandfather's coat of arms with that of her own family. Clio had loved the leather stretchings and panes because they had always allowed the light of the sun to come inside.

But now even in the morning the chamber was dark and stank of smoke and must. The furniture was huge, roughly hewed and hard.

There was nothing remaining that had belonged to her family.

No tapestries. No fur rugs. No chests or fine linen sheets or goose-feather ticking. The bed was hard wood and thick rope and had a prickly hay tick tossed on it for a mattress. Atop it was one rough woolen blanket that still itched even after she had rid it of fleas.

Sparrows and pigeons had been nesting in the window sills when she arrived and had flown freely in all the rooms from the looks of the filth on the floors. It had taken a few days for her and the few servants who had returned to the castle to clean it all out.

There was little a woman could have pride in. Her children, perhaps her husband, and surely her home. For the sake of the women before her, she wanted Camrose to be as it had been. She wanted it to be lovely. But it wasn't, so she kept to her old rooms, attending her own business while she waited for her betrothed to arrive.

She tried to dispel the fear she felt deep inside of her at the thought of finally meeting the man face to face, a man known as the Red Lion. 'Twas not a name that conjured up a pleasant and tame image.

But try as she might, she could not will her apprehension away. It was there, in her mind, clear and real and seeming like a bad dream from which you wanted to hurry and awaken so you could forget it. Though she could not forget, anymore than she could forget that her life and her future rested in the hands of a complete stranger.

So she had decided to meet him on equal ground. She wanted to walk toward him with the same graceful swanlike motion of the ladies at the queen's court, without fear, with only confidence. Her pride made her want to show him exactly what he had chosen to callously ignore.

She tapped her finger against her mouth, closed her eyes, and thought about those elegant ladies. She tried to picture them in her mind, to capture the right image.

After a moment she took two steps back, then two more. One deep breath and she lifted her chin, cocked her head for that confident and slightly arrogant air, then she slid her feet forward in "the glide," a motion that resembled a swan atop a glassy lake.

A few steps and she winced. The soles of her slippers grated against the stone floor and sounded like steel against a grindstone. She could hear it from her ears to her teeth.

She clasped her embroidered robe daintily in her hands, bowed her head, and said, "Welcome, sir knight." She started to sink into a curtsy, then straightened, tapping a finger impatiently against her cheek. "No, no, that is not how 'tis done," she muttered with a frown.

She backed up again, squared her shoulders, and raised an outstretched hand, then let it fall—suitably limp for an aura of feminine frailty—before she slowly moved forward.

"Sir Merrick. 'Tis wonderful to meet a knight of such renown." She did her curtsy, then rose with a surprising amount of grace.

"You must tell me, sir, what has kept you occupied these past four years? Lopping off heads?" She drew her hand across her neck in a slicing motion and made a face with her tongue sticking out of the corner of her mouth.

"Boiling people in oil?" She picked up a water jug near a window and poured it over the ledge while she feigned a wicked laugh.

"Or..." She spun around with both hands clenched high over her head holding on to an imaginary weapon; then she did her best male swagger and twisted her face into a grimace. "...merely cleaving"—she swung her arms down and grunted loudly—"the sorry infidels with your battle ax?"

She straightened once again to her courtly pose, faced the column, and smiled sweetly. "A mace, you say? With spikes? Why, no, I have not seen one used." She fluttered her eyelashes like a dolt. "What is that you ask?" She threaded her fingers as if in prayer and raised them to her cheek. "Aye, sir knight. I can see your fine thick muscles."

Pausing, she widened her eyes in mock wonder. "Would I like to touch them? Certainly, but you will have to kneel, since I cannot reach your fat head from here. I am but a small, weak woman, good for nothing but waiting for to wed."

Clio heaved an exaggerated sigh and clutched her hands to her breast. "Waiting for a man is such a trial. Say you, sir knight, whenever did you decide to deign to come and wed me?"

She looked beseechingly at the column.

"Perhaps you were concerned that I might out-grow my childbearing years." She nodded, raised one finger high in the air as if she were speaking to all the world; then she spun around. "Aye, 'tis so. A man must have an heir, now, mustn't he? A male child, of course. And what, pray tell, will you do with our girl children?"

She waved her arm around in the air as if she were swatting at a bothersome fly. "No doubt toss the useless creatures into the moat—until you have a son you can train to be as insensitive and boorish as yourself."

Clio raised a hand to her cheek in mock con-cern. "Oh dear, I did forget. How very foolish of me. Of course you will foster your sons out to some other churlish oaf so that they will learn nothing of a mother's love. For surely 'twould make them sniveling cowards and certainly not true *men*."

She gripped the seams of her woolen robe in each hand. "We women being such flighty and useless creatures, good for little else but childbearing and female sport." Shuffling on her tiptoes, she spun in a circle, holding her robe out as if it were a gown of silken velvet, then sank to her deepest curtsy.

It was at that very moment that she heard the applause.

The loud applause.

She shot upward and whipped around so quickly one of the rush lights flickered out, casting dark shadows in the room from the one light still burning.

40

Two tall knights stood in the chamber doorway. One of them was leaning against the doorframe. He was laughing.

The other man looked as if he had never laughed a day in his life.

She stood there, her feet suddenly feeling like boulders. She looked from one man to the other, finally choosing to keep her eyes on the handsome man with the reddish hair who was laughing and walking toward her.

He took her hand, then bowed gallantly. "Sir Roger FitzAlan of Wells, my lady." He straightened and gave her a wicked wink. "And my companion—" he nodded at the other man— "the earl of Glamorgan."

Later when she thought about this moment, she supposed when she heard the title "earl," she had made some sort of a small courtesy dip, but she could not be certain. For it was a horridly embarrassing moment she would have liked to have forgotten. So she had kept her gaze on the handsome red-haired knight.

Still smiling, he turned to the other man and said, "She won't need your razor." He kept grinning.

The other knight was not amused.

She tried to hide her apprehension. She did not know who these men were nor why they were here. Unable to look away, she stared into the hard, ridged face and the icy blue eyes of the tall black-haired man, looking for answers, for something.

"You are the earl of Glamorgan?" she asked, almost wincing when her voice caught a little.

She thought she sounded frightened and so she raised her chin and tried to look regal and fearless.

"I received the earldom this past year."

Now that he finally spoke, it was in a deep, clipped voice that was as icy as the look in his eyes. He slowly walked toward her, looking taller and bigger with each step he took. She refused to move, even though instinct told her to run as fast as she could.

He stopped when they were barely a foot apart.

Everyone and everything seemed to melt away. The room grew suddenly thick and stuffy, as if the shutters had been closed and all the air sucked outside.

A second later there was movement at the door. The earl spun around so quickly she almost fainted. His hand was on the hilt of his sword and he had drawn a dagger in his other hand.

Thud, in all his clumsy glory, scrambled into the room, clad in a woolen nightshirt. His thin legs and knobby knees stuck out like a chicken's, and his oversized bare feet looked like long loaves of shepherd's bread.

He stopped, standing stiffly with his bony chest stuck out. "I shall protect you, my lady." He waved a wall torch as if it were a sword.

Sir Roger raised a hand. "There is no need to make bonfires of us, lad. No one will be harmed."

For a second she thought she heard the

earl grunt something under his breath, and she stared up at him. His eyes were still on Thud, but he had sheathed his dagger.

Thud looked at both men skeptically. "Why should I believe you?"

"The earl of Glamorgan does not lie." He spoke for only the second time.

"An earl?" Thud had only seen one knight in his life, an event about which he spoke constantly. He stared up at the earl with the same expression a pilgrim would have had looking at his first holy relic.

"Aye," Sir Roger said. "But 'tis a new title, lad."

Thud was still staring at the dark knight. "Did you receive the title for valor, my lord?"

Roger reached out and tousled Thud's brown hair.

"He did. The king seldom bestows earldoms on cowards, lad."

The earl said nothing this time, just turned those icy eyes down at Thud with an unreadable look.

The moment seemed to stretch out for an eternity.

If he hit the boy, she'd kick him, then dart behind the kind-looking Sir Roger for protection. She doubted he would kill them. He wouldn't be here unless he wanted something. He looked like a man who would easily take whatever it was he wanted.

There was no doubt in her mind that this tall, dark knight could earn ten earldoms on the battlefield. When she looked at him, she wanted

43

to disappear. She could well imagine what it would be like to face him when he was astride a huge warhorse and had a weapon in his hand.

She sank into a fine curtsy, with her head deeply bowed. Then she rose and looked up at him. "What brings you to Camrose, my lord?" When he did not answer her, she offered her own. "Shelter?"

He gave a sharp nod.

"I see." She paused, but he was silent. "Provisions?" she added.

Another nod.

She did not know if she wished him to speak or to just leave. "I have only been at Camrose for a few days, my lord. I know not what we have stocked and ready." She started to take a step, but he reached out and clasped her arm.

He stared down at her. "There is no hurry. We will be here for a long while."

She glanced down at his hand on her arm and looked back up at him from narrowed eyes. She raised her chin but did not pull away. "What makes you think you are welcome, my lord?"

He released her and crossed his arms over his chest. He looked from her to Sir Roger, then back to her. "This castle is mine."

"This castle belongs to the lord of Camrose and my betrothed. I believe that neither Sir Merrick nor the king will allow you to take Camrose, my lord."

There was glint in his eye that she could not identify. For all she knew, he could draw his sword and chop off her head at any moment.

"I am Merrick de Beaucourt."

Thud's eyes grew even bigger. "The Red Lion? *Himself?*"

"Aye." He turned from Thud and pinned Clio with a dark look. "The Red Lion with the 'fat head.'"

She wanted the stone floor to split open like the bowels of hell and swallow her.

He took a step toward her.

Sheer instinct made her take two steps backward.

He followed her.

She took two more and more, and he moved with her as if stalking his prey.

She took one more step and backed against the cold wall next to the window. She flattened her hands against the stone and braced herself as she looked up at him.

He raised his hand toward her face.

"Do not strike me."

She heard Sir Roger swallow a laugh and her gaze flashed toward him. His look was kind, not cruel, and he shook his head slightly, saying with a gesture that Merrick wouldn't harm her.

Her betrothed stared down at her, silently, his hand near her cheek. "I do not strike defenseless females."

Instead of reassuring her, his words annoyed her, made her sound weak and stupid and capable of doing little without his help. For the briefest moment she almost wished he had slapped her instead. A whack didn't seem so bad compared to the condescending words he spoke.

He used his knuckle to raise her chin, so she had no choice but to look into his face. He was not a beautiful man. He was a warrior. A man whose life was armor and war and weapons. And one look at him left no doubt that his manhood had been molded on the battlefield.

His hair was black as one of Old Gladdys's prophetic ravens, and his brows looked like angry slashes across his broad and weathered brow. His nose was long and straight; his jawline and cheeks appeared as if they were sheared from the hardest flint. A thin scar sliced downward from his brow to his earlobe and was shades lighter than his skin, which had been baked brown by the desert sun of the eastern lands.

He was dark. Everything about him. From his coloring to his black expression. Except for his eyes. They were blue. Not the deep blue of a summer sky. Not the bluegray of the sea at dusk. But light blue, and clear, like the icicles that hung from the stable roof on the coldest winter mornings.

Once when she was small, she had peered through a long, sharp icicle that poked down from the eaves of the buttery. What she saw through the ice was a twisted view of what lay beyond. Blurred images that showed things misshapen.

So who or what was this man in whose hands she must place her life and lands? It was obvious he was a man to be feared. She had seen a few warriors like him before, but she knew them little. He appeared to be nothing but a warrior, all cold mail and sharp as the edge of a battle ax, someone with no human emotion. She wondered if she would find a heart inside him or only a blurred and twisted vision of what a person should be.

He shifted closer to her and planted his hands on either side of her, pinning her between arms that were the size of a smithy's.

She just stood there with her back against the cold stone walls, unable to move as she fought for something to say.

"You are by the window, woman."

Her mind seemed to have deserted her.

"Don't stand too close to the opening." He gave her a humorless smile and traced her cheek from temple to chin with one callused finger. "I've not had nearly enough practice tossing useless creatures into the moat."

CHAPTER 5

He didn't throw Clio in the moat. But he certainly looked as if he had wanted to. Instead, he arrogantly informed her that the following morning he planned to acquaint himself with the castle. He expected her to accompany him.

She had no chance to give her reply, aye or nay. By the time she had found her voice and realized he had been toying with her about the moat, he and Sir Roger were gone from the solar as swiftly and as silently as they had come.

So it might have seemed odd that the next morning Clio went toward the great hall with a small jig in her step. She finished her wedge of cheese with one big bite and hummed with her mouth full as she glanced back at the water clock she'd bought from a Venetian merchant at the Michaelmas Fair.

Time was dripping away.

She closed the door to her bedchamber and moved toward the stairs. She did a little dance down the stone steps, three steps down, one back up...three steps down and one back up, all the way down the circular staircase.

At the bottom she hummed a nonsense song, off-key as usual, spun around, and tossed a shiny red apple in the air. She caught it with a snap of her wrist and took a huge juicy bite.

Hmmm. So good.

She glanced up at one of the high windows in the wall, where an iron-studded shutter stood open. The high sun sent bold yellow light spilling onto the gray floor stones and made them appear as if they were made of pure gold.

This morning was one of those rare mornings when everything felt right with the world. Yes, it was a very good day.

Because she was two hours late.

During her sleeplessness the previous night, she had concocted the most wonderful idea! Rather like her own version of the delay tactics of Fabius the Cunctator. Only Clio's Hannibal was her betrothed, the earl of Grim, who had seen fit to leave her in a convent to languish for two years longer than promised.

Just to keep things fair between them and to wield her own sense of power, Clio decided she needn't rush to do his bidding. By her calculations, she could be two hours late every day for the next twenty years and still not have evened their score. Although she certainly intended to try.

She wanted to see the earl's face when she came into the hall. She went along a dark stone hallway where only one stub of a candle was lit and past a niche where a huge Flemish tapestry had once hung. Now there was nothing there but an expanse of plastered wall and the old iron rungs for the tapestry rod. Chips similar to those in the Conqueror's likeness pocked the smooth plaster wall, as if those who had stolen Camrose had practiced their battle-ax skills against it.

She mourned for the tapestry her grandmother had been so proud of. No one knew where the tapestry had gone, but she had vowed to make certain her home was restored with the fine things that had always made it a home, the furnishings so cherished by the women in her family.

And if Sir Merrick turned out to be a nipfarthing, no matter. She would use the profits

49

from the sale of her Welsh ale. She would not grovel to a man for the things she wanted. Should she master the recipe for heather ale, well, she need not apply to her husband for anything.

She brushed the cheese crumbs from her saffron yellow tunic; the color made her look so pale the abbess had once asked her if she was ill. Early that morning she'd made a fillet of old marsh reeds by twisting the twigs together, and she'd fixed her hair in the same way as the ladies in the queen's court.

Clio had so much hair that the knots by her ears were huge. She yanked on her sleeves, which were too long and made her look smaller and weaker.

Just like a "defenseless female."

For the final touch she fixed her face in an expression of careless innocence—that "What? Me late?" look. In an utterly nonchalant manner, she rounded the corner and faced the great hall.

She stopped cold.

The room was empty. No languishing men-at-arms. No meal laid out. No servants running to and fro like caged birds. No clink of the platters, no spilt wine and beer. No irate, red-faced earl.

She planted her hands on her hips and looked around. There was not even a hound snoozing at the hearth. Did they not know how she had planned? Humph!

A moment later she marched through the great hall and down the stairs, where she went out the huge wooden doors and into the bailey. The geese and chickens pecked at the ground while a rooster with a red plume strutted and crowed and behaved in manly fashion along the gutter drains near the wall. The chickens ignored him.

She could see Cyclops hiding behind some broken staves near the abandoned cooper's hut with Pitt perched on his feline head, wings spread and looking like the gaudy plumed helm of an ancient god.

She wondered what those two were stalking now. With all the mice to be caught, she'd hardly seen them since coming back. But both her pets looked plumper already, and their eyes had the lazy and overly satisfied look of the kitchen hounds after a Christmas feast.

In the bailey, there was no one. She walked through to the outer bailey and met the same emptiness. It was almost as if she were the last person in the world.

The portcullis had been cranked open and she could hear noise from beyond. She moved through the gates and over the long wooden planks that spanned the moat.

Every member of the castle, every villein, every serf, and a huge horde of men-at-arms were assembled in what looked like battle lines along the rolling grassy fields, where, toward the rear, a huge tent stood in an encampment.

At each corner of the tent flew silken pennants marked with the earl of Glamorgan's distinctive charge blazoned *sable a cross argent a lion rampant*

51

gules—a black field, white cross, and rearing bloodred lion. Whenever the breeze picked up, the flags rippled and waved and made the red lions look as if they were prowling.

She tried to see what was happening, then spotted Sir Merrick walking along in front of the lines. He wore no helmet or battle armor, only mail under a long black tunic that was belted with leather trimmed in thick silver chain. His sword and its sheath hung at his side.

A light breeze picked up the thick black hair that hung down to the back of his neck. For just an instant, that dark hair flashed silver in the bright sunlight; then the light shone off the silver sword sheath.

It hurt her eyes and forced her to shield them with her hand. His hands were locked behind his back as he walked in front of the lines, stopping to speak with each person. The servants did not appear to be cowering...yet. None were on their knees, nor were they prostrated before him.

Clio moved toward them and felt the stares and glances of some of the people and caught a few of his men turning their heads in her direction. Ignoring those looks, she searched about the crowd for Sir Roger's golden-red head, but it was nowhere in sight.

So much for a spot of high dry land in a flood, she thought.

Stopping a few measures away from Sir Merrick, she stood there, expecting some response from him. A snarl. A cold glare like the night before. Or a roar might be more in character for someone called the Red Lion.

She kept waiting.

What she did not expect was him to ignore her. Which was what he did.

Some perverse part of her wanted to march up to him and kick him, but she wasn't stupid, just annoyed because her wonderful idea was not working as she decided it should.

She stood there for the longest time, so long that people started looking at her out of pity and shared embarrassment, which made her feel even more conspicuous, more humiliated. Her betrothed was speaking to a villein, Thomas the Plowman, who held the most acreage and every year planted barley, wheat, and hay. Thomas was telling his lord about the land, about the water, soil, and the best crops to plant.

She kept waiting, and waiting. She shifted her weight, then forced her chin even higher so no one would know she was feeling embarrassed.

Lord Merrick would have paid more attention to a fly.

She sought to occupy her mind with something, anything. She began to do ciphers the way she had learned in the convent, only with new variables. If she had two maces, four battle axes, and a war hammer, how many hits in the head would it take to get the earl of Grim's attention?

If she had a jar of hungry fleas or a pot of sticky honey, which would be more amusing to put inside his armor?

If she had three frogs or a pitchfork—

"Lady Clio, my lord." Thomas the Plowman said her name and all eyes turned toward her. All eyes except her Merrick's.

She saw him stiffen, but he did not act as if he knew she was there. Perhaps he didn't. Perhaps he was deaf from battle. Perhaps he was thick-headed from too many blows to his helm. Perhaps...

"What need has *my* Lady Clio for your crops?"

"Not all crops, my lord." Thomas looked from the earl to her, then back to the earl.

Oh, God's feet! Merrick was about to find out about her brewery. She shook her head, but Thomas was no longer looking at her.

"Lady Clio only needs the barley," Thomas continued, never looking back at her. "She made provisions to purchase the villeins' own plow-shares for brewing her ale, my lord."

"Her ale?" Now Lord Merrick turned and looked directly at her. So much for thinking he did not know she was there.

"Yes, my lord. Lady Clio told us how she had learned to brew ale at the convent and how very special the ale would be. How there would be plenty of ale at Camrose, enough for those of us who only have cider or mead."

It was not a simple task to stand there and look calm and collected beneath his piercing blue stare and his cool detached manner.

"Our lady has great plans for the castle brewery," Thomas said proudly.

"Does she, now?" Merrick nodded, watching her with an unreadable expression.

"Aye, that she does."

Clio wished Thomas the Plowman would be silent.

"Come, my lady." Merrick raised his hand toward her. His tone made it clear he was not offering her a choice.

Her feet moved of their own accord while her mind screamed, "Where's your pride! Stay there and ignore him the way he ignored you!" Then she was standing before him, her pride in tatters. Her mind was calling her a coward, while her sense said, "Don't cross him before all and sundry."

She placed her hand in his, because she had to. When his hand closed about hers, she felt the calluses on his hand, calluses from gripping the hilt of his sword, from the reins of his warhorse, and from lances and maces and other such weapons of war.

It was a simple gesture, an honor to ladies that was supposed to be a courtesy. Many times a man had held out his hand to her—her father, the king, and others.

Yet with this man the act seemed intimate, private, and unsettling. As if he knew her thoughts, he turned and drew her with him to face the crowd, their hands held up for all to see. And they stood together, hand in hand; it felt as if they were one. This stranger and she.

His hand closed more firmly around her fingers, like the manacles that held prisoners to the walls of a cell. With a sense of doom more foreboding than any black omen Old Gladdys could foretell, Clio saw her identity slipping completely away from her.

CHAPTER 6

Merrick led his betrothed toward the castle. She walked beside him as if he were leading her to the gallows, silent, stoic, and looking as if she stared death in the face. She bore little resemblance to the spirited creature he'd watched twirl and dance in such enchanting circles around the solar.

Today there was no silver-gold hair that hung past her knees. No deep green robe that made her eyes look like a rich dark forest. No innocently wicked spark in those green eyes or charming, elfin grin on her lips.

Her face was pale, almost gray. She wore a tunic the color of a cesspit. Her hair was scraped back from her face and knotted in two coils that made her head look like an egg ...with handles.

The circlet on her head was twisted pieces of bramble; his first thought was of a crown of thorns. Worse yet, it was perched atop a scrap of sheer silk so ugly a grayish blue it must have been a waste of work for the worms.

He had the absurd thought that she might be like those spirits of legends and wives' tales, the kind of enticing creature who comes alive only by the light of the moon. His gaze fell on her again.

Sunlight certainly didn't enliven her.

He waited a moment longer for her to speak,

to question him, to say something. Anything. But the only sounds were those of their feet on the ground and the background noise of the castle going back to work once again.

She was silent as a rock.

He looked ahead of him, then said, "Tell me about the ale."

Her head shot up. "There is nothing much to tell." She spoke quickly, as if she had to get all the words out in one breath. Then she looked away, staring off at nothing. "The convent sold ale. Since I was there so long, the abbess sent me to help Sister Amice in the brewery. She had a special ale recipe."

"What kind of recipe?"

"Oh, just one for a stronger brew. It was very popular and sold well."

"Since you are familiar with the process, I shall make it your duty to hire a brewer."

"No!"

He froze. That was the most life he'd seen in her that day.

"I would like to brew the ale." She placed her hand on his forearm, and he stared down at it for a confused moment.

"Why should you wish to be bothered with the task?"

"I want to, my lord. Please. I enjoyed brewing. Sister Amice and I were working on some new ingredients when she died."

"What kind of ingredients?"

"Spices and herbs. Nothing too unusual." She kept her hand on his arm; then she gave him a direct look.

"You will have many duties here."

"I know, but I promise Camrose will have the finest ale in the land. And you have my word I will not shirk my other duties."

He heard the pride in her tone and he thought for a moment he understood her. He looked down at her hand and found himself saying, "You may do the brewing."

She stood before him and meekly bowed her head.

The nuns' influence, he thought.

"Thank you, my lord."

To tease her, he said, "Just don't try to serve my men any heather ale."

"Heather ale?" She snatched back her hand and gave him a look that was not meek or submissive, but startled.

"I can see by your face that you've never heard the tale. Some claim the Picts brewed an ale so potent that it helped them defeat Julius Caesar. Of course such a thing cannot exist, but fools still try to make it and usually end up poisoning ale-drinkers with their feeble efforts."

She must have had a weak stomach; her smile looked as if it were slapped on her face. "I give you my word I will never poison your men, my lord."

"I was jesting with you. And I believe, Clio, that you should begin to call me Merrick."

She said nothing. They walked together, in a castle that would be theirs and their children's, yet now at this moment they were nothing but strangers.

He stared down at her and wondered what

she was thinking. He looked straight ahead, then said, "It was foolish to leave the protection of the convent."

" 'Twas not too far to travel."

"The traveling distance was not my concern."

"Apparently neither was my existence for two years." She looked as if the words had slipped out before she could stop them.

For the longest time he said nothing, but instead only watched her, almost trying to look inside her head. She was silent, too, but averted her eyes as if she did not want to give him a chance to see what she was thinking.

"You are peevish because I did not come and wed you as agreed."

She didn't respond, just continued to walk beside him as if he had not spoken.

"You are too quiet. Have you nothing to say?"

"I have said enough."

"I don't think you've said half of what you wished to say to me."

" 'Tis over and done now." Her tone was clipped.

"Aye. It is. There is no going back. I cannot change what has happened."

"I know that." She couldn't hide her annoyance and it looked as if she was not even trying to. She sounded impatient and snappish. She did not understand.

He knew enough to know she wanted him to respond. Even if she did not realize it. Deep down inside of her, she wanted him to know that she was angry. "I am a man of war, Clio."

She met his look when he spoke her name. "I have been a knight for a long time, almost fifteen years. Before that I was fostered and trained to be a warrior. It is the only way I know. I obey my liege lord, my king, in all things. He came first. It is a matter of honor. Had I not been there, he would not be alive today. Likewise had he not been there, I'd have rotted in some desert hell and you'd be betrothed to nothing but a pile of bleached bones."

He made certain that he did not sound angry, or sorry. He wanted it plain from his tone he was not apologizing or trying to make her understand.

He was not placating her. He spoke to her the same way he spoke to his men and to the servants—a matter-of-fact way that allowed for no argument, but said that this was the way things were.

She seemed to accept his words, because she nodded, but within a moment she had lapsed back into that same awkward silence.

He stared down at the top of her head with that ugly headdress. "I do have news I believe you will find welcome. Edward has given me license to crenellate Camrose."

She stopped and looked up at him and frowned in puzzlement.

"It means I am to refurbish the castle. Along with the license comes a rich allotment to pay for the changes."

"You mean the king gave you money to restore and rebuild Camrose?"

"Aye."

Her manner changed so quickly he had to look twice. She no longer trudged toward the wooden bridge as if she were carrying the sins of the world. Her step was light and she stood a little straighter as she walked beside him.

But it was her face that made him almost have to look away. Joy and relief and something he could not name shone from her.

He'd never seen the like, and it struck him odd that things could change so quickly between them. He continued to watch her, stunned. And leery because he could barely believe his eyes.

To think he'd thought her plain in the daylight.

Her smile was the daylight.

Amid his confusion something touched him deeply, the idea that he could make her smile like that, a smile he found he was not immune to.

She became pensive a moment later, this changeling of a woman. His first thought after he'd watched her expression of wonder fade was that he would like to see her smile at him again.

They crossed the wooden bridge and he stopped and inspected the wooden planks. "Here is something that must be replaced. See there?" He pointed to the places where the wood was cracked and split. "The bridge needs to be stronger. I will replace it with strong stone blocks cemented with lime or perhaps build a wooden drawbridge and reinforce it with iron."

"Aye." She nodded, agreeing with him. *A miracle.*

"I can see it." She stood back and eyed the entrance.

The drawbridge would be the best for defense, he decided to himself. The bridge could be pulled up to thwart an attack.

"The stone would be lovely."

She was right, he thought absently. A stone bridge had its merits, since it would not burn.

She leaned over the old wooden railing and made a face at the water. "The moat is filthy. It should be drained and refilled."

"Aye. We'll have it drained." She was a practical maid and he was pleased with her and with himself for choosing her six years ago. "The moat should be enlarged, two to three times the size."

He paused in thought, imagining the size in his mind's eye. It would be wide and deep, too deep to fill and difficult to tunnel under. No siege tower would be able to scale the outer wall of this castle.

With a wider moat, burning the bridge would be more difficult. He could have the drawbridge, which still appealed to him. He liked the idea of having the power to control the entrance.

"Then we can have swans," she said with enthusiasm.

Swans?

She was already walking ahead of him.

He followed her, frowning as he watched her enter the gate ahead of him with a bounce in her step. There would be no swans atop his moat. Unless she could find swans that spat poison or devoured their enemies.

She had stopped underneath the barbican and was frowning upward by the time he joined her.

"That's disgusting," she said, her hands planted on her hips.

He looked up.

"Those are murder holes, aren't they?" she asked.

"Aye." Even he couldn't believe it. It was disgusting. There were only two murder holes chiseled into the roof and those were small and thin and looked useless. He shook his head in disbelief. On a castle in the borderlands where the Welsh came raiding regularly. Two puny holes. "I agree. 'Tis stupid."

He would build a stronger higher gate tower and pepper it with plenty of holes from which to drop missiles and rain arrows on their enemies. No man would slip past his gate.

For the next hour they moved through the castle. She insisted on showing him where every tapestry had hung, where carpets had been, and telling him how the windows' panes had been polished bone. He tolerated it, knowing it was difficult for her to return to the castle that had been her home and see it in such shambles.

Also she was a woman. He supposed she had different priorities and saw most things differently than he did.

So when he talked of the arrow slits and she

wanted glass windows, he said nothing. When he mentioned adding more chimneys and she talked of the queen's decorated fireplaces, he just moved on. His lady had not been trained in war. So he tolerated her interest in furnishings and glass windows and decorated fireplaces.

Most of the time Merrick had expansion on his mind. He had decided to double the size of the keep and replace the roof with iron tiles. She thought it a splendid idea until he informed her that the iron tiles the castle blacksmith would forge were to protect them from fire arrows, *not* to allow them to hear the patter of the rain in the solar.

By the time they sat at the high table in the hall and were quenching their thirst with wine, his patience was thinning. She refused to eat the bread and kept shoving the platter out of his reach, while she prattled on about things that were unimportant.

"I can just imagine the moat, Merrick. Black swans and lily pads, perhaps some marsh marigolds along the borders and a small boat."

"A what?"

"A boat."

"Would you have the Welsh raiders float across our moat to the honking of swans and the scent of flowers? Why not give a feast for them and lower our drawbridge to the sound of trumpets?"

She scowled up at him, not looking the least meek and submissive. "You needn't make me feel foolish. I was thinking about the beauty of the place, not about the Welsh."

"A castle is for defense. A place made to keep those inside safe."

"I was only daydreaming aloud," she snapped, watching him.

He leaned across the table and snatched up a chunk of bread before she could move it from his reach again.

"I understand you clearly, my lord."

"Daydreaming." He snorted. "A foolish and female pastime." He ripped off a hunk of bread with his teeth and chewed the bloody hell out of it.

She watched him swallow the bread and her expression lit with something akin to victory. She lifted the platter with a suddenly sweet expression. "More bread, my lord?"

"No," he barked, not liking her sudden sweetness or her clear use of his title instead of his name. A moment before he had been "Merrick."

She waited a moment, as if she were savoring something tasty, then set down the bread platter. "So you contend that men do not daydream."

"Aye. We have better things to do."

"Oh? And what about you, my lord?"

He looked up. "What about me?"

""You claim daydreaming to be foolish and female."

"Aye." He almost laughed. "Men do not have such a weakness."

"Ha!"

"What are you implying with your 'ha!'?"

65

"Only that you aren't female and your mind can surely wander as well as mine."

He could no longer hold back and gave a sharp bark of laughter. "Me? Daydream? What foolishness. A warrior whose mind wanders is a dead warrior."

She placed her palms on the table and leaned toward him. "I think I must be speaking to a ghost."

"Explain yourself."

"Shall we lower our drawbridge and invite the Welsh in for a feast?" she repeated in the same impatient tone he had used, which annoyed him more.

He stood up then, not liking her boldness or her argument. She was a woman. She should defer to him in all things. He planted his hands on the table, too, and leaned over, glowering down at her.

"You must have been daydreaming, *my lord.*"

"I don't think so, *my lady.*"

"Oh? Ha!"

He was learning to hate that word.

"We don't have a drawbridge," she announced, then spun around with her nose so high in the air she would have drowned if it rained.

A moment later she was gone, her angry footsteps tapping up the stone stairs. He stood there with his hands still planted on the tabletop and he felt as if he were struck dumb. A moment later he asked himself, what in the bloody hell had happened?

He straightened and stood there feeling as if he were waist-high in the midst of a marsh, sinking. He shook his head, then downed another glass of weak watered-down wine.

It did not help.

He reached up and massaged the tenseness in the back of his neck, wincing when he squeezed too hard. 'Twas not his own neck he wanted to choke.

It dawned on him then that any thoughts of that ideal and peaceful life he'd sought for so long had just gone straight to hell.

Before him was his future, a future with one small woman. Lady Clio of Camrose. And at that moment he knew with surety that she would be more trouble than every rebel Welshman in all of Wales.

Bragawd Ale

Soak barley and allow to sweeten,
Dry until malted,
Mash with yeast and water for fyne wort.
Mix fyne wort with:
Honey, cinnamon, ginger,
Cloves, pepper, heath flowers and galingale.

—Medieval Welsh Ale Recipe

CHAPTER 7

The castle brewery had been a mess. Dirt and mud on the floors and rats in the rushes. The vats were old, rusted, and filled with stale ale and mold, and the iron pipes that fed water to the cistern in the corner were not siphoning from the castle well, but instead came from the filthy moat.

It took a few days to clean up and that was with Clio, Thud, Thwack, and Old Gladdys all working hard. But by midday on the third day, the spicy scent of herbs and dried flowers was all you could smell if you happened to pass by the open shutters.

Inside, Lady Clio was perched on a wobbly wooden stool before an oaken table with two legs that were shorter than the others. Pitt, the goshawk, had the end of her long blond braid in his beak. His wings were spread out as if he were in flight, and whenever the stool would wobble, he would swing back and forth, back and forth, like a cradle, while Cyclops watched from his one eye, his paw batting at him every so often.

The hard dirt floor had been swept clean with a long and thick willow broom that Brother Dismas handed Old Gladdys as a means of transport when she threatened to leave Camrose to the Fates.

But a dirt floor in a brewery was not a good idea. The first small testing of ale she'd brewed had been gritty with dirt and sand, and she would have to lay down cloth to protect the malt.

So, early yesterday morn, Clio and her helpers had pilfered flat slate stones for the floors from the freemasons who were working for the earl. In the last week, the road to Camrose had been busy with the arrival of masons, smithies, sawyers, and other building craftsmen.

There were so many piles of floor stones that the stacks were taller than the earl of Bluster himself. Clio decided the few tiles they needed to floor the brewery would not be missed.

Like most of the thatched huts in the two baileys, this one in the upper bailey was long and narrow, and the walls were of wattle and daub that was cracked and needed patching. But the inside was usable now. The dried herbs and small bags of spices she'd brought from the convent were scattered haphazardly in a corner near the window.

Bundles of sorrel and rue, toadflax and hyssop, sat atop cloth bags containing willow bark and rowan leaves, acorns and walnuts. Foxglove, marsh reeds, and cattails poked out of the wide mouths of earthenware jars, and a row of small hemp pouches with unraveled drawstrings held fat nutmegs and brittle cinnamon sticks, black cloves, and saffron-colored cumin seeds.

Mortars and pestles made of brindled stone, hardwood, and glazed pottery were stacked in every size from those small enough to cup in your hand to large ones that you could only hold if they sat in the crook of your arm. There were three pepper horns and two brass coffers with small locks that each held precious pale sugar and fine granules of pure white salt.

Clio glanced down at the parchment on which Sister Amice had scribbled her list of herbs. "Hmmmm. What is next?" she muttered and dragged a finger down the list. "Milkwort? No...I did that one. Fennel powder. No, I added that one. Ah-ha! Here it is. I need three gills of salix..."

She crumbled willow bark and leaves into a stone mortar and vigorously mashed them into a fine powder of salix.

Old Gladdys had quietly spent the last hour or so moving about the room and arranging the herbs, oils, and tinctures into positions corresponding to those of the moon and stars during the spring equinox.

Brother Dismas had come inside only once, hiding behind his crucifix, which he'd wrapped in dried holly. It seemed God had warned him to do this, since the Lord knew that witches were afraid of holly and there would be no way for the old Druid to give Brother Dismas the evil eye.

Old Gladdys looked perfectly capable of giving anyone the evil eye. She had frizzy white hair that stuck out from her head like carded lamb's wool. Her nose was so hooked that Thomas the Plowman had once claimed if he ever misplaced his scythe, he could use Old Gladdys to cut grain. Her eyes were sharp and ageless, but they were dark, almost black, and they looked even darker because the only color she would wear was black.

So as Brother Dismas faced her, peering uneasily around his raised cross, Old Gladdys had turned around, stuck out her bony jaw, and closed one devilish eye. Suddenly she began to wildly wave her scrawny arms in the air, then pointed at the monk while she chanted:

> *Eena, meena, mona, mite,*
> *Basca, tora, hora, bite,*
> *Hugga, bucca, bau,*
> *Eggs, butter, cheese, bread,*
> *Stick, stock, stone dead!*
> *O-U-T...Out!*

Every bit of color drained from the monk's florid face. His gaze shot to Clio. "What is she saying? A curse? Did she say wart? Will I awake in the morn with warts?"

Old Gladdys hunched over and stuck her wrinkled neck out like a vulture. "Ancient words, they are."

She wiggled her bony fingers at him. "All Druids use those words"—she paused—"to choose their sacrifices."

He gasped.

She gave him a long and calculating look.

He raised his crucifix so close to his face that his nose was pressed to the back of it. He began to back out of the room. At the doorway, he hollered, "Lady Clio! Lord Merrick is searching for you!"

A moment later he had fled, leaving nothing in his wake but a muttered "Hail Mary, Mother of God."

Clio shook her head. "Shame on you, Gladdys."

" 'Tis true," the old woman said with a certain gleam in her black eyes that looked suspiciously like amusement.

"You know he'll be out of sight at least until evening mass," Clio said with a sigh.

"Aye." Old Gladdys crossed over to the huge black pot with the ale mash, wearing the same look Cyclops had when there were feathers sticking out of his mouth.

As for the earl of Hardheads, Clio could not have cared less whether he was looking for her or not. With each grind of the pestle, she pictured her betrothed, wasting away his time looking for her the way she had wasted away while waiting for him.

Clio began to giggle a little wickedly. Her father always said she had never learned to win graciously. But truly, this was a fine bit of vengeance she had concocted. Learning to wait for her was an experience the earl needed to become familiar with. 'Twould be a part of his life for a long, long time.

She laughed out loud, then caught Old Gladdys spying at her out of the corner of her eye.

" 'Tis nothing." Clio waved her hand around.

Cyclops picked that moment to bat Pitt with a paw, then began to circle the stool, rubbing up against her foot and then circling

72

again. Clio looked down at her cat. This was the most life she'd seen in him in days.

He kept bumping and rubbing against her foot. She reached down and scratched him behind the ears.

The fat devil tried to bite her.

She snatched her hand back and scowled at him. "What's wrong with you?"

"A restless cat." Old Gladdys nodded knowingly. " 'Tis a sure sign that a storm is brewing."

Clio glanced out the small window. The sky was blue and cloudless and the sun was shining through, casting broad amber light on the floor.

There was no storm brewing.

She shook her head and then went back to work. A few minutes later she was immersed in her recipe.

Thud had gone to the cooper to fetch some new ale barrels, but Thwack was puttering with a water cistern in the corner.

"Thwack?" she called out absently as she leaned over the huge black ale pot. "I need your help."

"Aye, my lady?" The lad turned around.

"I need you to fetch something for me," she said and looked up.

At that very moment Thwack took one step-right onto the blade of a fallen shovel. The handle sprang up and whacked him right in the forehead.

An odd, empty clunk rang through the room.

The boy wobbled for a moment, then rubbed his head, frowning.

Clio slid off the stool and rushed over to him, Pitt still swinging upside down from the end of her braid.

She looked into Thwack's squinting eyes.

He stared back at her.

"Are you hurt?"

He blinked as if he were seeing double. "No. I'm Thwack. Hurd works in the stables, my lady."

She tried again. "How is your head?"

His expression was confused. "I don't know. We haven't made the beer yet. Have we? Do you have a head on your barrel?"

"Your forehead, Thwack."

"Do I have foam on my forehead?" He stretched his neck and jaw out trying to see his own head.

"We haven't made the beer yet," she explained slowly.

"Good. I thought I missed the brewing when I stepped on the shovel and conked my noggin."

Clio studied him to see if his eyes looked glassy. Well, at least more glassy than usual. "Your noggin is fine, then?"

"Aye, but my head hurts."

She had the sudden urge to bury her own head in her hands and begin to count very slowly. But by now she was too familiar with Thud and Thwack, and though they could test the patience of a saint, there was nothing in them that was the least mean-spirited. They were sweet and simple lads.

Both boys had been brought to the convent when they were only six. A wandering minstrel found them in the King's Forest, where they had been living as wild as animals.

The good sisters had taken them in, bathed them, fed them, and helped them understand how to live among their own kind. The nuns had christened them Peter and Paul, but the boys would only answer to the names they had formed for each other—Thud and Thwack.

Thud was so anxious to please that he would scurry like a small forest animal, except that his feet were so huge he had trouble scurrying anywhere. It was almost as if he forgot his feet were attached to his legs. Inevitably, down he would go with a thud.

Thwack was just the opposite; he never scurried. He was slow and methodical and could only concentrate on one thing at a time. That was his problem. He would concentrate so hard and so completely that he would not look where he was going and thwack! He'd run right into something.

He tried so very hard to please, but tended to become confused easily. If someone asked him to do more than one thing or if he became distracted, he could spend hours in utter confusion.

One time Sister Margaret, who was in charge of candle-making, had asked him to fetch a bucket of well water so she could cool the tallow candles. On his way to the well, Sister Anne had asked him to look for her prayer book. The next day they found the prayer book in the well bucket, and when the abbess opened the candle cabinet, she almost drowned.

While at the convent, Clio had taken the time to teach them their letters. After that they had followed her everywhere, like little guardian angels who were eagerly grateful to do whatever she bid them to.

Thud and Thwack were good lads, kind and true. They just didn't think or behave as did the rest of the world.

Clio brushed a stringy lock of brown hair from Thwack's red and swelling forehead. "Would you like to help me with the newest ale recipe?"

"Aye." He nodded vigorously.

"Good. Then you can start by bringing me the honeycomb on the other table."

The young lad rocked on his toes for a moment, scratching his head as if he was deciding which table she meant. This was not too difficult, she thought, since there were only two tables in the room.

"Which table are you working at, my lady?" he asked her, frowning.

"This table?"

"Aye."

"The bowl with the honeycombs in it is on that table." She was back on her stool and counting out a number of cinnamon twigs. She didn't look up, but just pointed in the direction of the only other table in the room.

There was complete silence. When she realized it, she glanced up at the boy. "Is something wrong?"

"I'm confused. You said the 'other' table. Where is the 'other' table?"

"*That's* the other table."

"But you said that was 'that' table not the 'other' table and the table you are at is 'this' table, not 'that' table or the 'other' table."

"Thwack." She kept her voice calm and even.

"Aye?"

"How many tables are there in this room?"

He pointed at the table in front of her, raised his thumb, and mouthed "one." He looked at the other table, raised his first finger, and mouthed "two." He stared intently at his hand, studied it for a long moment, and looked back at her. "Two."

"Aye. So...if I'm working at *this* table"—Clio patted her hands on the tabletop in front of her—"and I need the honeycomb, where do you think it would be?"

He thought for a stretch of minutes; then his expression brightened. "In the beehives?"

"I meant I need a honeycomb in a bowl on a table. Now try again."

Thwack frowned, then raised a finger and guessed, "In the kitchens?"

She shook her head.

Old Gladdys craned over and muttered something at the boy. He looked at the old woman, then shrugged as if he couldn't believe it. His gaze went from one table to the other and back to Clio. He chewed his lip for a second, then said, "On that table?"

"Aye. On that table." Clio smiled and went

back to work measuring and sorting her spices and herbs.

He must have stood there for a long time, because she felt him tap her on the shoulder a good time later. "My lady?"

"Aye?"

"Why did you tell me to look on the 'other' table instead of 'that' table?"

Clio looked from one table to another, then sighed. "Don't fret over it, Thwack. " 'Twas me. I was confused."

"Aye." He agreed. "That you were, my lady, that you were." He shuffled over to the table with all the speed of a passing eon, then spent a few minutes foraging through the jars and bowls and other containers on the table.

Each item had his full attention for a good few minutes. Finally he found the bowl, examined it for the longest time, then moseyed back across the stone floor.

He handed her the bowl. Inside was a deep amber wedge of sticky honeycomb. "Do you suppose someone stole the 'other' table?"

Clio shook her head.

Thwack walked away mumbling, "Perhaps Sir Merrick replaced the 'other' table with 'that' table."

Before long he would forget about the tables. But now she had her own work to do. She mixed the salix and thyme, then ground a pinch of heather flowers together and added them to the mash that was cooking in one of the huge black pots lining the eastern wall.

Beneath the hanging pot, a low, banked fire sent smoke curling up through one of the crude smoke holes in the thatched roof.

Later the ale was bubbling and steaming. The room had grown moist and warm. The pots boiled brews that filled the air with the scents of herbs and malt.

Clio took a wooden bowl and dipped it into the ale. She let it cool slightly, then stuck her thumb in to test the temperature. She turned her thumb up, judged the consistency by the texture and the way it coated her thumb with a light frothing.

The ale was done.

She took a sip from the bowl and swallowed. Like a bubble of beer, a small giggle burst from her mouth. Surprised, she licked her lips, then realized she was just happy because she had brewed the first of her Camrose ale.

Surely that was something that would make her feel like laughing out loud. She proudly took another sip and and got another giggle.

'Tis wonderful, she thought, and lifted the bowl to her lips, downing the rest.

She heard Old Gladdys cackle wickedly, and Clio lowered the bowl from her lips.

"I told ye there was a storm brewing," Old Gladdys announced, then rushed out the door in a flash of white hair and swirling black wool robes.

Clio covered her mouth to stop another bubble of laughter and turned back around.

Her urge to laugh died as swiftly as it had come.

Merrick stood in the doorway, his expression blacker than any storm clouds she'd ever seen.

CHAPTER 8

"The castle well collapsed," Merrick barked, and took two steps into the brewery, searching for the source of his problem.

He found the source.

Lady Clio stood with her back to him before an ale pot, giggling.

Merrick fixed on her with a dark look that matched his black mood.

She spun around suddenly and faced him. Her happy expression quickly melted away, which annoyed him. The fact that he was affected by something as foolish as her smile annoyed him even further.

He looked away from her expressive face and crossed the steamy room in a few long strides to a water cistern and tangle of old iron siphoning pipes that sat at the far end of the hut.

Lined up along the wall near the pipe drain were large ale pots filled with liquid, some cooking on small wood fires, others sitting cold. But even the cold pots had bright flower petals, dark green leaves, and earth-colored powders floating on top of the contents, like some desert sheik's bathing pool.

He turned and studied the cistern. It only took him a moment to see what had gone wrong. The siphoning pipes were too wide and too strong for a small cistern. So the iron pipes had pulled at the well water with such force that the walls of the well had caved in, leaving the castle with absolutely no water.

He leveled a pointed look at Clio. "I gave you my consent to brew ale, *not* to suck the well dry." He studied the pipes again, shaking his head. "I'd like to flay the skin from the fool who did this."

When he faced his betrothed, she had that stubborn stance he was beginning to find all too familiar and all too irritating.

She swiped a strand of stray blond hair from her face and said, "There was plenty of water in that well." The challenge in her voice did nothing to cool his anger.

"There *was* water. Until the walls of the well collapsed. Now there is nothing but a mud hole."

She blanched slightly.

He took a step toward her. "There are hundreds of men at Camrose. The castle workers, builders and masons and craftsmen, and my own troops. All those men are here and the castle has no working well."

She looked from him back to her steaming vats. "The men can drink ale until a new well is dug. I've made plenty." She waved her hand at the pots. "See?"

"And shall I order the horses and oxen, the chickens and pigs, to pull out their ale tankards? Shall the cows give milk tainted with malt?"

From her face he could see she hadn't thought of the animals.

He crossed his arms over his chest. "What? No quick answers, Clio? And how do you propose the stonemasons mix the lime and sand to cement the new walls? Should they use your ale? How do the sawyers cool their saws? The rough masons their stones, and the blacksmiths their iron?"

She was quiet, chewing her lip for a long time while she twisted a ring on her finger. Then her face lit up so suddenly it looked as if she had stepped before a bonfire. "They can use the foul water from the moat," she said, then gave him a smug look.

"The moat was drained into the fields this morning."

"Oh." She bowed her head.

'Twas the first sign of feminine meekness he'd seen from her. He looked at the floor, too, where he saw the flat, thin flagstones the master mason had reported were missing. There had been a fight that morning between the stonemasons and the rough-masons over the missing tiles.

Someone cleared his throat behind him, and he turned around. One of those inept lads that followed his betrothed like guard dogs was standing a few feet away from him, rocking from one bare, dusty foot to the other. He looked as if he needed to either speak or visit the privy.

Watching the boy was enough to make him dizzy. "Have your say, lad, or stand still."

"I have a question to ask you, my lord."

Merrick gave him a nod.

"Did you take a table from here?"

He heard Clio utter something and frowned at her. She was shaking her head and waving her hands at the boy.

"I have no idea what you are talking about. What table is missing?"

"Not a 'what' table, but a 'that' table." The boy paused, frowning, then muttered, "Or was it the 'other' table?"

Clio was suddenly at the boy's side, guiding him toward the doorway. "Never mind the tables, Thwack. You go along to the coopers and see if you can help Thud."

A flash of brown sped through the doorway a second later, and Merrick spun toward it, his hand on his dagger.

The other boy scrambled to a clumsy stop in front of his mistress, who grabbed his shoulders to keep from being plowed over.

"My lady! My lady! We have trouble! You must hide from the Red Lion, for they say his anger is fierce. Those siphoning pipes you put in the castle well have—" The boy suddenly noticed Merrick and cut off his words so quickly there was almost an echo.

Merrick did not say a word. He just looked from one pale face to another and another, then turned and stared out the window, searching for something. Patience. Wisdom. Divine intervention.

What he got was the sight of a head covered with fuzzy white hair; it slowly rose up over the rim of the windowsill like a giant dandelion. A pair of wizened black eyes peered right at him. 'Twas the crazed old hag who kept burning bonfires on the nearby hillsides. The sky above that hill was beginning to look like that of London, where the burning coal fires ate the freshness from air and turned it gray.

As Merrick stood there, a rare sense of defeat swept him; it was something he was not used to feeling. He crossed the room to one of the brewing pots, took down an ale horn, and filled it.

Without another word he left the brewery. As he walked out, he could feel the surprised looks of Clio and those lads. He had no idea what they expected. Perhaps they thought he truly would flay the skin from her.

What he truly wanted to do was start this day all over. Or perhaps start his life all over. No. He was lying to himself. What he wanted was to see Clio smile up at him again as if he had just given her the world.

He drove a hand impatiently through his hair as he moved across the castle yard, going somewhere, anywhere. Confusion seemed to fill his head, and he crossed the bailey without stopping or speaking.

When he reached a newly built section of the inner wall, he halted in the shade, moving aside as a caravan of lumber wagons passed by him. Still feeling confused and power-less, he lifted the ale horn to his lips and drank deeply, then wiped his mouth with the back of one hand.

The ale was good, which surprised him. He stared at the horn, then took another swig. It had a flavor he'd never before tasted, even after being in the East, where drinks were spiked with spices and flavors that were exotic and rich and unlike any other.

He rested his back against the wall and drank again, until the ale horn was empty and his thirst quenched. And as he stood in the shade, the cool air grew heavy and heated, as if the sun had come to find him.

Merrick took in deep breaths of air that was dusty from the traffic in the castle yard. He was not feeling himself. Perhaps it was a fever that had entered his blood.

A second later, he had the strangest sensation. As if birds were inside his stomach, a whole flock of them.

He shook his head a few times to shake off an odd and uncharacteristic sense of light-headedness that had swiftly overwhelmed him.

Not much time had passed, and he thank-fully felt somewhat more like himself, so he moved over to where a group of his men were digging a new well. He stood there, watching, then opened his mouth to say something to one of his men.

'Twas then that the oddest thing happened.

Merrick de Beaucourt, the earl of Glamorgan and the famed warrior known as the Red

Lion, did something he had never done in his battle-filled life.

He giggled.

CHAPTER 9

Mornings at the convent had begun with the pleasant chiming of a prayer bell at Prime. Each day dawned for the villeins and townspeople with the predictable crowing of a cock. But at Camrose, the new day started with the incessant pounding of a blacksmith's hammer, the cracking split of a stonemason's chisel, and the recent occurrence of giggles from Earl Merrick's men-at-arms.

Clio sat up in her straw bed and stretched, reaching her arms high in the air and yawning. Cyclops was wedged against her hip, sound asleep and wheezing the congested sound that was his usual snore. Pitt stood perched on the iron rung of a bedside candlelamp, one yellow foot bent up like a child getting ready to hop and his speckled head tucked safely under the down of his left wing.

When she moved, the cat snorted a couple of times, then rolled over on his back, paws curled into the air. She scratched his plump and furry belly and chest. He began to purr so loudly he sounded like a bumble bee.

After a few minutes she pulled her hand back. His eye shot open and stared directly at her with the annoyed look of someone used to having his way. Rather like her betrothed.

The racket from the courtyard below echoed up the keep like summer thunder bellowing in the sky. She glanced at the arched window slit, where a pair of white doves sat on the stone ledge as if they were eavesdropping.

She threw back the woolen covers and got up, then padded across the cool flagstones to the window and sat down on a rough wooden stool. The doves cooed and whirred at her like pets, then suddenly took flight, skimming into the morning sky like two plump white arrows.

The birds were perfectly matched, like the lovebirds she had seen in a cage made of gold at Queen Eleanor's court. They had been a gift from some foreign diplomat. Although Clio's court experience had been brief and unpleasant, she had not forgotten those birds. She recalled how she had imagined her marriage would be like the life of those birds, days of cooing and cuddling and sweet song.

Clio leaned into the window, placing her arms on the ledge. She rested her chin atop them and drifted back to those girlish dreams she had thought abandoned, those times she had sweet-talked herself into believing dreams could come true.

Nothing had been said about a wedding. Merrick never mentioned it. He did not occupy the castle. He camped outside the wall and was busy supervising the rebuilding of Camrose. In the order of things, she assumed the castle was more valuable to him than a wedding. And it hurt her deeply, though she wished she could feel nothing.

Her pride refused to allow her to ask about the marriage herself. She decided to act as if it did not matter to her.

But it did.

She still ached with an intense human need. An emptiness, because she wanted to be cherished and loved. She wanted a husband who was kind to her and who would be her friend. She wanted someone to whom she could tell her darkest secrets and dreams without worrying about being thought frivolous or foolish. She still wanted a family, longed for that kind of life bond. The deaths of her mother, father, and grandparents made the lonely ache in her worse.

Even her old nurse had died, a few years after Clio had gone to the convent, leaving her feeling sucked dry. Like a lone flower in a field. Thud and Thwack were devoted to her, and she cherished that devotion, but it wasn't the same. She needed a stronger bond of love, the kind of love a woman needed to give and receive.

What she wanted deep inside her romantic heart was a knight who would wear daisies for her favor. For when a knight wore an emblem of two daisy blooms on one stem, he was declaring to all the world that he loved a lady and she loved him back.

She sighed with a wasted bit of longing, then turned her attention toward the castle below. The bailey was already bustling. Yet the sun was just creeping over the east hills, where the trees looked like the black teeth of a saw and where curls of smoke still lingered in the tree-tops from one of Old Gladdys's bonfires.

She caught sight of Thud and Thwack moving toward the stable. Thud raced to the entrance, tripping only once, and swung open the wooden gate, twitching with restlessness as he waited.

Thwack moved at his own pace. Behind him was a trail of pigs with their snouts poking at the ground. She smiled. They trotted along behind the lad like favorite dogs.

A small scratching sounded from the heavy chamber doors, and Clio turned just as a young maidservant entered carrying fresh water to the ewer that sat on a small table in the corner. The girl said nothing but crossed the room and opened the door to leave.

"Dulcie?"

The maid turned.

"Has Lord Merrick asked for me?"

"No, my lady."

Clio frowned. Now, that was odd. Every morning he had sent someone to fetch her. She used that demand as a daily beginning for her Fabian plan. It was the marker by which she would calculate her lateness. She glanced up and saw that Dulcie was still waiting at the door.

"He has not been to the keep yet this morning."

"Oh."

"Shall I send someone to find him?"

"No!" Clio snapped. "I mean, no, I do not need anything else. You may go now."

Dulcie closed the door.

Clio washed quickly and dressed in a gray gown that made her skin tone look the same color. She braided her hair and wound it up in those giant coils, then topped it with an ugly pea-green veil with a fillet of bright bloodred and silver ribbons. She looked wonderfully dull and awful, so then raced down the stairs.

As she moved through the great hall, she heard laughter and stopped. A group of Lord Merrick's knights sat at table near her, breaking their fast and giggling like silly goose girls. She had come to the conclusion that Merrick's men-at-arms drank too much. They seemed to become laughing drunkards rather easily.

Ignoring them, she moved into the yard and hurried toward the nearby kitchen, where the transom above the doors was the one she remembered from her past. Her grandmother had had craftsmen carve roses over the doors for good luck.

There was so little left of the Camrose Clio had known. Her life seemed displaced and out of step. She did not feel she was truly home, until she saw these intricately carved roses.

Her step and mood were lighter when she left the building that housed the kitchens, and she carried a cabbage leaf filled with plump wild strawberries, the juicy deep-red kind that always stained her mouth.

Geese fluttered about the hem of her gown as she moved through the yard, sucking on the tangy, sweet berries. A tinker's cart rattled past on its way toward the kitchens, where the cooks would haggle and bargain until the poor man took less for his shiny pans and cast iron pots then he could get from selling a dull knife at the local fair.

As she stepped into the cart tracks, she heard a squeal and spun around. Two of the castle pigs were inside willow cages in the back of the tinker's cart.

Something was wrong. She could not imagine Thud or Thwack giving up two of those piglets.

She headed straight to the stables. She entered the gates and went past where some of the cattle lowed in the cow shippen. Merrick's horses had been stabled inside and were munching on hay and oats from wooden troughs that had been nailed up inside each stall.

From the other side of the building near the equerry that had become the gathering place of the squires came the sound of loud voices and the banging clank of swordplay.

She marched past the beasts and rounded the corner.

There inside a circle of older boys was Thud. He had a tin pot atop his head like a helm, except the handle stuck out over his left ear, and whenever he moved, the pot slid down into his eyes. Strapped to his chest like armor shields were metal pastry sheets, and in his hand he clutched a long roasting rod, which he was using to fend off the polished sword of a squire who was twice his size.

The squire brought his sword down hard on the roasting rod, and metal clanged so loudly she flinched and had to shake her head to clear it.

She wasn't the only one. Thwack was on the ground with leather straps and baking sheets around him. He was pounding the heel of his hand against his ear while he blinked. Next to him on the ground was a tin pot like Thud's, only the whole left side was dented.

The squires jeered and hooted and harassed the poor boys so loudly no one heard her cry of protest. She shoved her way into the circle, grabbed the dented pot, and flung it right at the bully who was fighting with Thud.

The squire glanced up and ducked.

The pot sailed past him.

'Twas unfortunate timing indeed, for at that very moment the earl rounded the corner.

The pot bashed him right in the center of his forehead.

CHAPTER 10

Someone was calling his name.

"Merrick?"

Ah. 'Twas his betrothed. She sounded far away. Had he indeed locked her in a tower?

"My lord?"

His squire, Tobin.

"Dominus vobiscum."

Who was this speaking? A priest. Latin. Last Rites? Who had died?

Merrick opened his eyes.

'Twas raining.

He blinked and his vision cleared.

Brother Dismas was sprinkling holy water over him and praying for his wretched soul.

"God's feet!" Merrick bellowed. "I'm not dead, you fool!" He tried to sit up, but a thousand wee candle flames flickered before his eyes, and his head felt as if someone had tried to cleave it in two.

He lay back down with a pithy string of curses. His head throbbed now, so he winced, then gave a low moan.

Water dribbled on his face.

He opened one eye. "If you shake that water in my face one more time..."

"My Lord God says that his holy water 'twill make you pure of heart and protect your vile human soul."

A growl escaped from Merrick's mouth and he reached for the monk with his huge hands, but someone pulled the thick-headed man safely out of his line of vision.

The next thing he saw was Clio's face staring down at him. Her skin looked almost too pale.

He dropped his arms to his sides and felt the dry dirt beneath him. He was lying on the hard ground.

"What happened?" he asked her.

"I hit you in the head with a pot."

He was not surprised. He heard the worried whispers of his men. The squires and many of his men-at-arms formed a ring around them.

Lady Clio was still searching his face for something while she chewed on her lower lip.

His gaze locked with hers. "Was I good?"

She frowned, clearly startled. "Good at what?"

"Whatever it was that made you fling a pot at me."

He heard his men laugh. Yet she did not. She looked angry. She had hit him with a pot and there was no contrition in her expression, nor in her manner.

There was no fear. No apology. Instead she grew haughty again, that chin came up and her mouth thinned into a familiar stubborn line.

He stared long and hard at her lips, for they were the only color on her face. They were stained red and looked sweet and inviting and as if she had reddened them to torture him.

'Twas time.

His hand shot up and pulled her head down to his so swiftly she fell across his chest. His mouth closed over hers, hard and open, and his arms clamped around her, holding her where he wanted her.

She struggled against him, squirmed and made muffled sounds against his mouth, so he rolled over, pinning her under him in the dirt.

The air erupted with the whoops and whistles of his men. She opened her mouth and tried to cry out, so he plunged his tongue inside.

Her struggles ceased and she grew still as stone. He opened his eyes as he kissed her, as he stroked her mouth with his full tongue.

Her startled gaze was staring back at him. And in those eyes he saw desire and passion and more.

Then she bit him.

Clio shoved at Merrick's shoulders and he rolled off of her with a muttered curse. She could hear the men behind them laughing quietly.

She scrambled to her feet and glared down at him. "You had no right to do that."

He seemed to grow before her eyes. A moment later he was standing before her, tall and intimidating and truly angry. They stood barely a foot apart.

"No right?" he asked with lethal quietness.

"Aye." Her response was clipped and firm and meant to spite him.

"You are mine, Clio." His voice was measured and even, the kind of voice that brooked no argument. "You seem to have forgotten that."

"No. I did not forget, my lord. You are the one who forgot." She paused, then said exactly what she was thinking, "For six years."

For an instant there was no sound. Nothing. Her words just hung in the air to taunt him. The men began to back away, mumbling. She heard someone speak fearfully of the Red

Lion and his reputation. Another man called her a fool.

But she would not back down. She had lost so much already. Her home, her pride, and now her dignity.

All round them the men began to disperse.

"Tobin!" he called out to his squire, never taking his gaze from her. "I would speak with you."

The squire who had been beating on Thud stopped near the corner of the stables. He no longer looked so cocky. Thud and Thwack had scrambled away the moment Merrick awoke.

Merrick broke his gaze from her and moved toward his squire.

She exhaled.

He stopped and glanced back at her. "Wait here."

They were a few strides apart when she said quietly, "You seem to have a penchant for leaving me to wait, my lord."

He ground to a halt and stood so still he looked rooted to the ground.

Immediately she wanted to take the words back.

He turned very slowly and looked at her from narrowed eyes. "I did not think waiting here a moment would so tax your spirit."

Since she was already sinking into a deep hole from which she would have no easy time escaping, she decided to go down fighting. "I am well used to waiting for you. I do not like it."

His look was long, hard, and seemed to

see into places she wanted hidden. He crossed his arms. "Why do I have the feeling that at any moment you will stamp your foot?"

She could feel her face flush with embarrassment. She remembered her father speaking to her in such a way when she was a small child. It galled her that he was right; she was acting foolishly.

But pride was such a hard thing to give up, especially when her pride had been so terribly wounded by the way he had neglected her.

Those two years had seemed like a lifetime to her. The daily looks of those who knew she'd been forgotten or perhaps even abandoned. The pity in their eyes had pricked her pride more than any chiding could have.

She'd had such wild dreams of what love and marriage should be. But those dreams had slowly died, hour by hour, until every day that she waited for him stretched out before her like a long and endless road to nowhere.

" 'Tis not important." She waved a hand loftily in the air. "Go about your business as you will, my lord. I shall wait." She paused, and some devil inside her made her add, "I'm becoming so good at it."

He closed the distance between them with a few long strides. "Forget what I said." His words came through gritted teeth.

He took her arm in a firm grasp that made her gasp.

"I have changed my mind. I should like to have your company, *my lady*."

He spun around with her so quickly she

became lightheaded; then he headed for the keep.

She had to quicken her steps to keep up with those long strides of his. As she trotted along beside him, the silken coif and circlet covering her coiled hair slipped to one side.

Muttering, she slapped her hand down on it and struggled to keep up with her betrothed—the earl of Quickfeet.

CHAPTER 11

Merrick did not care to be reminded of his faults, particularly in front of the whole castle, and especially by Clio, someone who he wished would see him as a man. Not as if he were ready to kill her at any moment. She seemed to be trying with a strong purpose to force him to react that way. 'Twas as if she were trying to goad him into something.

He did not know what she wanted from him. He had always found women to be odd creatures whose thoughts were so different from his. He was trained to speak openly, honestly, as frankness was revered in men.

Yet women seemed to say one thing and act as if they wanted something else. He had the hardest time trying to understand them. He never knew whether to listen to what they said or watch the way they acted.

Frustrated, he half dragged her with him to the great hall, behaving like the brute she had implied he was.

He sat in the high-backed chair meant for the lord of the castle. He waved a hand toward the smaller chair next to him and looked at Clio. "Sit."

She did not move swiftly, but his squire did. The lad sat down on one of the lower benches.

"Not you, Tobin!" Merrick barked at the young man, who shot to his feet.

Tall and blond and muscular, Tobin de Clare was a strapping boy of sixteen, and nephew to the earl of Chester, one of the most powerful noblemen in all of England. The lad would make a good knight, if he ever chanced to learn some humility.

Clio was still standing near Merrick. He turned back and gave her a pointed look that made the knot on his forehead throb. She finally sat down with a loud sigh that sounded as if she was annoyed.

For just one instant he felt a flash of understanding for those men who had locked their wives away in a tower. More than likely it was not to protect the women from their enemies, but from their husbands' anger.

He studied his squire for a long time, a calculated move to make the lad squirm.

The silence dragged on, and finally Merrick spoke. "I heard some tale of a fight between you and those puny lads. 'Twas the reason I happened to be rounding the corner when my lady, here, sought to crack open my head."

" 'Twould take more than a tin pot to crack open that rock you claim is your head," Clio muttered.

He scowled at her. "What was that?"

"Nothing," she said blithely. "I was only praying."

"A good idea, especially if you said what I think you said." His tone should have warned her to keep quiet. Experience, however, convinced him she would probably not heed such a tone.

"I had little else to do *but* pray for all those years at the convent."

After he counted to fifty and made it a point to sit on his hands, he managed to ignore her. He turned back to his squire. "Have you nothing to say, Tobin?"

Clio shot to her feet and planted her small hands on the table. She glared at Tobin. "He can say nothing that would justify what he did. He was beating up on those poor boys for amusement."

"That is not true." Tobin gave Merrick a direct look, then turned to Clio and made a small bow. "Begging your pardon, my lady, but they wished to fight. 'Twas their idea."

"I see," Merrick said, resting an elbow on the table and rubbing his chin. "Two young orphan lads who have no training experience, who must use kitchen tools for arms, and who barely have enough sense to come in out of the rain, challenge you, a trained swordsman, to a mock battle, and out of the goodness of your heart, you decided to beat the holy hell out of them?"

Tobin blanched.

Merrick bellowed for the guard. The man ran over from his post at door and made a quick bow. "Aye, my lord."

"Bring those two young lads here." Merrick paused. "Thump and Thwart."

"Thud and Thwack," Clio said indignantly, which seemed to be the only way she spoke to him.

"Bring them here," Merrick repeated. "Now."

The guard hurried from the hall. From outside he could hear the bustle of the castle yards, the constant sounds of building, and the barking of a dog. Then the heavy doors closed and the noises were muted.

Within the great hall there was little sound, something Merrick wished to use to his advantage. He sat there with his lady, both silent, while Tobin stood before them.

Merrick had not invited the young man to sit. He wanted him standing and wondering and worrying.

Beside him, Clio wiggled slightly; then from the corner of his eye he felt her look at him. She wanted to speak. He could feel it, like a live thing between them.

Lord, but she was a stubborn one.

"What are you going to do to them?" Clio finally asked.

He turned to her. "Do not fret over it, my

lady. There are other things that should be worrying you."

"Such as?"

"Your mouth for one."

"It did not seem to bother you, my lord, when you had your tongue in it."

Tobin made a choking sound, and Merrick whipped his head back around. His squire had turned away and had his hands locked behind his back and he was engrossed in examining the roof beams.

The doors to the hall creaked open, and the guard came back with the boys in tow. He stood before Merrick, holding them by their tunic collars, a lad in each hand.

Clio stood. "Release them."

The guard's eyes never left Merrick's face. It was as if she had not spoken. He trained his men well and they were loyal and true.

He placed his hand over hers. "Sit down. I will handle this."

She started to snatch her hand away, but his fingers held on to hers firmly. She looked as if she wanted to say something, but she did not. She sat.

"Tell me, lads, why you challenged the squires."

Thud straightened and took a brave breath that made his bony chest puff out like a pigeon's. "We wish to be knights, my lord. We wish to fight, for practice."

"I do not want to fight anymore this day, Thud." Thwack was still nursing a knot on his head. "My head hurts."

Merrick felt a jolt of sympathy for the lad. His own forehead was beginning to hurt like hell.

Thud jabbed the lad with his elbow. "We *both* want to be knights, sir. We wish to train with the pages and squires."

Tobin burst out laughing as if the idea were the most amusing thing he'd ever heard. "Those two? Knights?" He howled.

Clio's fingers tightened within Merrick's grasp.

He waited for Tobin to stop laughing. "You find that amusing."

"Aye." Tobin was still grinning, the cocky fool.

Merrick was quiet for a long time, thinking, then he looked at the boys. Thud was tousled-headed and had a nose like a spaniel—wide and covered with brown freckles.

Thwack was snub-nosed and had a wide mouth and serious brown eyes. Both boys had dirt smudges and bruises and scrapes on their faces and necks. They were a sorry pair, but there was something about them, an eagerness to please that made him think long and hard about what he should do.

"I have a rule about my men fighting amongst themselves. You are all aware of this rule."

All three of them suddenly wore expressions of dread.

"If I do not punish you, others will believe my orders can be disobeyed." Merrick stood. He turned toward Clio and extended his hand. "Come, my lady."

She looked at his hand as if it were a coiled snake.

"I would not dare ask you to wait again," he added with a cutting tone, then turned to the lads. "You will follow us."

They left the great hall. Clio walked by his side. When they were in the bailey, he could feel her watching him.

"What will you do to them?"

"You shall see."

"I do not want them harmed. I will not let you beat them."

"I do not beat young boys." He paused. "Only women who do not know when to hold their tongues."

"I am not afraid of you, Merrick."

She called him by his given name. Finally. He stopped by one of the towers and gave some instructions to a guard.

Tobin and the younger boys stood there, trying to look brave. Merrick could see and feel their apprehension, something he wanted them to feel as part of the lesson he wanted to teach them.

The guard returned with a cart and shovels.

Merrick stood tall before the lads, then pointed at a wooden trapdoor near the base of the tower. "You will clean out this latrine pit."

Their faces grew tight with horror.

"And every latrine pit. At every corner of the keep and at the gates."

"Every pit?" Tobin repeated. "But, my lord, there are ten pits."

Merrick crossed his arms over his chest. "I know how many there are."

The lads all looked green. 'Twas hard to keep from laughing at them. "I suggest you start now. 'Twill take a few days if you work hard and work together."

He turned to Clio. "Come now, my lady. Let us leave them to their work." He led her back across the bailey. As they walked she kept looking back over her shoulder.

"Thud and Thwack did nothing to deserve this," she said as they neared the inner gate.

"They disobeyed the rules. They have to be punished."

"But it was your bully of a squire who fought with them. He is older and wiser and more experienced. He could have wounded them. They could have had serious injuries."

He stopped and leaned against the stone curtain wall. He looked down at her. "Like getting hit in the head with a pot?"

She did not know when to cease her argument. "They are only boys. Special boys. Do you know where they were found?"

"Under a rock during a full moon?"

"It is not an amusing tale, my lord. They were abandoned in the forest. When they were found, they spoke but only single words. They ate raw meat and crawled on the ground, sniffing at it."

"I can do nothing about their past."

"You can be gentle with them. They need kindness."

"And what will happen when they grow up being treated like babes? You think that will help them?"Merrick gave a sardonic laugh. "You do them no favor by coddling them."

"And you do by punishing them?"

"I will do as I think best." He held his hand out to her. "Come now."

She didn't move, but stood there glaring at him.

He looked away for a moment. The thought crossed his mind that he might need to have one of the castle blacksmiths make a strong lock for the west tower.

He counted to ten. When he looked to her again, she had her back to him. Exasperated, he exhaled and closed the short distance between them. "Turn around, Clio."

She did not move. It looked as if she were not even breathing.

He took her by the shoulders and turned her around.

She glared up at him, her expression all stubborn pride. His gaze left her eyes and moved to her mouth, set in a firm line that said, "I will not let you break me."

He had no patience left this day; it had been taxed to his limit. He pulled her against his chest. "You push me too hard. I will not take this from a woman. I will not take this disrespect from you." He grabbed her chin and forced her to look up at him.

"Don't!" She struggled in his embrace,

wiggling and squirming while her hands pushing against his chest.

He swore to himself that he would not force a kiss on her again. He wanted her to come to him of her own free will. He released her and stepped back so swiftly she stumbled. He grabbed her arm to steady her.

She scowled at him, then gave his hand a pointed look. "Do not touch me."

He did not release her this time, but stood there, holding her arm. Their gazes were locked in a battle of wills, and with each second that passed their breath came in short, angry pants.

She was looking at him as if she expected something, as if she almost wanted him to react.

"I will not ravish you, Clio."

She gave him a long hard look, then raised her chin. "Why not?"

He stood there, dumbfounded. Surely she hadn't just asked him that. "What did you say?"

"I asked you why not?" She planted her fists on her hips in that way she had and added, "Do I not appeal to you, my lord?"

He drove a hand through his hair and looked away, asking heaven for patience with this woman, which was like asking to find the Holy Grail.

She stood just inches before him, her chin jutting out and her hands on her hips as if she were not barely half his size.

There was a challenge in her eyes and she said, "We shall have an interesting marriage

if you cannot even bear to consummate it."
She shook her head the way his warhorse did
when he reined him in too quickly.

"Annulments have been granted for such sit-
uations," she foolishly continued, having no
idea of the dangerous line she had crossed. "Perhaps 'tis a good thing that you find my looks
not to your taste, my lord earl."

Her tone was too casual, as if she spoke about
something menial, like fleas or firewood or a
meal, not about his manhood or something as
important to both of them as a blood bond of
marriage. Very quietly and slowly—with much
control—he spoke, "I have said nothing of your
looks nor of my reaction to them."

"I am aware of that fact. Certainly you do
not wish to wed me for myself, but for Camrose and the king's favor."

"My motives for marrying you are none of
your concern."

She laughed at him without humor.

"Do not worry yourself over the consum-
mation, my lady. I promise you our marriage
will be consummated so often the servants will
have no time to change the bed linen."

"Ha!"

There it was. The one word that could
make his blood boil. His anger was so strong
it almost clogged his throat.

He stood barely a foot away from her and
fixed his darkest look on her defiantly upturned
face. "One more word from you, mademoiselle,
and I will consummate our union against this
castle wall."

CHAPTER 12

"I'm glad to find you surrounded by peace and quiet, my friend."

Merrick jerked his black gaze away from Clio at the sound of Roger FitzAlan's amused voice.

Roger stood in the shadow of an archway, a shoulder resting against the wall of the gate tower and one foot propped casually on one of the stone steps that led to the tower parapet.

He stepped out of the shadows and looked at Merrick with a wry gleam in his eye and an irritating smile that broke too brightly through his neatly clipped red beard.

Merrick glanced down at Clio. She was standing toe-to-toe with him, glaring at him the same way he had been glaring at her. To anyone watching they must have looked like two angry bulls ready to butt heads.

His anger had been so consuming that he had not thought of where they were or who was near. He had been that angry.

Yet all around them were the sounds and motions of the castle's renovation. Men shouted orders to workers while guards directed the building materials and supplies that seemed to appear an endless line into the castle.

Blacksmith's hammers rang in the distance and sounded like war swords clashing together on a battlefield. Rope winches with gears that needed oiling squealed as heavy tubs of lime mortar were raised to the upper battlements, where freshly hewn stone girded with long iron posts made the new walls at Camrose stronger than those of any other castle on the Marches.

Supply carts squeaked and rumbled through the gates, their teams goaded by men who whistled the oxen forward. Broad and sturdy stone wagons with long lines of huge draft teams lugged stacks of smooth square slate tiles that would line the new arrow loops. As those wagons rolled over the old wooden bridge that spanned the newly emptied moat, the studded cart wheels made constant creaking and tapping sounds.

Roger closed the distance between them and clapped Merrick on the shoulder. "All you need now are the Welsh."

There were times when Roger could be damned obnoxious; this was one of them.

Roger turned to Clio, gallantly taking her small hand and bowing low over it while he praised "the beauty of the rose-petaled flush in her lovely cheeks." Pinning her with a heated look, Roger slowly raised her fingers to his lips, kissed them, then turned her hand, and kissed her palm.

Merrick had seen his friend perform this same gesture whenever his mind was bent on a sly seduction. He also knew Roger well enough to know he did this with a purpose in mind. Something that had nothing to do with Clio and everything to do with goading Merrick into a spate of jealousy.

It was working.

Merrick had the sudden urge to plant his boot on Roger's leather-covered ass and shove. Hard.

Clio smiled brightly the way she seldom smiled at him, completely taken in by Roger's romantic ways, which did nothing to cool Merrick's temper.

Then she sweetly asked Roger to join her for late mass and their supper meal following.

Roger looked at Merrick over the top of her blond head and winked.

Since Merrick had arrived at the castle late that first night, he had yet to take any meal with her. She never came down, even when he had made a point of saying he would see her there. He scowled down at her, unable to stop himself.

She quickly made some excuse about leaving her lord earl to his well problem, and before Merrick could stop her, she hurried off toward the keep.

Roger looked at him. "So what is happening with your well?"

"Nothing I cannot handle easily."

"Are you certain? I can help. I don't mind being a part of this."

"I don't doubt it," Merrick groused. "Since you think you're a part of everything."

Roger laughed. "Not everything, my friend. Just that which you are too hardheaded to take advantage of."

But Merrick only heard him with half an ear, for he was intently watching her weave a path through the bustling outer bailey, around horses that were twice her size, past honking geese that had nipped at his ankles, and dogs that yapped at the rolling carts.

He was well aware that Roger watched her as he did, and he felt his friend's puzzled look. But Merrick could no more look away than he could act as if he did not see the sun. He stood there silently, feeling unsettled and restless, the way he felt just before a battle.

She moved past an oxcart that carried huge stone grinding wheels for the mill and some iron gears for the new portcullis. Their size made her look even smaller, farther away, like something he sought that was just beyond reach.

After the cart passed, Merrick lost sight of her. But his mind had not lost her image, nor had he lost the powerful effect one small woman could have on him. He could still see her small straight back, the proud lift of her head, and the long blond braid that hung down her back so thickly and brushed over her body, back and forth, back and forth, whenever she walked.

The image took him on a moment's journey back to that first night at Camrose, when he and Roger had come upon her in the chamber off the solar. The night she had been dancing out that sprightly charade by the golden light of a burning candle.

His first sight of Lady Clio had hit him like

112

a war hammer. Fate had given him a lady so fair, so full of life, that he had only stood there, dumbfounded, watching her performance.

He had told Roger the truth when he'd said he'd never pondered her looks. But the moment he saw her, he changed how he thought.

She was small. The top of her head did not even reach his shoulder. Yet her presence in a room affected him more than he could fathom. 'Twas as if some giant had entered the room and the walls had suddenly begun to close in. A tight feeling he could not explain.

The first thing he had noticed when he stood in the arched doorway was her hair. It hung clear to the backs of her knees and was a light silver color he'd only seen once before— when he'd been lying under a purple night sky in the desert, waiting for a battle that would begin at dawn.

That night had been filled with shooting stars, hundreds of them. None of the men there had ever seen the like. Some fell on their knees, confessing all, for they feared the world was ending.

Others drank too much wine and later did not remember the spectacle. But Merrick had lain there most of that starry night, on a pallet outside of his tent, and he'd watched the brilliant twisted star-trails above him.

Like now, when he watched the lost image of one small woman.

CHAPTER 13

At the high table in the great hall that eve, Clio sat between Merrick and Sir Roger, and fought the urge to fall asleep facedown in her trencher.

The spiced rabbit and wild truffles had been served with flaming quail on swords. But the two men did not notice. Instead, they debated how many rocks would have to be heaved from a standard mangonel to smash a hole in the four-foot-strong curtain wall.

Along with dishes of golden leeks and braised greens came the trumpeting of the castle heralds, while Sir Merrick and Sir Roger discussed the perfect dimensions of the new arrow loops—splayed on the inside so the archer could take aim, taller than before for longbows—horizontal slits were a must for a broader ranger of fire, and finally they agreed they must add circular oeillets to accommodate the larger crossbows.

A few delicate glass panes or the old polished horn held no practical value for strengthening Camrose, according to Merrick. The two of them laughed at the foolish thought. For anyone would know that they would break when hit by an enemy's missile.

Clio found herself thinking longingly about missiles.

She dropped her chin onto her propped-up fist and imagined how her betrothed would look with leeks dripping down his head.

When Sir Roger's own squire rose to play the lute, the servants came parading from the kitchens with rich frumenty and almond cream with fresh pears pickled in cinnamon cider. Yet the two men on either side of Clio did not notice.

They had moved on to discuss *ad nauseam* the types of foul loads for the trebuchet, the latest mining techniques, and the proper widths and lengths of trees from which to make the strongest battering rams and locating those trees.

Clio stared at the lump of pudding on her silver spoon with the falcon-shaped handle. If she gripped the handle in her fist, then took her other hand and pulled back on the bowl of the spoon, the cream should arc through the air...

"Perhaps Lady Clio will sing a song for us," Sir Roger said suddenly, turning to took at her.

She dropped the spoon in her lap. "Me? Sing?" She picked up the spoon, then swiped at the cream on her gown.

She glanced up once to see Brother Dismas backing out of the room with a face that was pinched and pale. He suddenly had candles to light and prayers to recite that could no longer wait.

Thud left in his usual rush—"to feed the swine"—and even Thwack moved more quickly than Clio had thought he could. Out of the corner of her eye, she watched some of those who remembered her make their quick excuses, while the old servants were sneaking out of the room.

They knew her well. Too well.

Singing was not something Clio did with any amount of expertise. In fact, her father had forbade her to sing, and eventually, to even hum in his presence.

"I know no war ballads," she said, giving Merrick a direct look.

"For our entertainment only, my lady," Sir Roger said, smiling. "Surely you will bless us with a song. Any song."

Merrick watched her intently, as if he hadn't been ignoring her throughout the meal. She almost declined; then the last couple of endless dining hours flashed through her head.

'Twould serve them right if she did sing. She slowly scanned the room and saw the bully squires looking up at her expectantly. In fact, now that she noticed it, every man in the room wore that male look of overweening and pride-filled expectation—as if they were saying, "I'm ready now to be pleasured and amused by *the woman*."

She could feel the slow warmth of satisfaction spread through her. She stood slowly and with great dignity, then gave a small curtsy. " 'Twould be my pleasure to entertain you good knights."

She walked to a seat near the large fireplace, where the lute player was sitting, strumming a quiet tune. She leaned down and told him the song; then she began:

There were three men came down from Kent
to plow for wheat and rye...

The men sat still as stone; their jaws hung open like those of village idiots. She could hear her voice, loud and screechy, like the sawing of metal upon metal. Each word echoed up in the broad, arched rafters of the hall. From the corner of her eye, she could see the lute player flinch as each higher note scratched forth from her throat.

And these three men made a solemn vow.
John Barleycorn should die.
Then with a plow they plowed him up
and thus they did devise to bury him
within the earth and swore he would not rise...

Sir Roger looked as if he wanted to slap his hands over his ears, but he managed a sick and weak smile when she walked near him and hit a purposely high note.

Outside, the birds were flying away from Camrose in flocks. The swine shoved their snouts into the hay in the stable, snorting and sniffing and making whining sounds. The cattle bawled, and the horses battered the gates, trying to get away from the noise.

Inside, Clio had moved to stand behind her betrothed, and she raised her voice higher, sharper, and louder.

Amazingly the man did not flinch. Seemed 'twould take more than her screeching to pierce his thick head. But Clio was never one to give up.

She went right into the fifth verse.

It was, after all, the longest song she knew.

At verse ten, when one or two men had finally succumbed to a few groans, and one brave lad had rested his head on the table, she stood in the middle of the hall and threw her voice as far into the air has she could.

> *Barleycorn is the very best seed*
> *That ever was sowed on the land.*
> *For it would do the heart most good*
> *In the turning of man's hand.*

Clio finished the final verse. The lute player had stopped two verses before.

She gave them an innocent smile, then sank to a deep curtsy. "Now that you have been properly entertained, I shall take my leave."

She turned around and, with her head held high, slowly and gracefully left the room.

There was stunned silence in the great hall, the only sounds the distant tapping of Lady Clio's feet on the stone steps, the snapping of the thick green logs in the fireplace, and the dull ringing in every man's ears. Each one of them wore the same expression—one of absolute befuddlement...and pain.

There was a sudden clatter in the entrance of the hall and the front door flew open with a loud bang—a pleasant sound to those who had been witness to the song. Three of the parapet guards, the lookouts, came rushing inside.

The largest man stopped before the earl. "We have a problem, my lord." The man was out of breath.

"What?"

"The castle walls, my lord."

Roger leaned toward Merrick, whispering because he probably could not hear himself. "Perhaps your lady's voice cracked the curtain wall."

"I wouldn't be surprised." Merrick winced, his own hearing still tender. "I think she cracked my ears." He looked back at the guardsmen. "What is the problem?"

"Wolves, my lord."

"Wolves?"

"Aye." The guard had a look of horror. "There are wolves at the walls."

Both Merrick and Roger were silent for a moment; then Roger gave a loud bark of laughter, and Merrick felt his own lips curl with the start of a smile.

"There are packs of them, my lord."

Roger was laughing so hard he was pounding the table with a fist.

The guard was perfectly serious when he looked at Merrick and added, "The wolves are howling at us as if we were the moon."

Only a day later the earl of Warmongers turned Clio's plans for a herbal workspace into a storage room for arrow quarrels and empty firepots. She stood at her chamber window and glared out at the tent in the distance. She was surprised there were not pointed stakes poking through the tent cloth, just to make certain he had a good defense.

He was meeting with Master James of St. George, the architect and master mason, and had sent one of the servants to fetch her. The two men were probably plotting how they could use her clothing pegs to display Welsh heads.

She placed her hands on the window ledge and scanned the sky. Not a rain cloud to be seen.

Cyclops was sound asleep in the corner. No restless cats either. Pitt was perched on the cat's head.

With a huge sigh, Clio looked at the tent, imagining it in a downpour. 'Twas a shame the sun chose to shine so brightly this day. Rain would have made her happier.

She plopped down on the lumpy hay tick that topped her bed and spent a while fiddling with her prayer beads. Bored with that, she set them down, then moved around the room, reciting Greek letters: *Alpha, beta, gamma, delta...*

Just for good measure she sang the French alphabet: *Ah, bay, say...*She danced the *capriole* while she conjugated French verbs, then memorized some verses of the Gospel according to John in Latin.

Over two hours after the servant had come for her, Clio left her chamber.

120

CHAPTER 14

"Sir Merrick has left, my lady."

Clio stared up at Sir Isambard, a stocky man with long curly brown hair and a broad nose under yellow eyes that looked like a wolf's. His stern face never showed what he was thinking; he always wore the same serious look.

He was in charge of Merrick's men-at-arms, and though he was not tall like Merrick and Sir Roger, he was stocky like the dairyman's prized bull and looked as if he could take on an army all by himself.

"He has left?" Clio leaned and stretched onto her toes so she could glance around Sir Isambard and out at the field beyond. The tent was gone, along with some of the men and horses. "Where?"

"He did not say, my lady." The burly knight stood in front of the castle gates as straight and solid as an old rowan. His huge sword was extended across the open section of gate to keep her from passing through.

She stepped back, then asked, "Where is Master James?"

"Inspecting the curtain wall, my lady."

"Fine, then I shall meet with him myself." She grabbed her gown in her fists and moved to step around the sword.

The knight shifted with her, still blocking her way.

She gave him the same look she had received from Eleanor, now the queen mother, and the abbess, Eleanor's cousin.

"Let me pass."

"The earl gave orders that you were not to leave the castle."

"He did what?"

"He said you were to stay inside the castle walls."

"I certainly will not." She started to duck under the sword, but the knight lowered it. "Remove that weapon from my path." Clio waved a hand as if she were swatting away a pesky fly.

"I'm sorry, my lady, but I cannot. I have my orders."

"I just gave you an order."

"Aye."

She took a step toward the gate.

He moved the sword. "I'm sorry I cannot obey your order."

Clio stared up at him. 'Twas like conversing with a stone wall. She waited a moment, but no idea popped into her head, so she spun around and marched away, her mind whirring like a spinning wheel. She slowed her steps, her hands clasped behind her back. She stopped, then casually turned back. "Do you like ale, sir knight?"

"Aye," he answered, his face stoic.

"Good." She smiled. "I'll have one of the maids bring you a tankard."

"I would be grateful, my lady."

Ah-ha! Clio thought, and bit back a smile

of utter satisfaction. Sometimes men could be so easy. One just must find their weakness.

"Just as soon as my watch is over," Sir Isambard added.

She mentally groaned, then tried again. "Are you not thirsty, sir?"

"Aye."

"Good, I'll fetch—" She turned around.

"But I'm not thirsty for ale, my lady. Not while it's my time on guard."

She stopped. The man had integrity. Amazing. She began to walk away in frustration.

"My lady?"

She paused and peered back over her shoulder.

"A cup of water would be welcome."

"Water," she repeated in a dull tone.

"Aye. Water from my lord's new well."

She nodded. Water, she thought. From his lord's new well. She walked back toward the keep, then sent a servant for Sir Isambard's water.

A few moments later she was inside the hall and walking up the steps to the upper chambers. She paused and looked down at the gate. The old knight was still standing guard, stiff and straight and immovable as the portcullis behind him.

So his lord gave orders that she was not to leave the castle. She scowled out the loophole. She was a prisoner.

Not a happy prospect. And she resented the high-handed way he treated her. There was no reason why she could not go outside the gates. She had left plenty of times to gather herbs and roots in woods. What did he expect? A troop of infidels to come thundering to their walls and snatch her away?

This was not the East. He'd been too long in the sun and too long at war. Did he think the world was at war with him?

Sighing in frustration, she crossed her arms on the loop opening and rested her chin atop them. She stared at the gate guard. There was no way he would let her pass.

Frustrated, she tapped her fingers impatiently on the stone ledge. "I wonder what would happen if I were to stand on the barbican wall right above the guard and tip a bucket of...*hmmmm*...a bucket of fresh eels? Perhaps. A pail of week-old flounder tails? Maybe...

As it turned out, Clio did not have to pour fish parts on the loyal knight's head to gain her freedom.

Instead she had concocted a truly wonderful idea!

She wrapped her hair in a length of heavy linen and twisted it into a fat turban. On her face and hands she smeared fine black sap from the outer shells of some walnuts that were stored in the granary.

By the time she was finished, she looked. like a Turk. Almost. The final touch was a long striped robe she pilfered from the castle laundry.

Then Clio had set out to blithely ride through the castle gates on Lord Merrick's favorite Arab horse, with its white blaze and stockings blacked over with more walnut sap.

No one had suspected. She was just congratulating herself for her most brilliant of plans, when she happened to glance back over her shoulder.

Pitt was swinging on the horse's tail. "Pitt!" she hissed. "Get off."

But he clung to the tail with his beak and talons, swinging back and forth the way he loved to swing on her braid.

She looked ahead of her. The late gate was only a few paces away. Fortune had been with her that no one had seen him yet, since her pets were the subjects of jest with the men.

She slid from the horse, pretended that she was checking a hoof, then stood and strolled to her mount's tail. She whipped open her robe and whispered, "Get in here!" She snatched up Pitt and hid him inside the robe.

After remounting, she prodded the horse forward and could feel Pitt nestle comfortably into her side. She rode through the gates with ease, and into the market crowd.

'Twas almost too simple, she thought. Once she was out of clear sight, she leapt off the horse and opened her robe. She let Pitt perch on her shoulder and walked over pillowy downs of rabbit warrens and grasses so springy they made the movement easier and gave a light bounce to her step.

Pitt walked off her shoulder and down her arm. He hopped onto the Arab's head and perched there, perfectly happy. She laughed at him. Pitt seemed to feel the freedom of the outlands as she did.

Mere moments later she tucked up her skirt and ran barelegged in the warm sunshine.

Free! She was free!

With a sense of pure joy she kicked off her shoes and ran in carefree circles around the Arab horse that had followed her and was grazing in a lush little dell between two gently sloping green hills.

There was still dew deep in the spongy grasses; it was cool and tingled the soles of her bare feet. She laughed aloud and spun 'round with her arms out like a quintain.

Her laughter was free and easy and seemed to rise up with the air the same way a breeze would capture and lift the tiny feathers of a dandelion puff. She looked up high into the heavens, closed her eyes, and savored her freedom.

'Twas quiet this day, peaceful. The sky was blue as a hedgesparrow's egg and the clouds thin and puffy and the color of lambsdown. You could taste the out of doors, clear and clean and so alive. There was only the barest of sounds: the tinkle of a sheep's bell. The flapping wings of wild swans flying overhead. The distant cry of a plover.

Over the next hillside she went with the horse following behind her like Thud's suckling pigs. Here, near the forest, the grass was

126

thicker, sweeter, freshly mown and edged with harebells.

At the rim of the Great Forest, woodpigeons hovered in the sessile oak trees and sparrows and larks flitted from branch to branch. Insects hummed a constant tune from deep within the forest depths like mysterious sirens calling out and saying, "Come, come...come, come...

She tied Lord Merrick's fine Arab horse to the limb of a giant chestnut tree.

A horse chestnut.

She found that terribly witty. She held out her hand to Pitt, but he ignored her. He was happy as could be, just perched on the horse's rump. "Fine, my feathered friend. You may stay here."

She gave him a stroke, then did the same to the Arab's muzzle, and took off into the woods, her skirts held high in her hands and a jaunt in her step while she hummed an off-key song about a woman's wicked cleverness.

It was cool in the forest and the air damp; the mosses and lichens smelled savory and verdant and as if they could give her ale the rich touch of magic. From the base of a massive tree, she gathered some medicinal plants and pungent weeds for flavoring and stuck them in a leather pouch that hung from a delicate chain of silver on her belt.

She then moved onward, deeper into the forest.

Here, the trees were so dense they blocked

out the sun. In the dark, dank corners of the woods, wild mushrooms with lacy edges grew beneath oak and beech trees, and the elms had huge thick crowns that made it seem as if it were night and not just a little past Sext.

She paused when a copse of leafy bushes thinned and beyond stood a dark bower where the ground was overrun with pale heart's ease and white mignonettes. She bent down and picked some pretty yellow honeyflowers, then plucked their lush grasses with nothing on her mind but her romantic dreams of Sir Merrick, the famous and brave knight who would sweep her away. She had truly thought he would be a man of poetry and fine words, a man who would give to her his heart.

Had she only known then that he was not a man of sweet words and gallantry. He had few words, except orders or questions. He was not cruel, but neither was he gentle and kind and attentive.

He did not open up his heart and talk to her. She did not know who he was. She only knew that he was so terribly different from her. She wondered now if he even had a heart to give.

She sighed for what might have been, for dreams dashed in reality and for her worry about her future, a worry that sometimes appeared as dark as this deep forest.

She stopped dallying and moved on. Soon the darkness began to disappear. The path between the trees and bushes grew lighter, the air grew warmer and less still. Shafts of yellow sunlight broke onto the path ahead. Spindly willow trees arched over the narrow path and were twisted with clematis on one side and wild guelder roses on the other.

Between the vines sunlight broke through in golden chutes, and falling blossoms floated down like fairy favors. It was almost mystical.

She moved through it, as though it were a bridal bower. The trampled path led into a broad meadow clove in two by a stream that flowed down from the purple mountains in the distance, where small caps of ice still remained.

Under the shade of a spreading hawthorn tree, she sat down near a tuft of privet and listened to the sound of the water bubbling over the rocks.

She hugged her knees to her chest and dug her bare toes into the lush green grass while she watched a small brown water rat scurry up the bank and lose itself in a thicket of lush drooping ferns.

The sound of the water rushing over a mound of scattered rocks was as soothing as a cool drink of mountain water on a hot summer's day. Through the breaks in the leaves of the tree, bright sunny rays warmed her shoulders. She turned her face toward the sun, then remembered the blackening sap.

Laughing at her success, she unwrapped her hair, then knelt at the edge of the brook. A pink speckled trout broke the surface and snatched a fly from midair. The thought crossed her mind that trout would make a fine meal that evening.

Clio bent over the peat moss that fringed the bank and washed her face and hands in the cold, clean water. With her eyes squeezed tightly shut, she groped around on the grassy ground, trying to find the linen so she could wipe the sap and icy water from her eyes.

She turned, now on her hands and knees, and she moved to where she had tossed the cloth. Her hand touched the linen and she grabbed it, then moved back and bent over the stream, her loose hair failing all about her.

Humming off-key a ballad about a mystical knight with a green horse who claimed the heart of his lady, she vigorously scrubbed her face, then tossed the cloth aside and placed her hands flat on the river's edge.

She leaned over and peered down at her reflection in the silver water. Her hair was in the way, so she tucked it behind her ears and stared back down at the silvery water.

Over her right shoulder appeared a man's dark face.

Clio took a deep breath and screamed.

CHAPTER 15

Welshmen rushed out from the bushes and trees like ghosts appearing from thin air. They were a wild-looking lot, stocky and rough, with no helmets and hair that hung past the leather quarrel slings on their backs.

Cocked over their shoulders were long-bows that were almost as tall as a man, and not a one of them wore armor.

Their leather jacks and braies were weathered, smudged with dirt, and appeared to be the same color as the forest, brown and deep green. The men wore no spurs, rode no horses, and like the ancient savages in a troubadour's ballad of war, they were barefooted and their eyes empty like those of the just dead.

They stared at her and laughed without humor, a cruel laugh that warned they could not be kind.

She screamed again.

But it wasn't their appearance that frightened her. Wild and wolflike, though it was. They moved with such menace, in a pack, closing in slowly like predators going for the final kill.

The man whose face she had seen in the reflection suddenly gripped her by the shoulders. Another prowled toward her with a double-bladed Welsh knife, hooked in deadly angles at the blade tips.

Her eyes locked on the dual blades, and she went completely limp. Still.

The man behind her laughed with victory.

She twisted suddenly, catching him off guard. Kicked at him once, then she ran. Right between two of the men.

"Rhys! Grab her!" Someone shouted.

She didn't look back. She darted in and out of the woods and trees, her gown clutched tightly in her fists. Birds scattered from the brush as she ran past, flapping up into that clear blue sky and telling the men exactly where she was.

Her feet crunched on the fallen leaves and fir needles, and her breath came out in hollow pants and gasps; the sound of her breathing, like the birds, was giving away the direction in which she ran.

Her heart pounded in her ears. Her breath came harder and more edged. She could hear them behind her, grunting like savage animals as they chased her.

So near.

How near?

One man shouted. It sounded as if he were right next to her. Running. Shouting at them to follow her. "Don't lose her! Owen! To the west! There!"

Oh, God...

"Do not let her escape!"

Her chest burned and her feet felt like rocks.

"Kill her!" One of them called out.

Kill her?

Fear gave her speed, made her strain her legs for longer strides.

Her small size let her race through narrow openings that the bigger men had to run around. She ran and ran, faster and faster.

An arrow whizzed past her shoulder and thumped into a tree trunk.

She ducked down, hunching as she moved. Then she hit another clearing and raced across it, turning sharply to the left when she saw the river and open land in the distance.

Another arrow sped by her head, a third past her feet. She glanced over her shoulder. A mistake.

She stumbled and straightened to keep her balance.

An arrow hit her. In the back of her shoulder. Sharp. Piercing.

She cried out and looked down at her shoulder. She saw the hard shaft protruding from her back.

'Twas the strangest thing. It hurt terribly, yet at the same time she felt distant, as if this were happening to someone else and she was just watching it all unfold.

She kept running, driven by little more than instinct. They would catch her. She could not stop. She would die. She glanced back at the arrow in her shoulder. She could die from her wound.

Her feet slowed of their own accord, as if her strength were being sapped away. She tried to will her herself to run, but her body refused to obey her. Her breath was fast and labored. She could not hear them behind her anymore, but then she could hear little but her racing heart; it thudded like death drums in her head and ears and chest.

She had nothing left but spirit. Her body would not mind her. She had no choice but to face these men.

Let the last thing she did be to face them with a look in her eyes damning them to hell. She stopped and turned around, her head high. Proud.

There came a loud and eerie sound so terrifying the world around her seemed to freeze. It was a war cry, human and real, that blew through the air louder than any herald's trumpet.

"A de Beaucourt!"

There it was again, echoing upward to the very crowns of the trees as if cried out by a thousand men of war.

But in truth, there was only one hard voice. One she recognized, like a sound you hear from far away when you are standing at the edge of a cliff with nothing around you but wind and air and water. A call of rescue at the one time when you are out of hope and luck.

Horses' hooves suddenly pounded the ground so hard it was as if the earth were about to crack apart.

A man screamed out, *"Er cof am Gwent!"* Then he was oddly silent, his last words a hail to an ancient Welsh kingdom.

Clio stood dreamlike.

A massive gray warhorse reared up at the edge of the clearing, its hooves pawing at the air. The rider was a knight in full armor. With another cry he drew a long and shining battle sword that caught the light and made the knight and his mount look like God's wrath.

Even without the war call it would have only taken her a moment to recognize the red lion emblazoned on the trappings of the knight's huge mount.

Merrick was here.

An instant later he swept through the band

of Welshmen with deadly intent. His sword glinting from a shaft of sunlight as he raised it high above him, then slashed downward to cut down her attackers.

A man cried out and went down, then another, and another. Arrows clinked uselessly against his protective armor plates and fell to the ground, where they were crushed and splintered by the huge and deadly hooves of his warhorse.

She stood half in awe, half in horror as she watched him take on the outlaws. All of them. Until finally the last few Welshmen fled back into the forest, running for their lives the way they had made her run for hers.

Then, there was only the two of them, all alone in the small clearing. He turned his mount toward her and spurred it forward.

She was acutely aware of the sudden lack of human sound. The silence from this man who had saved her. The air around her seemed to make her weightless.

Inside her head, her reason spun slowly away, out of reach in flashes of half thoughts. She closed her eyes to stop the world from swimming before her very eyes. She concentrated on what she could hear. The creak of his saddle, the clinking of a harness and spurs, and the lathered breath of his mount.

She knew he rode toward her. His horse pounded the ground with each step closer; it was a dull beating sound. Just like her heart.

Finally she gave in and opened her eyes.

The horse was barely a foot from her, and he reined it in and did not move, but sat there saying nothing, only looking down at her from the dark slits in the visor on his helm. His rapid breathing slipped out in misty threads through the small breath holes.

He still held his sword in his hand.

Blood dripped off of it and onto the mesh fingertips of his gauntlet. She understood his purpose. He wanted her to get a good look at the bloody sword before he sheathed it. As if it stood as an image for a lesson to her. Something horrible to be burned into her memory.

His tactic worked.

He had no idea how tremendously it affected her. She could not look away, even though the sight was the most gruesome thing she had ever seen.

'Twas as if she were rooted there, an ancient tree forced to see only that which passed it by. Unable to move or look away.

Her life had been sheltered, and the tales of war she heard were tales of the romance of war, sung in pretty melodic ballads of bravery and chivalry by men who had never killed another.

There was nothing glorious in what she had just witnessed. Nothing romantic. Her stomach rose in her throat and seemed to stick there.

He flipped open the visor and stared at her with a look that did not bode well. Cold and blue, with barely contained anger lurking on the edge of his expression.

His free arm rested on his saddle pommel

as if he were 'relaxed. But she could see he was tense and tightly sprung, so taut it was almost as if he were ready to snap in two.

"I am gone but a few hours and yet you manage to almost get yourself killed." His voice was gritty and low and unpleasant.

She searched for something to say, but no words came to her. She just stood, frozen, dizzy, hugging herself and looking past him to the bloody scene beyond. She closed her eyes and remained stiff and numb and sick inside.

A moment later she sank to her knees and bent forward so her hair shielded her burning face from him.

For the first time the arrow showed from her back.

She heard his vicious curse, but did not know the reason. She just knelt there shaking and weak and hurting, hidden by her hair. Then she did the only thing she still had the strength to do.

She cried.

CHAPTER 16

Merrick swelled with sudden rage. Impotent, paralyzing rage. His hard gaze hit the deadly looking arrow. He knew at that instant that the Devil could take him to hell and through all the trials of purgatory, yet it would not be punishment enough.

He had failed her.

With slight pressure from his knee and a tightening of the reins, his warhorse knelt to the ground. Merrick awkwardly slid from his saddle, his motions made stiff and restricted from the armor that protected him.

Nothing had protected her. Nothing. And 'twas his duty.

He had seen men die. He had seen bloody wounds. He had been cut and stabbed and shot with arrows himself. But the sight of that arrow in his lady's back made him feel as if he had been cloven in two.

He moved toward her as swiftly as he could; sounds of the armor rattled and clanked and scraped into the air. The sound was harsh, but not nearly as haunting as her quiet sobs. Part of him wanted to rip off every last piece of plate metal he wore, so that he had to stand there as defenseless as she had been.

Beside her, he fell to one knee and slid his hands about her waist. Even through his gauntlets he could feel the shaking of her small body. He drew her onto his bent knee. "Easy. Easy, Clio. I'm here, now."

She sobbed his name, a shame-filled half cry, and her face was hidden against his shoulder. He had to close his eyes to stop some foreign and massively overpowering emotion that suddenly burned behind his eyes and deep within his heart.

He held her there for the briefest of moments. Because he could do nothing else.

He was a warrior, yet he felt weak and cowardly and angry all at once. He stood up then with her in his arms. She had one slim arm slung around his neck and the other arm, the side that dripped with new blood from the arrow, hung limply at her side. He moved toward Aries stiffly. She moaned once when his arm accidentally grazed the arrow shaft.

His warhorse knelt on command, and Merrick remounted, settling her gently in front of him. As Aries stood, Merrick looked down at Clio. Her sobs had stopped, but her breath was as ragged and tattered as his pride.

"Take a deep breath," he whispered in a hoarse voice that did not sound like his. He looked down at the long arrow protruding from the back of her shoulder and slid his arms under hers.

He gripped the stiff shaft in both hands and broke it off.

She moaned.

The sound was like a dagger in his gut.

Her breath came in uncontrolled pants of pain. Then she whimpered and it about killed him.

He cupped her head protectively beneath his chin and said, "I'll take you home, Clio. You're safe now." He paused, then added under his harsh breath, "You will be safe. I swear this to you."

She muttered something he could not understand against his neck; then he felt her sag against him. He turned his mount with only the pressure of his legs, then spurred them forward.

They rode from the dark forest out into the sunny field beyond, heading for Camrose, which sat on a hillside in the distance, looking peaceful and strong and gleaming white against the horizon. As if nothing dangerous could possibly happen within its proud sight.

He wanted to shake his fists at it. He wanted to shout and curse at the heavens over the irony of it all.

For years he had been able to look down upon a battlefield and know easily from where to mount the best attack. He had finely honed senses that could almost feel his enemies' presence before they ever showed themselves. He could forsee a trap coming, and he could easily judge if a man would make a true soldier.

Yet when he had stood before this woman in the small forest glen, he had felt helpless. It was as if he had been in the middle of a battle and had just had his mount and his sword taken away.

Now, as he sat on his horse, he tried to control the turmoil inside of him. He could not feel any life from her. There was no warmth. No touch of skin against skin. Nothing tangible. But then, he wore his armor, so between his and her touch there was nothing but cold hard metal.

Then, as he had that empty thought, her body began to shake, quivering like an arrow when it just hits the target. He looked down, and even though her head was bent, he saw the tears scoring her cheeks and dripping over her mouth and chin.

She was crying again. Silently. Her tears dripped onto the coude of armor at his elbow and trickled down the hammered metal vambrace that covered his forearm. She settled even closer against him when he clamped his arm possessively around her small body. He found it a sudden struggle to find air to breathe.

Aries climbed a small hill of freshly mown grass, and her head fell back against his shoulder. A second later her tears dripped onto his breastplate, where they slowly traced down in a path across his heart.

Merrick raised his head, slowly, and gazed straight before him, his jaw clenched the way it did when he saw a blow coming.

He stared out at nothing for a long time. It seemed a lifetime, forever, especially when his thoughts were so confused.

Strange how his armor could fend off arrows and slashes of swords. It could deflect the blow of a mace or the jab of a dagger. It had saved his life too many times to count. Yes, his armor had never ceased to protect him.

Until now.

At that instant, a moment of time that was no more than a flicker in the face of Fate, he learned something that would change his whole life. No matter how thick the metal or

141

how masterfully crafted, no matter how many men-at-arms he had or how many weapons he drew, nothing...no nothing would ever protect him from this one small woman.

Clio sat on the lumpy straw tick in her bedchamber, where Merrick had carried her. She remembered little of the ride back to the castle, only the security of his arm around her and the embarrassment of her tears.

Almost before they rode through the castle gates, he had begun to shout orders. She wasn't certain which was louder, his shouting or the loud clanging sound of his armor as he awkwardly climbed the stairs with her in his arms. He stumbled once and swore countless times before he kicked open her chamber door and laid her on the bed.

"Do not move," he ordered, then watched her as if he thought she would disobey him.

She returned his dark look with a weak smile. "And to think I intended to run up and down the stairs a hundred or so times."

He did not find her humor amusing, just shook his head. " 'Twould not surprise me. God knows, woman, what you will do next."

"Walk to London." She had tried for a sprightly tone, but her words sounded drained, even to her own ears. She sagged back on the tick, then flinched from pain when she accidentally hit the arrow stub.

Stars swam before her eyes and she clenched her Jaw so tightly her teeth should have cracked.

"Here," he said with sudden gentleness. "On your side." He helped her lie on her good shoulder. "Stay still." He turned and clanged across the stone floor, then braced his hands on the doorway and bellowed "De Clare!"

For the next few minutes all Clio heard was Merrick repeatedly calling for his squire and shouting orders to everyone and anyone who happened to be nearby.

She could picture the scurrying belowstairs almost as if she were standing and looking down at it. Servants running to and fro like confused pigeons. His men trying to obey seven orders fired at them at once.

"You! Stop!" Merrick's loud and rough voice echoed off the stone walls.

Wincing slightly, Clio glanced up at the doorway. There was poor, sweet Thwack.

He froze mid-step, staring in the direction of Merrick's voice. "Aye, my lord?"

"Come here...Thump."

The lad stepped out of Clio's line of vision. "Aye, my lord?"

"Bring some heated water and towels now! De Clare! Tobin! Where the hell is my squire, damnit!?" Merrick's voice echoed like a cathedral bell through the keep, "*Someone. Anyone.* Get some bloody hot water and fresh linen up here *now!*"

"Oh!" Thwack took some backward steps. He glanced into the room, then paled. "I'll fetch the water, my lord! I will."

"Then get moving, lad and be quick about it!"

"Aye, my lord. You can trust me."

"Where the hell have you been, de Clare? Get this armor off me!"

"Yes, my lord," came Tobin's harried voice.

Another muttered curse came from just outside her door, and a piece of armor sailed past the door to clang onto the stone floor and roll into a corner where Cyclops had been sleeping like the dead.

The cat opened his one eye and glared at the armor, then stretched, stood up, and prowled close to it, making that gurgling sound he made whenever he had something cornered. He sniffed at the armor piece, then meowed loudly.

He spent the next few seconds batting it around as if he expected it to grow legs and run at any moment. But the piece of armor didn't move, so he butted his fat backside against it. His long tail thumped on it a few times; then he yawned once, plopped down on it, and went back to sleep.

Merrick was still grumbling in the hallway.

"Please, my lord," Tobin said, his voice filled with forced patience. "Can you stop pacing? I've almost—"

"God's eyes, de Clare! What in the name of St. Peter is taking you so bloody long? Unfasten the blasted thing. Stop dallying here and there and everywhere! Lady Clio could bleed to death before you even get moving."

A gauntlet flew across the hall.

Lady Clio could bleed to death. 'Twas a very good thing she was not prone to hysteria, else his tactless words would have sent her into a fit.

She cupped a hand around her mouth to be heard over his cursing and called out. "I'm fine, my lord."

Merrick's armor-covered feet clopped to the doorway. He poked his head around the corner, scowling so hard his dark brows almost came together.

His helm was off and his mail hood was gone, too. His black hair stuck out as if he had driven his hands through it a thousand times. His narrowed gaze went from her face to her upper arm.

"I'm fine," she repeated, nodding at him. "Truly."

From his expression she could see he did not believe her. He grunted something she could not hear, then disappeared again.

"My lord, please..." came Tobin's frustrated voice. "If you would just hold still a moment longer."

"For godsakes man, be quick about it!"

There was another crash. Clio heard Tobin swear softly. Then there was the rattling sound of mail hitting the stone floor, and the squire muttered, "Thank you, God."

"Where in the bloody hell is that water?" Merrick yelled so loud they could have heard him in London. He began to pace in front of her door. Back and forth he went, ranting and grumbling.

She stared at her betrothed with sudden fascination.

He was wearing only a loincloth.

Clio had seen a few naked men. She had seen to the bathing of her father on occasion and a visiting diplomat once. But neither of them, nor the skinny castle and village lads that bathed naked in the streams, had looked anything like Merrick de Beaucourt.

His arms and chest were thick and sturdy. His skin was darker than her own pale skin. The color of it made hers look pasty. Beneath the black whirls of hair on his body, muscles rippled like tight steps down his belly to the edge of the loincloth.

That one small scrap of thinly-tanned leather covered his male parts, which, as she stared at them with complete fascination, looked like huge knotted fists.

When he would turn his back to pace, she could see scars, both white and purple, across his back and his right arm and shoulder.

His buttocks looked incredibly tight, tighter than hers, she thought with no little disgust. But his thighs were heavy with strength and snaking muscle, and she understood immediately how he could so easily control his horse with only a slight leg motion.

She had stopped listening to his words, because they were only muttered curses and male talk. Looking at him was much more interesting.

But before long his pacing began to make her lightheaded. She shook her head slightly, but it did not help. The room spun a little, as if she had drunk too much wine. She took a deep breath, but it made her wound ache so much she had to close her eyes to block her tears of sudden pain.

Certainly it was not fair. She didn't want to close her eyes when the view before her was so spicy.

But nothing seemed to help her light-headedness, so she lay down her cheek atop one hand and tried to keep her eyes open. They grew heavier and heavier, until she knew they were only open to small slits.

A moment later she closed them completely. 'Twas the last thing she remembered.

CHAPTER 17

They hovered about Lady's Clio's chamber like black harbinger ravens sitting in a hanging tree. Thwack and Thud, their wide and worried eyes locked on Lady Clio, who was lying so still on the bed. Tobin and Sir Isambard stood near the door along with three maidservants, two old and the young, plump teary-eyed village girl called Dulcie.

Brother Dismas stood by the bed praying in Latin and dabbing oil in the sign of the cross on her brow. He suddenly switched languages. "My Lord God! Save this poor daughter of Eve!" He flung holy water over Clio, the bed,

Merrick, and everything else within five feet. "Use your divine wisdom and grace, dear Lord God. Let her stay here, where she is needed by...by..."

The monk scanned the room frowning. He glanced quickly and fearfully past Merrick, whose jaw was so tight his neck ached.

"...By these wretched souls, who need all of your divine help and..."

At that moment Old Gladdys came inside the room. She took one look at the monk, hunched her shoulders, and raised her bony hands high in the air like a witch about to cast a spell. She chanted some Druid song and danced around the room, her black clothing flapping about her like bat wings.

The monk's mouth clamped shut faster than the king's castle gate and he held the cross at the end of his prayer beads in front of him like a shield.

"Out!" Merrick shouted. Not even for Clio's sake could he take any more. He pointed at the door. "Every last one of you! Out! *Now!*"

Seconds later all were scrambling to get out the bedchamber door at the same time. All but that fool Brother Dismas, who was tying a dried piece of holly threaded with garlic to his cross, and the Druid witch, who was hunched over, cackling and blinking at the monk as if she had something stuck in her eye.

"I said out!" Merrick pinned the monk with a menacing look meant to send him anywhere but there. Straight to hell for all Merrick cared.

"Me?" Pompous Brother Dismas looked stunned, but raised his cross higher. "But surely since I have God's divine ear, I should stay. Get this heathen witch out!" He scowled at Old Gladdys and raised his cross a little higher. "Before she gives us all the evil eye. Lady Clio needs my prayers on her behalf"

"She needs all of you gone." Merrick took a step toward the man.

The good brother quickly whipped the string of prayer beads back over his head, stuck his brass aspergillum under his armpit, and gathered his robes up in his fists. He stood there a moment, apparently waiting for Old Gladdys to stop chanting. He turned back to Merrick. "God says you must move her lady's bed."

"What?" Merrick scowled back at him. "Move her bed? Why?"

"Our Father just told me, my lord. You must move the bed to that wall." He pointed across the room. "There."

Merrick stared at the wall in a moment's confusion.

"To save Lady Clio," Dismas continued. "The Lord says her head must be pointed toward Golgotha."

The man was crazed. Merrick just looked at him blankly.

"Calvary," the good brother explained. " 'Tis the hill where Christ was—"

"I bloody well know where Golgotha is, you idiot! I've been there! Now get out of this room before I crucify you!"

The monk swallowed hard and ran out the door. His footsteps pattered frantically down the stone stairs.

"You too, old woman. Leave." Merrick stepped in front of Old Gladdys and stopped her from twirling in a hexagon-shaped path.

She looked up at Merrick, then scanned the room. The moment she saw they were alone, she straightened and returned Merrick's look with a wise and completely lucid look of her own. She handed him a small earthenware pot she took from a sack sewn to the hip of her robe. "Put this unguent on her wound."

Then she walked out, her back straight as an alder tree.

Merrick shook his head, then took the stopper from the pot. Inside was a lichen-green salve of strong-smelling herbs that looked and smelled as if it offered more promise than did moving the bed and aiming Clio's head toward Jerusalem.

He closed and bolted the chamber doors with an order to a guard that no one was to enter. He turned back and just stood there, one shoulder leaning against the wooden door.

She had passed out. He could see she was weaker than she had claimed. Her skin was pale and grayish and the color had nothing to do with her clothing choice.

He had seen that look before on wounded men. She might have thought she was fine, but she was not. He wrung out a cloth in the basin of tepid water. Then he washed the wound again. It was deep and still bleeding.

He cut her gown from neck to waist and stared at her body, unable to look too long upon the wound because of its depth. When he pressed on the soft flesh beneath her collarbone, he could feel the tip of the arrow just beneath her fine blue-veined skin.

He had removed arrows before. From men not women.

And not his woman. There were two ways to extract an arrow. One was to pull the shaft back out the way it had entered. But if the point was spiked with small prongs, it could rip the flesh away from the bone and make the victim bleed to death.

He used the second method and cut a cross in the front of her shoulder with a dagger. She moaned and twisted, and he had to hold her down. Fresh red blood the color of scarlet poppies poured out from the wound.

He watched her for signs of consciousness. There were none. Thankfully. As swiftly as he could, he used some narrow tongs to pull the arrow shaft through, pinning her with his other arm.

She tried to buck him off her and moaned even more pitifully. He had to take deep breaths of air that were hard to catch and hold. She cried quietly.

"I would take your pain from you if I only could," he whispered. After a moment that seemed like an eternity, she quieted.

He looked at the arrow in his hand. The shaft was spiked.

But now fresh new blood the color of poppies swelled swiftly from the wound. He dropped a cloth into a beechwood bowl filled with warm water and vinegared wine. Then he dabbed at and firmly pressed the cloth against her shoulder.

It had to hurt. Still she did nothing but give a small wisp of a moan that sounded as if she were farther and farther away.

No matter what he did, the wound would not stop bleeding. His anger, his frustration, was so strong at that moment he wanted to hit something.

All but a few of the Welshmen who had done this to her had already paid harshly for their sin. In his mind's eye he saw her running, saw them chasing her, and all over again he swelled with that rage.

He felt her look on him before he looked down and saw it. She was awake and stared up at him like a cipher, those bright eyes of hers empty and lifeless. She looked as though she were little more than human air.

Her eyes drifted closed, as if keeping them open were too much for her, but she placed her hand on his where it rested on his thigh.

He stared down at her hand while his thumb stroked one of her fingers. There was dried blood all over her arm, wrists, and hands from holding her wound while she was running.

He took the wet cloth and washed her as gently as he could. When he was done, he wrung out the cloth; the water in the bowl turned a deeper color, like the red-brown dirt of Cyprus, where they had buried too many men. He had seen so much blood in his lifetime that he had thought he was immune to the sight of it.

Apparently not.

Seeing her small hand covered with blood sickened him. Not since his first bloody battle had he felt the bile rise to his throat as it did now. He had forgotten he could feel this.

Still the wound bled on and on, and he knew he must do something drastic, before the wound could become putrid or before she slowly bled to death. He knew what to do, but it did not make the thought easier; it made it more difficult.

Don't think. Don't think. So you don't have to feel.

He stared at the rough oaken table near the bed. His dagger with the handle in the shape of a cross lay next to a squat tallow candle with a bright flickering flame.

Slowly he picked up the dagger and lifted its blade to the fire, watching almost sightlessly as the metal got hotter and hotter. The wound still bled, and to him, it looked as if her life were draining away in a bright red stream.

He took a deep breath and started to move the dagger toward her shoulder. But his hand froze. He could not do this. He could not. He waited, prayed, closed his eyes. He put the blade to the flame again, waiting longer while the dagger blade turned hotter and hotter.

He took another long and deep breath, then swiftly pressed the knife to her shoulder.

Her eyes shot open and she screamed long and loud.

It sounded as if it went on forever. Then she fainted.

He sat there staring down at her, her scream still ringing through his mind, in his head, his ears. In his heart. He dropped the knife as if he had touched the hot blade; it clattered onto the stone floor. He took deep breaths, but it did not help.

He slipped to his knees on the floor as the anguish swelled inside of him. He gave a muffled, aching moan that sounded as if it came from someone else, some wild animal or wounded beast; then he buried his head in his arms. And cried.

CHAPTER 18

Clio slept restlessly, feeling as if she were in between two worlds: The real world, which seemed a like a dream because it was nothing but a nightmare of pain. And her dream world, a place where it was safe and sweet and real, where it was night and the stars shone above her in numbers too many for one person to count.

Some of those stars were far away, as if they were closer to heaven. But others, just a few, were so near her she thought she could reach out and touch them with her fingertips.

She had never seen stars like these, some shooting west and others shooting east, while a streaky cloud of them just stayed in the same spot and twinkled like the bright sapphires in Queen Eleanor's crown.

In this odd dream, she was standing on the edge of a giant crevasse; it was so deep she could not see the bottom. Just a huge black abyss that was frighteningly empty.

On the other side of that deep ravine stood Merrick, astride his huge warhorse, which was stamping and snorting and looking like it wanted to jump. Behind him, lined up like men armed and ready for battle, were row after row of standards with distinctive waving banners—*sable a cross argent a lion rampant gules*—black field, white cross, and rearing red lions.

Suddenly the lions became real, alive. They jumped down from the pennants into live packs that prowled in circles on the ground, then leapt across the wide crevasse as if they had wings.

They landed on the other side, near Clio, and the moment they touched the ground, their paws changed into bare human feet.

They roared continuously, then all turned toward her.

She saw the intent to destroy in their eyes, and she ran.

Their roars became human shouts. *Kill her! Get her! Stop her!*

She stole a quick look over her shoulder and

saw the pack of red lions had changed into Welsh outlaws with longbows and leather jacks and looks more frightening than those of animal predators.

Er cof am Gwent! came their Welsh cries.

They shot bloodred arrows at her as she tried to escape. She dodged them and ran on. When the arrows hit the nearby trees, they stuck, then melted in bloodstains as if the trees were wounded and bleeding.

In the distance she could hear Merrick's voice. Far, far away, calling her name, again and again, but neither of them could cross the deep ravine. The further along its edge she ran, the more the wide black canyon between them seemed to widen.

Until finally, when her feet and her wind were giving out, the dark crevasse turned into a giant black hole that reared upward like an enormous black dragon and swallowed her.

Clio awoke with a shivering start.

Her eyes shot open and she stared at the rough-timbered ceiling of her bedchamber, blinking. She tried to sit up, propping up on her elbows as she did every morn, but pain shot through her right shoulder and back, then ran like fire down her side.

She moaned so deeply it sounded like a growl in the back of her throat, and fell back against the lumpy bed. A few moments later she opened her eyes again. Her vision was blurred with tears from the sharp pain.

Her eyes cleared as the pain in her shoulder changed to throbs, which soon dwindled to something tolerable, a deep ache that spilled and burned across the chest. She hurt, and she closed her eyes and felt her tears spill.

A cold breeze swept over her face, which was hot from nightmares and tears. The air ruffled the small damp hairs near her temples and cheeks.

She turned her chin slightly so she could look toward the loop where the shutters had been left open. It was night outside, sometime between Matins and Lauds. She could see the dark sky. No sign of twilight. No sign of dawn. Just night, deep and dark and almost as black as the chasm of her dream.

Beside the bed was a brazier. Nearby sat a small table with three wobbly legs. Atop it was a wooden basin strewn with cloths and some salve in the kind of hand-thrown pot that Old Gladdys made for her love potions.

Clio shifted closer to the opposite edge of the bed so she could feel the hot air drift up. She relaxed a bit more, then scanned the dark chamber.

A candle flickered golden light in the corner nearest the door, where Merrick was sprawled in a chair. His long legs stuck out in front of him and his elbows hung over the chair arms, while his head cocked over to one side.

He was sleeping, his hands folded at rest atop the thick silken fabric of a richly embroidered blue robe he wore.

Part of her was disappointed.

She liked the loincloth.

She could take in her fill of him, watch him without the tension of him looking into her eyes. There were times when his looks made her feel as if her eyes were windows, clear and open for him to see what she was really thinking.

A frightening thought.

A woman's mind was the only place she had that was truly all hers. There she could dream her dreams and make her plans. Make the outside world go away. There she could be the one who ruled. She controlled her thoughts and dreams, and there was no man inside for her to answer to, no man to tell her what she could or could not do.

She lay there and watched him sleep. Thinking, wondering, her fantastical dream still fresh in her mind.

There were some—Old Gladdys for one— who said dreams were signs, inklings of what was happening in your life. Clues to the future or doors that opened to the past.

They claimed that only in sleep could you look at things from a different perspective, in a fantasy that takes all your human fears and doubts away and leaves nothing but the purity of the issue.

'Twas true, she supposed, that she and Merrick were like two people standing on a giant ravine. They were on opposite sides of life with nothing to bind them together except the very impasse that kept them apart.

She wondered if all men and women were

so different from each other. Did war truly teach men to look at the world only in terms of defense and protection? Or were men and women different from the moment they were conceived? Did they naturally approach life from opposite directions?

The answers must be somewhere, in heaven or in God's hands. Perhaps there was a golden chest, a coffer with a bright silver lock, kept high up in the heavens that held all the answers to love and life and why God chose to make a woman so different from a man.

She gave a short, all-encompassing sigh, knowing these were questions for which she might never find the answers.

Her gaze drifted back outside, where the moon had slipped down the sky and shone through the loop, casting Merrick in its white light.

Moonlight turned his black hair silver, and she could see, even from the bed, how long and dark his eyelashes were when his eyes were closed. She was surprised she hadn't noticed before.

Probably because he was usually glowering at her. You can't give a good glower with your eyes closed.

In sleep, his features were not so taut and stern. He looked younger and she found herself wondering what his childhood had been like.

When she looked at him sleeping, she could imagine he was once a small boy, an image that was almost impossible when he was awake. It wasn't that sleep made him look weak. His jaw was still strong and as angled as the stone curtain walls, yet the tension was gone from him, as if he had been sucked dry as the castle well.

Black stubble covered his chin like powdered smudges from walnut shells; it spread up his jawline in a dark shadow and came up to daggerlike points near where his cheekbones were close to his ears.

His nose was long and straight and noble, like the beak of one of the king's hawks. His hands were tanned, and black hair swirled thickly from his forearms to his wrists and peppered lightly over those strong hands with clean and clipped nails.

She remembered his hands from the clearing, gauntleted, covered with blood. In her mind's eye she saw the whole scene again. The violence, the dispassion. Her fear.

Until she had seen him fight with that sword, she could not imagine what his life had been like. She remembered secretly wishing she could be a knight and travel off to strange lands and have the freedom to do as she wished.

What a youthful desire, the kind where you see the world from dreamy eyes instead of seeing how it truly exists. The kind that makes you feel foolish in retrospect.

She stared at her aching shoulder, now empty of its arrow. A cloth was tied about it, and she was glad. Part of her did not want to see it because she might have to relive what had happened to her.

Instead, she stared at the thick woolen cover on the bed, plucking at some threads. As if her eyes had minds of their own, her gaze rose to look at him.

Today, for the briefest of moments, she'd tasted a small bit of his harsh life. It had changed her. So it must have changed him over the years, again and again, each incident pounding away at him the way a battering ram slams against a gate until it splinters.

The violence he'd witnessed and lived through, the way life could become death in a mere instant, the apathy to both, must have influenced the way he was. His view of the world.

She was surprised how much a moment could alter a lifetime. It was like aging a few years in one single day. Things seemed clearer to her, because she had a small taste of how war and a knight's duty in life could taint a man.

And she could begin to understand Merrick now, to see why he thought of everything in terms of war and defense, why he felt the need for protection.

Because after all those years of war, Merrick knew nothing else.

Clio had been cooped up in her chamber so long she wanted to jump out the window and try to fly.

Instead she demanded a bath.

You would have thought, from the looks on the servants' faces, that she had asked for the English throne. After more clucking than

161

could be heard from the chickens in the stable yard, they decided they must "check with the earl for permission for her to bathe."

The earl of Orders had barred everyone but one maid from her chamber. After the first two days she had begun to feel like a prisoner. By the end of the week she had decided he was the meanest of men to keep her shut up like some outlaw.

Her shoulder felt perfectly fine. Well, except for when she fainted because she tried to go down the stairs too soon. And those two puny times her wound had reopened and the bleeding had started again.

Just because she had been shot with a little arrow did not mean she could not supervise some ale making. The servants had tattled on her and she never had the chance. With some ingenuity, however, she had managed to oversee the digging of an herb garden by sitting in the arched window in her chamber and hollering down to Thud and Thwack.

At least until Merrick saw her. And therein lay her problem. Merrick. Other than to come in, yell at her, or threaten to tie her to the bed, she had not seen much of him since that night she awoke.

The very next morning the chair he had slept in so quietly stood empty. For some reason she cared not to ponder, she felt a strange stab of loneliness.

But now it was midmorning, just past Terce, and Dulcie stood behind a squat wooden bathtub with a splintered rim and rusted joints. Clio sat inside, her knees pressed against her breasts and warm water up to her armpits. There was golden sunshine outside and she could hear the song of a meadowlark somewhere above her.

"Turn yer head, my lady." Dulcie was busy scrubbing Clio's long hair with a soft pungent soap made from lentils and mint. The scent was almost as soothing as the feel of soapy fingers scrubbing her head. It felt so good after days of sleeping and forced bed rest.

"So what is my lord up to this day?" Clio asked casually, imagining him pacing her room in a loincloth. Gagged.

"He is meeting with the master mason."

"Ah, yes. No doubt he has been busy adding more murder holes."

"Aye, my lady. That or looking for his horse."

Clio winced slightly. She felt some guilt over the horse. That fine animal had disappeared along with the Welshmen who got away. Had she not taken it, well...

But Merrick had said nothing about it. Nary a word, which ate at her conscience a bit. Deep inside, she wished he had ranted and raved because then she would not feel so guilty.

She paused, a sudden thought hitting her for the first time. She glanced at the perch near her bed. 'Twas empty. Cyclops was asleep in the corner, but Pitt was no where.

"Where is Pitt, Dulcie? I haven't seen him. He was with me when I left."

"No one has seen the bird."

She sat there for a long time.

"Perhaps he finally figured out how to fly," Dulcie suggested.

"Aye," she murmured. "Perhaps." Her bird was gone, like Merrick's prized horse. She supposed there was some justice in that. There had to be some kind of recompense for her rash actions. She just hoped that both of the animals were well.

Dulcie rinsed her hair. "I think my lord is busy because he spent so much time in here with you those first days."

"I know," Clio said blithely. "I awoke and saw him that one night."

"Oh, not one night, my lady. He would not let anyone inside until he was certain you would be well. He even took the arrow out himself. The earl nursed you himself."

That gave her pause, and shut her up.

She stood, her thoughts pensive, while Dulcie toweled her off, then she stepped from the tub.

Somewhere in her fog of memory she remembered him talking to her, softly, gently, those strong arms that held her in her shadowed dreams. Lips on her brow and a strong warm feeling when she was shivering.

Were they real? She had thought they were dreams. Tricks of her mind. She stared down at the floating soap foam in the water, and she felt ashamed.

"I see you are most recovered, Clio."

She whipped her head around toward Merrick's deep voice. Wet strands of long hair slapped her face and body and her poor maid, who dropped the towel.

"I'm sorry, my lady," she said, looking as flustered and as naked as Clio felt.

Clio snatched the towel from her maid and awkwardly wrapped it around her. It was not very large and she wasn't sure what to cover first.

"You have much color to your skin," Merrick said in complete seriousness, yet she felt he was laughing behind those blue eyes. Strange that now they did not look cool or icy.

His gaze lingered on her for a moment, traveled a hot path from the top of her wet head to her bare toes.

A stab of an odd hunger, something she had never felt before, overcame her. She had to fight the urge to place her hand on her belly.

With a boldness she thought bordered on madness she straightened, standing tall. She returned his look, then she dropped the towel.

CHAPTER 19

"Now 'tis you who have much color to your skin, my lord."

The imp stood there boldly, in all her naked and innocent glory, and taunted him with his own words. He almost congratulated her.

Instead he just looked his fill. Her skin was flushed from the bath and her hair was slicked back and shone like the sleek heads of the seals that played in the surf near Cardiff.

He had thought she was a small woman, dainty and petite. But her breasts were full and the pale color of a lamb's nose, her waist small and her hips lush. He wondered what the men of the Church would have to say about the golden color of her nether hair. He knew Roger would have plenty to say, perhaps even an ode, pretty words to make the earthy subject sound romantic.

But there were no pretty words in Merrick, just emotion, strong and fierce. He felt desire rise within him as sharp as a battle cry. Passionate and burning through his blood. His hands itched to touch her, his mouth to taste her, but it wasn't just hot desire that held him there. It was something stronger, a bond of some kind that told him he could have spent a lifetime just looking at her.

But her gasping maid, a plump country girl with ragtag hair the color of newly mown hay, jumped in front of her and blocked his view. "This is not done. My lady...My lord ...You are not yet wed. I...I—" she began to stammer.

"Lady Clio." Merrick made a gallant bow so well done he should have received another earldom for it. Then he straightened. "When you have finished, I would have a word with you." He turned to leave, but paused with his hand on the door. He looked back and smiled. "Do I need to come fetch you?"

"No." Clio said in a haughty tone, never once looking the least bit shy. "I'm certain I can find you most simply, my lord."

He gave her a quick nod and closed the door behind him.

By the time he had left the hall, gone outside, and turned the corner of the stable, he was whistling.

It was not simple to find him.

He was not in the solar, nor in the great hall. The baker had seen him with the smithy after he had broken his fast, but the smithy hadn't seen him since midday, when the master mason had needed him.

The master mason had gone to the nearby quarry for more stone, alone, but a guard had seen the earl with Thomas the Plowman, John at the Well, and William the Cooper. The earl had left Thomas, John, and William when Brother Dismas had complained that some of his men had been dicing in the nave and God's wrath was a truly frightening thing and no little bad luck for Camrose.

But, when she found Brother Dismas, he hadn't seen the earl since just before Sext, when Sir Isambard sought and found him. Now, no one knew where Sir Isambard was.

Finally she found the older knight at the stables, where Thud, Thwack, and Tobin were mucking out the stalls.

"Sir Isambard?"

He turned around. No smile. No change of

his expression, just the same gruff face. He gave a nod of his head. "Aye, my lady?"

"What are those boys doing?"

"Mucking out the stable."

"I can see that. Why?"

" 'Tis the last of their punishment for disobeying Sir Merrick's orders."

"They are still being punished?"

"Aye. This time for the herb garden."

She started to argue that it was not them but herself who should have been punished for that, but the two young boys came up to her, spades held proudly in their hands like battle swords.

"The earl told us... "—Thud held his head high and proud—"if we are to become knights someday, we must learn to obey his orders." He paused and looked up at her from eyes that pleaded with her to understand. "Even in defiance of you, my lady."

Thwack just nodded slowly. "Me too. But we shall become knights someday and protect you with our lives."

Tobin was foolish enough to snicker.

Sir Isambard gave the squire a hard look. "Lord Merrick has given you a special job, de Clare."

"I have served my lord for a long time," Tobin said with pride and pompousness. He stood over Thud and Thwack and said pointedly, "My lord saves more important service for those of us who have served him well."

He was so cocky Clio wanted to clout him with a spade.

"Aye, my lord earl rewards those who deserve it," Sir Isambard agreed with great seriousness.

"What, sir, is this important service?" Tobin swaggered in a circle around Thud and Thwack, then turned his handsome face toward the old knight. He wanted theold knight to announce his select duty in front of the younger boys just to make them feel bad.

Sir Isambard rubbed his chin thoughtfully, then said, "When you've finished cleaning the stable stalls, de Clare, you will be in charge of training."

"Training?" Tobin frowned.

"Aye." Sir Isambard planted his hammy hands on his hips, then added, "Thud and Thwack."

Tobin scowled. "Training them for what?"

"To be the newest de Beaucourt pages."

Thud and Thwack let out whoops of glee so loud they drowned out Tobin's curses.

Had Merrick been there at that very moment, Clio would have thrown her arms around him and done whatever he bid her. For a few minutes anyway.

She had never seen those two lads so happy. She almost cried. Sir Isambard clapped Tobin on the shoulder harder than Clio supposed was necessary. Merrick's squire had a sick look on his face; he looked as if he had just eaten bad flounder.

"Sir knight?" Clio called out to the older man, who still hadn't smiled. "Have you seen the earl?"

"Aye, my lady. He is up on the battlements, there." Sir Isambard pointed north.

She waved her thanks, turned with her

skirts clutched in her fists, and ran like a loose child toward the stone stairs. By the time she reached the topmost archway that led out to the wall walk, she was out of breath, so she stopped, placed a hand on her heaving chest, and leaned against the wall, waiting till her breathing slowed.

"Are you going to make me wait for you every time we're to meet?" Merrick stood in the outer archway, his hand gripping the carved rim of the arch. Half of his face was cast in shadow, but the half she could see was not angry. He looked amused. As if he was enjoying her.

She took a deep breath, raised her chin, and said with utter nonchalance, "Perhaps."

"Two long years' worth?"

So he'd discovered her game.

"Probably longer." She strolled toward him as if she hadn't been running so hard her breath could not keep up.

Together they walked along the battlements, where the stones were stained in places with the deep brown color of old blood. She was not certain she would have noticed those bloodstains before the incident with the Welsh. She had never been attuned to such things.

This section of the wall was high above the castle, where the wind blew stronger and the air grew cooler. Around them was nothing but the sky and the wind and each other.

Below, the castle was bustling, but up here, it all sounded very far away, another world below them, while they were like clouds that blew toward someplace far in the distance where their life paths would meet.

He was silent, so she turned and looked up at him to try to gauge his thoughts. He was leaning back against the stone tower, his arms crossed over his chest. One knee was bent, and his boot was propped against a stack of rocks piled below the crenellated wall.

He stared off at the horizon, where the green hills and clusters of trees met a blue and cloudless English sky. She leaned back against the yellow stone of the tower and wondered what the rest of her life would be like with this strange man who spoke and looked so gruff yet seemed to have a gentle side.

"I expect to be obeyed when I give an order."

So much for his gentle side, she thought.

"And especially by those whom it is my duty to protect."

He sounded like her father. She chewed her lip and listened.

"I do not give orders because I am cruel or selfish or to torment you, Clio. I do so for safety reasons or for what is best for your land, which has been given to me to safeguard."

When she said nothing, he continued. "You will not find me difficult to live with. But when I give an order, I expect to be obeyed. It matters not whether I give that order to my men, to my servants, or to my wife."

"I am not your wife yet." The words slipped from her mouth without a thought. It was all she could do not to rush and say, "Wait! I take them back!"

He didn't move or speak, and because of it, her rash words seemed to echo in her ears and made her feel foolish and sound childish. She was not petulant, usually, and to hear herself sound so was ugly.

The fact that she acted so in front of Merrick seemed to suddenly bother her even more. For some strange reason she cared not to think on, his good opinion of her mattered.

She stared at her hands. "I should not have said that, my lord."

"Perhaps your challenging tone was not wise, but I am getting used to it."

Her head shot up. The look he gave said he was teasing her. She almost smiled.

He continued, "And I would have you speak to me with honesty." He paused, his expression edged with a harsh tautness that said this question was important, and not simple. He searched her face. "Tell me now. The truth, my lady. Do you not wish to wed me?"

"I did not say that."

"While I was gone for all those years, did you give your heart away to another?"

"No. No." She shook her head. "There is no one else."

"Then you agree to the marriage."

She looked at him then, and found she could no more tell him no than she could flap her arms and fly around the watchtower. "I agree."

His face showed no emotion, but she felt something pass between them, something that felt like desire.

"I want you to come to me as a willing bride, Clio. So make certain you mean those words."

"I mean them. I will wed you, my lord."

"Freely."

She nodded and started to turn away.

He moved his head, bending down slightly so he could still see her face. "Look into my eyes and say it."

"It."

For just a moment she thought he might smile at her, this stern, but puzzling man, the warring knight and close friend to the king, a man who had nursed her and who was to be her husband.

The expectant and intense look he gave her said more than words. She sighed and wished her future husband had a sense of humor more akin to hers.

"Freely." She had repeated the word he wanted, then added words of her own, "I will wed you, Lord Merrick, of my own free will."

"Good."

She started to move again, but he stopped her with a gentle hand on her good shoulder.

She looked back at him.

"It is customary to seal the promise with a kiss of faith."

Her gaze flicked to his mouth, which was wide and still in that tense line. The dark smudged shadow of a beard surrounded his lips and lined the strong lines of his jaw and cheeks. His neck was corded with muscles, for it took a strong man to wear the weight of mail, especially the hood and collar.

She had lifted her father's once, when she got the idea into her head to become his squire so she could go to a tournament in Normandy. But she had given herself away the first night, when she had to use both hands to lift his mail hood.

Her father had laughed, claiming she—a woman—would make no squire. She told him that after lifting the hood, she understood why men were so thick-headed.

But now, as she looked up into the face of the man she had just agreed to wed, she saw that his eyes were that same cool blue under black winged brows. Yet this time they held no anger, no icy facade, but instead the same blue-hot gleam she had seen when he kissed her in front of his men and when she had dropped her towel.

She was level with his chest, so she crooked her finger at him. "Your cheek, please, my lord."

He did not bend down to her. A second later he lifted her off her feet and kissed her right on the mouth. His large hands held her only by the waist; then he turned and pressed her against the stone wall with his body while one hand slid up and cupped the back of her head, protecting it from the sharp edges of the stone.

His breath tasted fresh and green, as if he had recently cleaned his teeth with a hazel twig. She could smell the scent of the spring sun on him, that warm and yeasty smell. There was no odor of leather, road, or of horse about him this day.

His tongue flicked over her lips. She opened her eyes in surprise and found him watching her. He pulled back and dragged his lips softly over her brows, then down to her lids, so that she had to close them again.

He was so gentle. The kisses were like whispers, soft and breathy and warm. His lips moved to her ear. "Open your mouth to me."

This time he did not seek to take from her, but asked her to give, the same way he had made her admit she would wed him. He was giving her the chance to take control, and they both knew what that meant.

She could never claim she was forced by him.

Then his lips covered hers again; his tongue filled her mouth and played with hers, brushing it and licking and tasting her, running over her teeth and then slowly tracing each lip, only to thrust back inside and send her to a place where she had no thoughts in her head, where all she could do was feel, where her blood raced through her body as if it were poured from a vat of boiling oil.

He tasted of everything she had ever loved: of honeyed figs and sweet Sicilian oranges, of almond milk and wild black cherries, of raisin cream and rose pudding, and of a woman's dreams.

Her arms slid up his chest and around his taut neck. She clung to him, because she didn't know what it was she wanted. She was chilled one minute, then burning the next, as if she had caught some strange yet beautiful fever from the moon and the sun.

She pressed her body against his because she felt a restless need to move against him, to rub his body with hers, and to try to climb inside of him. It was as if there was something she needed desperately awaiting her there.

He groaned something against her mouth, started to pull away.

She gave a small cry of disappointment that came from deep inside of her and made her sound like a small bird that had fallen from its nest.

He pressed his hips against her and pinned her to the tower wall, then used both hands to cup her face. He kissed her again. His mouth was urgent and pressed harder than before, his tongue battering hers with strong and powerful strokes. It was almost as if he were being forced against her by some unseen hand, forced to kiss her to prove he had won her as his own.

This was no gentle lover's kiss. It was the kiss of a warrior. Her warrior.

He tore his lips from hers abruptly.

She had been so caught inside their kiss that she had to shake the strange lightness from her head.

It took a moment until his face no longer blurred before her. When her sight cleared, she could see that his eyes were on her mouth. His breath came in faster pants, as if he had been fighting or riding hard.

Her own rapid breath mixed with his, and the wind over the battlements swallowed it. Her heartbeat slowed first in her wrists, then her chest and her ears, until it beat once again with a slow, strong rhythm.

He gripped her by the waist and stepped back, setting her on the stones. She looked away, embarrassed by what had passed between them. She felt like a wanton, like the lush dairymaid with the white skin and rosy cheeks who used to seduce her father's men by pressing her body against theirs and luring them behind the hayrick.

This weak-willed, amoral Clio was foreign to her and she was frightened by what she'd done. She could feel her hands begin to shake, so she clasped them tightly and tried to hide them in the folds of her tunic.

"Are you afraid to look at me?"

"No." She did not raise her head, just spoke the word that blatantly denied exactly what it was she was feeling—fear.

Because she was afraid of what she'd see when she did look at. him. To complete her humiliation, she felt her eyes swell with tears.

Oh, no, not now. Don't cry.

She bit her lip, but it didn't help. The tears spilled onto her cheeks.

To her horror she felt his hands on her shoulders. He turned her around and pulled her against his chest. She kept her face hidden and tried to stop crying.

"Clio."

She couldn't respond because she knew he'd hear those tears she tried to hide, tears she hardly understood.

"You are crying?"

She looked away.

"Did I hurt you?"

"No."

"Tell me why you are crying."

"I don't know why. I just feel like crying." She pushed at his chest, but he refused to let her go. She slowly raised her face to his and saw his mouth descending again.

That kiss. Dear Lord, but she wanted that kiss again.

A shout sounded from the fields beyond the castle. He released her abruptly, and together they moved to the battlements and looked down. Riders approached escorting a long column of wagons. Pennants with red rearing lions waved in the breeze.

When he turned toward her, there was an odd glint in his eye, amusement with a snatch of arrogant pride, something that worried her a little.

He raised his hand toward her. "Come."

For just a moment she hesitated, then nodded toward the procession below. "What is this all about, my lord?"

"About?" he repeated, then took her hand in his and, without looking at her, only staring straight ahead, drew her along with him back toward the stairs. " 'Tis your bride-price, my lady."

CHAPTER 20

Clio had never seen a mechanical bird before. She had not known such a thing existed and never thought to own one. According to Merrick, this one had once belonged to the great Macedonian Alexander.

She looked at the brass bird, and thought of Pitt, then quickly prayed that he was well out there in the forest. Perhaps he was swinging upside-down from the branch of a willow tree or happily sitting atop the head of a fox or a badger or some such thing and picking out lice—his favorite sport.

The mechanical bird she held cupped in her hands was a strange looking thing. She almost wished it could talk. What tales it would have to tell!

She glanced at her cat, who had been listless since her goshawk disappeared. Clio placed the brass key in a small notch hole in the middle of the bird's back and wound it, 'round and round, the way Merrick had showed her.

The bird made an odd clicking sound, then its wings rose a little with each click, until they were spread as wide as those of a gyrfalcon.

Cyclops arched his back and hissed, suddenly awake—a miracle in itself—and squatting down on his haunches. His tail swung back and forth and he stared at the brass bird with his one eye.

The day before, Old Gladdys had placed a black eye patch where Cy's missing eye should be, which gave him a heathen air and had sent Brother Dismas into fits and cries about the cat truly being a familiar.

The mechanical bird with the illustrious past began to shuffle in a jerky circle.

Cyclops pounced. His fat belly landed right atop the bird, which still made a scratchy noise, like that of a broken bell. *Clank, clink, clunk!*

It inched out from beneath Cy's bright fur, jerky brass wing first. He curled his paws around the wobbly bird and pulled it against his furry chest.

There were loud pinging noises like flat chapel bells and a loud *boing!*

Cy screeched and whipped out the door so fast that if it weren't for spotting his tail, Clio might have thought the cat had just disappeared into thin air.

She glanced back at the mechanical bird.

It lay on its side on the floor, its wings at an odd angle and a bouncing wire in the shape of Dulcie's ringlets poking out of its back. She rose from the stool near her new bedstead, crossed the room, and picked up the pieces, then set them on a small table that was covered with small jewel chests, golden cups, thick plates, and assorted reliquary caskets.

When she turned back and looked around her, she was still unable to believe what she saw. The goods flowed from her chamber into the solar.

On the stone floors were hand-loomed rugs

with intricate designs of silken nightingales, winter roses, and white horses. Flemish tapestries were rolled and stacked along the solar wall, beside chests of cloth the color of jewels, some of the lengths made of threads' so shiny they looked as if they were spun from real jewels—sapphires, rubies, emeralds, and amber. There were others woven with metal threads of spun silver, copper, and gold, and a chest held braid and tassels and ribbons that shone like moonlight.

Atop an ornately carved ebony tester frame, with a rosewood truckle bed that slid underneath, was a plush wool-and-feather-filled tick made from rich woolen damask. There were pure linen sheetings spun from finely worked flax and bleached so very white that you could almost smell the sunshine in them. Scattered all over the bed were earth-toned pillows made of downy goat hair woven into a soft, thin cloth called Kashmir.

From the East, in the land where the mongoose weasel lived, came a wooden wheel used for spinning wool into the finest of thread; it sat in a corner by a golden strung harp and three fluted reed instruments that sounded as deep and as mellow as the midnight call of a lonely wood owl.

A small sloping scribe's desk for writing sat next to its matching stool with leopards carved on the base. Merrick had seen them moved near the highest and broadest open solar loop so daylight came inside and shone on the polished burl of the desktop.

And now, when Clio looked at it, glowing in the rich sunlight, the polished wooden top looked the same rich color as a warm summer sunset.

But like its giver, the delightful desk held deep, wonderfully surprising secrets hidden from the casual eye, for when she had lifted the desktop, there was a compartment beneath. 'Twas filled with parchment so fine it was as thin as the skin of an onion. Next to the thin paper was a polished wood box of writing quills with different-sized cut points and a horn filled with precious indigo ink—a gift from a sultan who was impressed by Merrick's riding skills.

There was more. So much more. Every corner. Every nook had something new, something more unique and pleasurable than the last. As she scanned the room, she felt over-whelmed and awestruck by all the riches that sat before her very eyes. Here. Inside Cam-rose, her home, the place she wanted restored to elegance. But this was more than elegant.

'Twas almost too much, she thought for a moment. But what was too much wealth, too much majesty?

Confused by her thoughts, she turned and stopped when she caught her reflection in a large piece of polished brass that Dulcie had hung near her new silver water basin and matching ewer with a handle in the shape of a prowling lion.

It did not escape her thoughts that these riches were given to her by the Red Lion;

they were his property and he had chosen to give them to her. Before, she had always thought scornfully of a bride-price as a purchase payment, like that for an auction slave being sold to the highest-bidding master.

But somehow, Merrick had made her feel as if these were gifts, presented to her and selected only for her. Special presents, not to buy her, but to provide her with pleasure and comfort. She knew that the thought sounded wistful and foolish, but it felt so very true.

She stared at the polished brass.

Was that she staring back? She cocked her head slightly. She did not look like herself. She reached up and touched the blue, teardrop pearls that hung from her headpiece, a gold and jewel-encrusted fillet with pearl drops along the crown that were the same color as Merrick's icy eyes.

Her skin was flushed as if she had walked in the hot summer sun, and there was a sparkle to her green eyes. She touched her red and slightly swollen lips with her fingertips.

Kissed. She had been kissed.

Not a groping old bishop's kiss in a dark corner of the stairs, or a stable lad's quick peck on the cheek, but a man's kiss. A real kiss. One so intimate she had not thought such a touch existed.

She gave a dreamy sigh.

The sultans of the East might be impressed with Merrick's riding skills, but Clio was rather more impressed with his kissing skills. She smiled a wicked little smile that made her belly flip and her blood tingle through her veins as if she were being leeched.

She had promised to wed Merrick. She had given her word.

She did not know what surprised her more, that she had agreed so readily, or that he'd actually asked. If she had said no, would he have accepted that? Some perverse part of her wanted to test the theory, but another part of her knew she never would.

She tried so hard not to care. She tried so hard not to give an inch to him. She tried and she failed. He won her, as surely as if she were the prize in a tourney.

And he did so not with brute force, not with bribery and the riches that now surrounded her. He did not do so with kisses that made her wits go walking or her heart throb. She supposed that his surprising kindness was part of what changed her mind, as was the gentle firmness she had seen in him the last week.

But the one thing that finally did win her was something so much more powerful, so remarkable. 'Twas the greatest gift he could have ever given her: the right to say no.

Sometime before Lauds, when Clio couldn't find a wink of sleep atop her plush new bed, she had gone up on the battlements and stood there, her back pressed against the cold, damp stones. She stared up at the night sky, where it was so clear that the stars looked as close as the fireflies in the Great Forest beyond.

Once when she was small, she had ventured into that forest and seen strange flecks of light spinning through the air in flitting circles that looked like flaming bees. They had frightened her and she'd run to her mother's arms, crying.

But her mother carried her back inside the forest, hugging her tightly so she wouldn't cry, and then had shown her what those flickers of light truly were. Caddis flies was what she had called them.

She had told Clio that the villagers called them firedrakes and believed they brought good luck to those who watched them. Like the eastern star that proclaimed Christ's birth, the fireflies were friends to the angels, and God himself decreed in those first days of creation that the Caddis would be so blessed that they could dance in the air.

Clio never forgot that day, because that was one of the few memories she had in which she could still see the clear image of her mother's face.

So she stood on that wall walk and watched the sky, feeling comfortable and easy. She pretended those stars that flickered like the Caddis were there to bring her luck. Her sleepless mind drifted back as if by magic to the wonderful kiss atop those battlements, and she stood that way until dawn came and the stars all melted away.

With a deep sigh, she turned to go back to her bedchamber, but a door in the courtyard squeaked like Thud and Thwack's piglets. Clio moved to the wall and braced her hands atop the stone, peering down.

185

In the dawn light she saw Merrick walking across the inner bailey, and her gaze followed him as if compelled to do so. There was something about the way he walked, the cock in his hip, the way his strides ate up the ground, the way his arms moved little yet his right hand rested on his sword hilt even though he was within safe grounds.

She saw that his shoulders stayed straight as he moved, his head high. His black hair gleamed almost silver in the new light and was getting longer and beginning to curl where the ends met his shoulders. He wore a leather tunic the same color as his hair and dark crimson braies that clung to the honed leg muscles of a true warrior.

His soft leather boots came almost to his knees, and golden light flashed from his knight's spurs. In the crisp morning air, the rowels jangled when he crossed the bailey and met briefly with the master mason and builders. She had the feeling he knew who and what was around him, even then.

For some inexplicable reason she hid in the shadows and felt her face flush and flame. He could not see her, yet he sensed her. She could feel it, this strange invisible bond that seemed to link them as one mind, one thought.

She felt sweat break out on her brow, and she did not move, even held her breath until her chest began to tighten. Slowly, furtively, she peered out from the shadows. She felt like a thief.

Merrick had turned back to the master builders, and within moments they all disappeared out the latest of the castle's new defenses: an inner portcullis that had been added last week to double protection.

She stood there feeling strange and somehow light, as if she were only half there. She glanced up at the golden dawn. Perhaps the stars were like the Caddis, there to bring her good luck. After all, she had gotten a good glimpse of Merrick.

Then she chided herself for being every kind of fool.

Of course that was silly thinking. If good fortune had truly been on her side that morn, he would have been wearing only that loincloth.

A few busy days later, Merrick was bent over the high table, his palms holding down the curling edges of one of the master builder's drawings.

"I spotted some Welsh devil on your Arab horse."

Merrick looked up.

Sir Roger stood in the archway of a side entrance to the great hall. His helmet was tucked under one arm and his mail hood had been pushed back and sat gathered at his neck like a yoke.

Leaves and sticky moss stuck out from his red hair, and grass and dirt peppered his mail tunic. There were great clumps of mud splattered all over his armor, so much so he looked as if he had been dipped in it.

He walked toward Merrick; water and mud

squirted out from the sollerets on his feet. With every motion of his arms or legs, water dripped from his armor joints in trickling trails all over the flagstone floor.

Merrick let his gaze slowly travel over his friend, from the wet weeds in his hair to the mud clots beneath his feet. "I'm surprised old Langdon didn't teach you that you cannot swim in armor."

Roger made a rude gesture and threw his gauntlets and helm on a bench. A soggy marsh marigold landed next to Merrick and he looked down, then picked it up and dangled it in front of him. "Lose this?"

Roger spat one of Merrick's favorite and most colorful curses.

Merrick had seldom seen Roger like this. His usual mood was light, sometimes insufferably so. Merrick turned back to the bridge plans. "You are not your merry self. The ladies will be heartbroken."

Roger sat down across from him.

The moment his ass hit the bench, there was a loud squish. He winced slightly, then caught Merrick's amused look. "I was chasing the cursed devil of a rider for you."

"For me." That bit of bunkum was even too much for Merrick. He gave a wry bark of laughter.

"Aye, for you. 'Tis your horse."

"Odd, I thought it might be because you have been trying to buy, barter, wager, or wheedle that mount from me ever since I've had him."

Roger was staring at his hands, shaking his head in disbelief. "I've been doing everything possible for over the last two years to get you to sell me that blasted horse."

"I know."

He looked up at Merrick. "That is all you have to say about it? I thought you'd be ranting the walls down over losing that horse."

Merrick shrugged. "I have other horses."

"Are you fevered?"

Aye, Merrick thought, ignoring Roger's puzzled look. His blood was hot, but the heat wasn't from any disease. 'Twas all Roger needed to know, that he way hot from a woman. He'd never hear the end of it.

He chose not to respond, but sat there in silence, pretending to examine the castle plans, which could have been upside-down for all he knew.

Roger, too, was silent for a few long seconds, then grudgingly admitted, "It took my squire and two men-at-arms to pull me from the river." He jabbed his dagger into a green pear that sat in nearby fruit bowl and took a huge bite, then chewed it as viciously as if it were tough and stringy mutton. "I about drowned."

"I can see that."

Roger just grunted. With an intent look on his scowling face, he was on to his second pear, jabbing and stabbing, poking and slicing it with his knife.

"Are you going to eat that fruit or kill it?"

"Both," he answered with his mouth full.

"Should I ask how a man of your famous horse skills ended up in the river?"

"No. Not if you value your life."

Merrick did laugh out loud.

Roger scowled at him, which made him laugh harder. Roger ran a hand over his filthy and mud-speckled face, then stared at his palm. After a moment his expression changed from angry indignation to one of sheepish amusement. "I suppose it would have been amusing to watch, were it not happening to me."

"Had it happened to me, you'd have been crowing and howling until I was ready to jam my fist in your face."

"Aye. That I would."

" 'Tis only your pride that is sorely wounded."

"No."

"You are hurt?" Merrick could hear the strain in his own voice. The memory of Clio and the arrow was still too fresh in his mind. He loved Roger like the brother he never had.

"Only my ass hurts." Roger shifted from one side to another. " 'Tis sore as Saint Apollonia's teeth. That river bottom was damned rocky."

Merrick tossed him a damask pillow from the lord's high chair, and Roger caught it and, to Merrick's surprise, used it.

When he looked at Roger again a few seconds later, Roger's gaze had drifted up to the rafter beams, his expression half thoughtful and half in awe. "You should have seen the rider, Merrick." He shook his dagger with a pear on it to emphasize each word. "I've never seen anyone ride like that. He looked as if he'd been riding that horse of yours all his life."

Roger turned and looked at him. "They looked like one whole beast when they rode up and over that craggy hill at Pwllycalch."

"They rode over Pwllycalch?" Merrick was surprised. The jagged and deadly hills of southern Brecon near the Usk Valley were infamous for their ruggedness. There was a local folktale that only the fey ones could traverse the chalky shale hills, because under the light of the moon they were said to sprout the wings of falcons and fly out of sight.

"Aye. They were up and over those rocks and halfway across the valley before I could make it past the first gorge. Made those desert riders from Damascus look like old, feeble women."

But feeble old women were the last things on Merrick's preoccupied mind. He was thinking of Clio, lost in an image of her face, that special face, and the earthy sweet flavor of her warm mouth.

And so it was that Roger sat across from him thinking of a different image—that of a horse and rider, the finest he'd ever seen, flying across the wild Welsh valley as if they were drinking the wind.

CHAPTER 21

Drinking was just the thing on Clio's mind. Not drinking the wind, however, but instead her duty to provide her own bride ale.

Bride ale was supposed to be special—a gift to the wedding guests from the mother of the bride. She had no living mother, but she certainly had pride.

What a wonderful idea she had hit upon! Of course she would make the best bride ale ever. She secretly hoped her recipe would finally be the magic one, the one she and so many others had sought.

What better wedding gift to give her husband and his men? The same invincibility as had the ancient Druid warriors, the ones who had sent Caesar and his legions running back home.

So she lay on her stomach across her plush new bed, her bare feet waving in the air impatiently as she thumbed through Sister Amice's notes and recipes.

Had she told anyone what she was planning, they might have claimed she was counting her eggs as hens. She could just hear them now. "That Clio! What a silly goose of a girl she was, making her bride ale when no wedding day had yet been set."

But Merrick had said they would wed within a fortnight. She had no cause not to believe him. He had not lied to her since his return.

Besides, she rationalized, he was the one who volunteered the information and in a casual, offhanded comment.

Chest after chest had been brought to her chamber. She had not known what to look at first. The closest one was filled with lovely cloth, the like of which she had never seen. She almost crawled inside the huge chest as she rummaged through bolt after bolt of fine cloth.

"There is only one more delay for our wedding," Merrick had said.

She remembered thinking to herself at the time, what was he saying now? She'd been almost impatient while looking in awe at fabrics so sheer and thin that she'd felt as if she were looking through the precious window glass at a cathedral.

"Wedding?" She'd paused. Did he say wedding? She'd poked her head out and asked, "Our wedding?"

Merrick had just disappeared around the entrance to the solar with the master builder running at his heels.

She'd dug her way out of the chest and stood quickly, slapping her hair from her face in time to see the top of his head disappearing down the stone stairs.

"Merrick! Wait!" She'd run to the staircase. "What thing is delaying the wedding?"

But she'd gotten no response. He had disappeared, called away by the master builder.

Once again.

So now, as she lay on the bed, she propped

her chin in her hands and scowled, thinking of the last few days. She had not seen him since she'd spied on him from the battlements.

She was beginning to wonder with no little irritation if she should disguise herself into a stone brick. Or a bucket for the new wells. A guard for the portcullis or the builder's drawings for the bridge spanning the wider moat.

Then she would have more of Merrick's attention. And she needed his attention if she was to pry some more of those wonderful kisses from him.

But after a moment her annoyance just drifted away. She should be more tolerant, more understanding. If for no other reason than to repay him for his kindness to her, his care and his gifts.

Sighing, she glanced back down at the notes lying on the bed before her. Within a few short lines she read where the good sister had written of Trefriw and the *chalybeate*, which Sister Amice translated as special spa waters of Wales that were rumored to have healing properties.

Spa waters? Healing properties?

She quickly turned a few more pages and found another suggested ale recipe. She read the ingredients slowly. When she was done, she raised her head and tapped a finger thoughtfully against the small cleft in her chin.

A moment later a small frown line appeared in her brow. She began to chew on her lower lip and nervously twisted her mother's ring on her finger. Her expression changed quickly, in a mere snap of the fingers. Her look became dovelike. Peaceful.

Then she smiled. My, my, my, she thought. Perhaps it was a good thing her betrothed was so very busy.

Merrick rode with a few men toward the coast. Roger was beside him, having no trouble keeping pace with Merrick's hard riding atop the best horse he could get saddled quickly.

After riding Aries and the Arab, the poor beast beneath him seemed a puny excuse for a mount. Had Merrick had the Arab horse, he'd have caught Clio by now.

"Why the hell did you give her a wagon?" Roger asked.

"I don't know." Merrick mentally called himself every kind of fool. The truth was he had given her the specially ornamented wagon as part of her bride-price. He had heard that ladies adored such things. He wanted to please her.

At the time he had been remembering how her body glistened in bath water while her defiant expression dared him to look at her. Even burying himself in the castle renovations for days had not driven the image of her from his heated mind.

He had been thinking with no sense, but with his nether head. He did not know whom he was more angry with, Clio or himself.

From the corner of his eye he caught Roger's

stare. "After being shot with a Welsh arrow I wrongly assumed that she would not be stupid enough to take off alone again."

"Alone? I thought that Welsh hag was with her."

"Aye. 'Tis the same thing. The old woman is mad."

"I've seen that old woman. She winked at me, blinking one black eye. I tell you, it scared the bloody hell out of me. I wasn't certain if she was flirting or giving me the evil eye."

"You sound like that fool monk Dismas." Merrick remembered when Clio was ill, he had seen that hint of intelligence and lucidity in those black eyes of Old Gladdys's. And there was that pot of salve, which had healed Clio so swiftly she had spent a good week causing him more trouble. "I think the woman is harmless."

"Harmless? Hell, Merrick, all she has to do is wink once and she could scare off even the Devil himself. Considering that, I suspect Lady Clio is safe with the hag."

Merrick wouldn't believe Clio was safe until he could touch her and see for himself. He kept picturing her running from those men, the arrow, the blood, and hearing her scream.

The memory just made him spur his mount harder, up and over a hillock and down a broad valley that looked out over the bay. He rode as hard as he could, getting every ounce of speed from the horse.

He was across the valley in no time and cantering down toward a brown ribbon of road that cut through the coastal cliffs. He caught a flash of red and slowed his mount. He reined in.

There, on the road below, was a lumbering red wagon shaped like a huge sausage. The driver was dressed in black robes and had a white dandelion fluff of hair that bounced in the breeze like carded wool.

Strapped to the wagon were what looked like huge water barrels. As the studded wagon wheels with their golden paint and ornately carved spokes rolled over the road, dirt and dust clouded up behind it, and all the way up on the ridge, he could hear the barrels banging like Celtic war drums against the wagon's hollow side.

In his anger, he hoped Clio was safely inside, getting a pounding ache in her head from the racket. He stared down at it and almost laughed at the image. There were so many water barrels it looked as if the poor oxen were pulling all of Cardigan Bay behind them.

Roger rode up and reined in, cursing him for a fool. "You're going to kill that poor beast you're riding."

"No," Merrick said through gritted teeth. "I'm not going to kill this horse." He drew his sword and used it to point down at the wagon, where a small and familiar blond head had just poked out of the wagon's window. "If I kill anything, Roger, it will be her."

CHAPTER 22

It did not take all of her wits for Clio to know that she was in trouble again. She clung to the wagon window and just stared out toward the east.

The way Merrick and his men were riding toward them gave her a small idea of what his enemies must face when Merrick and his men were bearing down upon them. If you were their prey, the sight was would be more than frightening.

Red Lion pennants waved in the sea breeze like flags of warning. Merrick rode hard, so swiftly he was halfway down the hillside, a good five lengths ahead of his men. You could not miss the bright bloodred lion on his surcoat. His dark cape billowed out behind him like dark wings and made him look like the Devil himself riding out of hell.

The ground shook with the thundering sound of horses running over the low coastal hills as if they had wings on their hooves. Dust clouded up behind them and shouts from their riders pierced the air like barbaric battle cries.

Clio looked out the wagon window toward the driver's box. Even Old Gladdys—who had more mettle than Eleanor herself, now the queen mother—didn't test the patience of Lord Merrick and his troops. She reined in the ox team with some Welsh babble before Clio could lean farther out the window and order her to do so.

Merrick rode straight toward Clio. At the edge of the coast road, he reined in. Before the mount had stopped, he leapt off and strode toward her, his look as black as the cape he wore.

She was half-hidden behind a huge water barrel with a plugged top that had taken both Old Gladdys and her a good hour to roll and grunt and stuff inside the wagon. Altogether that day, the two of them had gathered ten full barrels of spa waters, enough to brew the bride ale for the wedding of a queen.

Chewing her lower lip, she peered over the splintered edge of the barrel. Merrick was not a happy man.

He tore open the door with such force that the wagon rocked. The door slammed against the side of the wagon and Clio flinched. Her arm slipped and her elbow hit the barrel; it wobbled and the top loosened and tilted.

A small bit of water sloshed over the barrel rim. Merrick reached out with the flat palm of one of his huge hands.

He was silent, pointedly so. He just stood there with his arm braced against the barrel until it stopped wobbling.

Meanwhile he looked at her like a dog who had a cat treed.

His brawny body filled the doorway. He was breathing as if he had been running hard.

'Twas a sight, for sure.

She stared at his face. Odd, she did not know someone's jaw could be clenched that tight. She would wager his teeth ached.

"Get out."

She chewed her lip for a moment longer, weighing her slim options. She raised her chin and looked at him, then said, "I don't think so."

She settled back against the soft leather seat back and spent an inordinate amount of time brushing imaginary wrinkles and dust from her gown. After all, she was most likely safe; the barrel was a bit of a shield.

He stuck his big black head inside the carriage and bellowed, "Tell me, woman! Do you sit up in your solar and plot these fits of defiance to test me?"

"What fits? I do not know what you are talking about."

"This...This...nonsense!" Merrick waved his arm around in the air as if she should understand exactly what he was speaking of "God's feet and hair!"

She stuck her nose in the air. "You are swearing, my lord."

"I know." He glared at her, gripping the top of the door rim with white knuckles. "It feels damn good, too."

She turned away and looked out the other window, wondering what he would do next. She could not have more obviously ignored him.

After a moment she could hear the whispers of his men, the shuffling of horses, and Sir Roger's pointed whistling.

"Clio." Merrick's voice was sharp and clipped and strained when he said her name. 'Twas so very different from the tone he had used when he had kissed her softly and with such warmth and tenderness. She knew he could be tender, and because of that she believed he would not harm her.

She turned her head very slowly; her eyes met his for a flash. Something passed between them that was strong and elemental and made her belly flip-flop. Her heart sped up and she found herself breathing harder.

Strange, since she had not been running either.

But as she watched him, waiting for him to make the next move, she could see there was nothing tender in the manner of the man who stood before her. He tore his angry gaze away and drove a hand impatiently through his hair.

He began to pace in front of her, locking his hands behind his back as if he needed to keep them from encircling her neck and squeezing hard.

His anger seemed to be like a live thing. His neck was a deep dark red, just as her father's had been when she had been banished from court by Henry's angry queen, Eleanor.

Merrick paced faster and faster, his long strides turning more stiff and his manner growing more agitated with each step he took.

He spun around and stopped suddenly, then he was filling the doorway. "Do you not understand what you have done, woman?" His loud words bounced like thunder in the close confines of the wagon interior.

"You needn't shout," she said in the same arrogant and touchy tone that had always confused her father when he was angry. "I have ears. I can hear you, my lord."

"Do you? I don't think you can hear me. Otherwise you would not keep disobeying my orders."

She tried to look thoughtful and intelligent. She kept her voice even and calm to counter his bellowing and show that she was the more reasonable and sane party, the one in control. "I do not recall any orders you gave regarding the gathering of spa waters."

He just stared at her.

She gave him a clear and honest look. "How can I have disobeyed an order I never received?"

Merrick looked as if he was mentally counting...or praying...or cursing. His lips were moving, but no sound came out.

"You are very angry." Pointing that out only made his neck redder. "Did you tell me I could not gather spa waters?"

"Why," he hollered, "in the name of Saint Swithun's sword arm, would I ever think that you would be overcome with the sudden need to gather blasted spa waters?"

"For my ale, of course."

"Forgive me," he said with heavy sarcasm. "But I must have overlooked the dire need for spa water when I decreed that you were not to leave the castle unescorted."

"I brought an escort. Old Gladdys."

Merrick stared at the old Welshwoman with a look that said he thought she was about as useless as silk pillows on a battlefield.

Meanwhile, Old Gladdys was winking at him and mumbling in Welsh.

Sir Roger moved his mount closer to Merrick. "Watch yourself, my friend, or you might grow warts on your nose tonight when the moon is high." His voice was light compared to Merrick's dark and gritty one, the same one that had been yelling at her.

Clio smiled at Sir Roger. He gave her a quick shake of his head, as if to warn her not to push Merrick too far.

Old Gladdys, who was still sitting on the driver's box, seemed completely unmoved by anything anyone was saying. She was too busy trying to make them believe she was casting Druid curses. The meaning of Gladdys's lyrical Welsh words hit Clio and she gaped at her. The old woman had just said something about the warts growing someplace other than on Lord Merrick's nose.

Clio felt her skin flush.

Scowling, Merrick turned back to Clio. "What did she say about me?"

"I don't know," Clio lied. She would not translate those words.

Old Gladdys laughed wickedly and began to hum a Druid chant. With much drama she turned her blackeyed gaze on Sir Roger and stared at him the way Cyclops eyed a fat, tasty stable mouse.

Merrick looked from Clio, back to the old woman, then back to Clio, whom he pinned with one of those dark looks of his. "We have four new wells at Camrose. There is plenty of water to use for your ale."

""Not *Trefriw*."

He acted as if he had not heard her. She knew he did not understand her, so instead of showing his confusion, he did the manly thing—planted his hands on his hips and proclaimed an edict. "I can see this is a futile conversation. You leave me no choice, woman. I will strip you of the duties of brewing and hire an ale maker."

"No!" She couldn't stop her panic and didn't try to hide it with the arrogant tone she used when she was arguing with a man. "I need something to do, Merrick!"

His expression flickered slightly when she used his Christian name.

"I must have a purpose. Some purpose."

"You do have a purpose."

"No," she shook her head, "I do not."

"You will be my wife."

"I need something to do!"

"Believe me, you will have plenty of duties."

"But you do not understand. I must have my own purpose!"

"I believe, woman, that your purpose is to drive me mad!" He ran a hand through his hair and stared at the ground. "Perhaps I already am mad."

"You're starting to shout again."

"Do not change the subject."

"I am not changing the subject. You *were* shouting."

"Get out of the wagon. *Now.*

She was trying to think quickly, to find another topic with which to confuse him. But her wits left her. And his look was not pretty.

"Do not make me drag you out."

"You would not be so cruel."

"I promise you I will drag you out of that wagon, then tie you with that length of rope across my saddle, and make you walk home behind me." He paused, then moved his face closer to hers and gritted, "That is if I don't decide to drag you along behind me."

"You would not do such a thing."

"I give you my word, Clio. What I will do you will not take any pleasure in. Now get down or you *will* walk back to Camrose."

She sighed, loudly, to show him she still had some small amount of power. It worked. He looked annoyed.

"I cannot move from the corner with this water barrel in my way."

"Crawl over it."

"I cannot. Here, wait and I'll try to move it a little..."

"Don't push on it!" He bellowed.

He reached for the tilting barrel.

She saw the panic in his eyes. Too late.

He cursed viciously.

Clio slapped her hands over her eyes and flinched when she heard a loud thud and the sound of water rushing.

Then there was utter silence. For the longest time. She sat there, eyes covered.

After a few long and rather telling moments,

she heard Old Gladdys cackle like a hen. Over and over. That seemed to trigger laughter, because some of Merrick's men-at-arms were suddenly laughing.

However, Sir Roger's laugh was loud and distinctive; it sounded like the barks of the seals along the western coast.

Laughter was good, she thought. Safe.

Very slowly she spread her fingers and peered out.

The great Red Lion was in the road on his backside; he looked like a drowned cat.

Roger leaned an arm casually on his saddle pommel and grinned down at Merrick, who sat in a large puddle of water. More water dripped from his long nose and clenched jaw and rolled down from his wet hair into his eyes.

"Didn't Hereford teach you, Merrick, that you cannot swim in only a barrel of water?"

Merrick cursed under his breath. He was getting bloody tired of hearing his own words thrown back at him.

With all the dramatic flair of the lead actor in a miracle play, Roger flung his arm out toward the bay beyond. "There's a whole bay out there for water play." Then he laughed even harder.

Merrick stood up. His cape was so heavy with water that it almost choked him. He jerked the silver lion brooch loose and tore off the heavy wet cape. He began to wring it out, twisting it with vicious motions while he looked straight at Clio's white neck.

From somewhere she found the good sense to truly look worried. He gave the cape another hard twist, then tossed it over his saddle.

He turned back to Clio. "Get down. You will ride with me."

To his amazement, she quietly obeyed him and stepped around the barrel. He mounted his horse, slid his boot into a stirrup, and held out a hand to her. "Give me your hand."

She stood there staring at him as if she did not trust him.

"Do not fret, woman. I will not cut it off."

His challenge worked. That chin of hers shot up and she placed her hand in his. He did not smile, but the urge to do so passed over him. Perhaps she was controllable after all.

"Stand on my foot. I'll pull you up."

She did as he asked, with more obedience than he'd seen from her since he'd stared at her bowed head that first day and foolishly assumed she was convent shy.

He clamped an arm around her and pulled her back against his chest. She gasped slightly. Her breasts were soft and heavy against the top of his forearm, and he could feel the pressure of her small ribs as he kept her pressed against him. He could feel the water, cool and wet against his skin, and knew she, too, was getting wet.

The sun shone high in the sky, and despite the coast breeze he was not cold. There was heat between their bodies, and not a mild warmth but a hot feeling that could almost have turned the air around them steamy.

He looked down to see her face was aflush, and she shifted as if she was trying to put some distance between their bodies.

"Hold still or you'll fall off." He pulled her tighter until she froze, and her soft bottom pressed against him.

He looked at Roger, who was still jesting with his men. "You will take the wagon back."

Roger stopped laughing so swiftly it was almost as if his voice had been snatched away. His expression turned sick when he looked at Old Gladdys.

The Welshwoman stroked back her hair with her hands as if it were a mane of luscious youthful hair instead of white woolly frizz. She scooted over and patted the wooden seat next to her, grinning at Sir Roger like a dewy-eyed dairymaid.

Roger looked as if he wanted to turn and ride away. He gazed at Merrick in disbelief. "You are jesting."

Merrick turned to his troops. "Three silver coins to the man who knows what Sir Roger likes!"

The men all shouted merrily, "He likes his ale strong, his saints fallen, and his women willing!"

Merrick cast a pointed glance at the old woman, who was eyeing Roger with a hungry look. He turned back to his friend and said, "She surely looks willing to me."

Ignoring Roger's pithy curses, he pulled Clio even tighter against him and spurred his horse toward Camrose.

CHAPTER 23

There was no moon in the black sky the night they returned to the castle. They rode through the gates to the flickering glimmer of torchlight and the long and empty sound of the watch guard's blow horn.

Merrick released her only long enough to dismount, then swept her up into his arms, carried her into the keep and up the stairs to her chamber, shouting orders to the servants for food, dry clothes, and hot water.

"I'm too tired to bathe," Clio muttered against his shoulder.

He just gave her one of those looks of his that said he was the one giving the orders not she, and he kicked open the door.

She was too tired and sore from the hard ride to argue. He dropped her on the bed, none too gently, and she opened her eyes planning to scowl up at him. He told Dulcie to get her out of those clothes and he strode from the room.

She was too tired to care if she slept in the dust from their ride. "Dulcie, please. I'll sleep like this. I'm just so
very tired." She could hear her voice drift off, as if it were someone else's from far away.

"Lift your arm, my lady." Dulcie was flitting here and there, unhooking her gown, clipping the sleeve seams, and pestering Clio as if she had not spoken.

"I'll sleep in my clothes," Clio grumbled.

"The earl gave me an order," Dulcie said, pulling Clio's clothing off before she added under her breath, "I'm no fool. Unlike some, *I* know enough to obey my lord's orders."

Before Clio could think of an eloquent and biting argument, she was in a clean linen shift and Dulcie had left her chamber with her arms piled full of dirty clothes.

She sighed and closed her eyes.

Merrick was standing at the top of the stairs, still bellowing orders. 'Twas like trying to sleep in a bell tower at Matins.

She propped up on her elbows, ignoring the aching muscles in her shoulders, bottom, and back. Through the open doors she could see him. He stood at the head of the stairs telling everyone what to do.

As usual.

So she fell back with a huge sigh. She did so adore this new mattress. It was soft and warm and like sleeping on a cloud. She stuffed a pillow under her neck and sore shoulder.

But as she lay there, trying to sleep and ignore the noise, she noticed an aching in her shoulder—the arrow wound—for the first time since she had healed. It was sharp and tense and felt taut as woof strings on a loom.

Perhaps she had overdone things a wee bit. Those water barrels were terribly heavy. The next time she would bring someone strong and brawny with her.

Cyclops picked that moment to leap up on the bed. He pawed the covers, purring in that loud way that always made her smile. He walked in a circle and plopped down near her head as if to say, "Now we go to sleep."

She stroked his furry head with that ludicrous eye patch tied around it. Just looking at him made her smile.

Sighing with weariness, she wiggled around for a moment to find a better position, then clamped a pillow over her head to block out Merrick's voice. She drew her knees up until she was curled into her favorite position, pulled the coverlets over her head, and finally slept.

"What are you doing?"

At the sound of Clio's voice Merrick looked up.

She was sitting up in her bed and looking at him from sleepy eyes.

"Taking a bath," he said casually while he used a cloth to scrub the dirt from his arms and chest.

"I can see that." She stifled a yawn. "I am not an idiot."

"I could debate that point with you." He leaned forward and ducked his head under the water so he didn't have to hear what she had to say. His patience was stretched taut enough already.

His head broke through the water surface and he slicked his hair back with his hands.

She had not moved. "This is my chamber."

He scrubbed the cloth over his face and

two days' worth of scratchy black whiskers. He needed to have his man shave him. He laid the cloth on the rim of the wooden tub where a nearby brazier would keep it warm.

He looked back at her. "There is no soap."

The expression she wore was startled. And he was glad, for that was how she made him feel whenever she switched subjects on him. "I think, woman, you need to spend your time seeing to the castle needs and not running off to collect spa waters. Perhaps you should be making soap instead of ale."

He paused and let his words sink in. "No chatelaine with any pride would have a household without even one puny ball of soap."

"I do not need a man to tell me what I need, my lord."

"Someday you will take those words back, I promise you."

"I have soap."

She'd changed the subject again.

"*Camrose* has plenty of soap!" She threw back the covers and pattered across the stone floor, churning her arms like a soldier on the march. She opened a standing chest and pulled out a round ball of yellow soap.

She held it out toward him, her nose up again.

'Twas a perfect position. He could see right through her thin shift. He looked his fill and was reminded of his foolhardy conversation with Roger about her looks, and how he did not care. Words did come back to haunt you.

He found he did care what she looked like, probably because looking at her gave him such pleasure. And it was a different pleasure from his man's need for a woman, different from wanting a woman. Just any woman.

He wanted Clio. His body responded to her, but that was not unusual. Right at that moment beneath the water he was hard as the castle wall. But he was a trained knight taught to control himself, so he could control his response. He did not act foolishly.

But somehow, this intense need in him was different with her. 'Twas only for Clio. And he could not control that, nor what she did to him, deep inside his body and in his mind.

His gaze flicked back to her just as she threw the soap toward him. He snatched it from the air so swiftly she blinked.

She watched him in stunned silence, so he hid his smile and examined the soap; then he raised it to his nose and sniffed. He made a face. "Lye soap."

She whirled around, which was good because he needed a moment to fix his face into a serious frown. She opened and closed a few compartments in the cabinet, then turned and said, "Thyme soap!"

She threw a new piece of soap to him.

Or perhaps at him.

"Rose oil!" Then came another. "Chamomile!" And another piece flew across the room.

He caught one with one hand and one with the other.

"Sea heather! Lilac!"

Merrick tried not to smile while he dodged

balls of herbed and essence-oil soap that flew at him like rocks from a catapult.

"Sandalwood! Myrrh! Spikenard! Clove!"

The clove soap hit the wall with a smack and rolled along the floor. That ugly one-eyed cat leapt off the bed and chased the soap ball, batting it with its paws before the ugly beast cornered the soap and pounced atop it.

"Musk! Patchouli! Lavender and spearmint! Almond, citronella oil, frangipani, orrisroot, honeysuckle, woodruff, attar of roses..."

A few minutes later, as Merrick sat in the tub with soap balls everywhere, he had to agree that Camrose castle had plenty of soap.

And its mistress had plenty of fire.

She stood in front of a chest, her fists planted on her rounded hips in a cocky "so there" way. One thing was certain. She was now wide awake.

God's feet, but she was beautiful! She tossed her head the way his mount did when he reined it in too quickly, then strolled toward him like a conqueror, swaggering pridefully.

He wondered if she was even aware that she was clad in only her shift. But he remembered her dropping the towel and thought proudly that she was not one to cower and hide her fine body.

Whether she knew how she was clad or not didn't matter.

The view did.

She did not look away, and he didn't either, since the oil bowl on a nearby table cast light that limned her shape beneath the fabric. She might as well have been naked.

If she was aware of how she looked, or how little she wore, she gave no sign, but stared at him instead from eyes that sparked with a challenge. And something else, something more elemental, that made him want her more than he'd ever wanted anything in his entire life.

"Come here."

She took her sweet time obeying him, but she did come to stand beside the tub. She stood above him, the glint of a devil in her eye.

He held out five balls of soap. "Which would you prefer to use?"

"To do what? Heave at you?" When he didn't respond, she said, "The biggest one, then."

He leaned forward. "Wash my back with one of them."

"You have servants to perform such tasks."

"Would you have me wake them at this time of night after working hard all day just to do what you could do so easily?" He had her and he knew it, but he decided to prick her pride, too. "There was time when a woman took honor in her duties, including bathing a knight."

She stared at him. He could see her thoughts cross her expression, flashes of panic and anger, curiosity and wounded pride.

Time seemed to stretch out between them the way it did when diplomats were wary and kept their tongues silent.

But just because there was no sound did not mean they did not understand each other. They did.

You push me too far, my lord.
You ask for it, my lady.

With a disgusted snort she snatched the cloth from the side of the tub and scoured a soap ball across it until lather was foaming and white and spilt over her hand and onto the stone floor.

"Lean forward," she snapped, and slapped the cloth on his back with a *smack!*

Solely to irritate her, Merrick casually rested his elbows on his raised knees and bent his head, then moaned as if he were in ecstasy; it did feel good after riding all over Wales hell-bent to find her before she got herself killed or raped or maimed.

She rubbed his back harder and harder.

Her movements were so vigorous that he glanced back at her, wondering if he were the one being maimed.

His timing was perfect, for at that exact moment she gripped the cloth in two hands and pushed it over his skin the way someone shoved a heavy chest across the floor. Her lower lip was tucked under her teeth and her face was strained, as if she were scrubbing as hard as her puny woman's strength would let her.

Any moment he expected her to grunt.

He waited a count of ten, then stood suddenly, water sloshing about him and onto her. His own bit of vengeance.

She gasped and fell back on the floor with a muttered curse to Saint David.

Acting perfectly natural, he turned and faced her, then purposely stood there longer than necessary, while she was on the floor, forced to stare up at him. Her gaze traveled down the length of his body.

He watched her eyes grow wide and her skin flush. Then he stretched, twisting this way, then that way before he sat back down in the tub.

There was long telling silence.

This was almost too easy, he thought, resting his arms on the rim. With a relaxed sigh he leaned his head back and closed his eyes.

She said nothing.

He opened his eyes and gave her a long searching look. After a moment he tossed her a ball of soap and said, "Now my chest."

CHAPTER 24

I wonder if the king would have me beheaded for throwing one of his earls out the tower window?

Clio slowly looked from Merrick to the arrow loop, and back to Merrick again. She tapped one finger thoughtfully against the cleft in her chin.

No. 'Twouldn't work. He would not fit; his head was too big.

Which also ruled out bashing him a good one.

She had scrubbed his skin until it should have been red and raw, but all he did was moan the way Cyclops did when she scratched his belly.

Thick skin, thick head, so went the saying.

In his case, a whole hive of Old Gladdys's bees couldn't have stung Merrick's skin. So, she thought it was doubtful that even a solid oak battering ram could dent his thick skull.

He picked that exact moment to crack open one eye and say, "I'm waiting."

For the briefest of moments she relished a few of her usual visions of dire retribution. Of course, after their wedding she would have a lifetime to get even.

Quite a pleasant thought.

She rose to her knees and smiled sweetly, lathering his hairy chest with the cloth and watching his eyes slowly slip closed again.

Men, she thought, were almost too easy.

Merrick stood at the side of the bed, looking down at Clio, who was curled on her side in the bed.

She looked up at him from over her shoulder, frowning. "What do you mean move over?"

"I'm tired and need to sleep."

"As I told you earlier, my lord. I allowed you to bathe here, but that is all." She pulled the covers tighter over her shoulder and turned her face away from him.

" 'Twas not a simple task spending the last few days chasing you from Brecon Beacons to Cardigan."

"This is my bed and my chamber."

"Not any longer."

That got her attention. She ceased trying to ignore him.

Her ugly cat was asleep on the bed, snoring. It sound like it had lung fever. He picked up the thing and dropped it onto the floor. The cat looked up at him from its one eye, then it looked at the bed as if he was contemplating leaping up again. "Do not even think about it, cat. I do not sleep with animals."

"Neither do I," Clio snapped, glaring at him.

Merrick stared down at her challenging eyes and planted his hands on the bed, bending over so his face was close to hers. "Unless you wish to see what kind of animal I can be, I suggest you don't test my patience any more. I will tell you this now and you will understand it. I will not waste any more precious time following you all over the countryside, fending off Welsh arrows and water barrels and God knows whatever other trouble you can manage to find."

She started to speak, but he shook his head, warning her.

"I will know where you are, Clio, at every hour of the day, and especially at night. I will sleep in this bed."

She opened her mouth to argue, and he jerked the coverlet from her clenched fists, which shut her up.

He crawled into bed and pulled the covers over him with a hard yank. "I am not in the mood to argue with you."

She scooted over to the very edge of the opposite side where there were no covers and sat up. A moment later she pulled the coverlet off him and up around her chin.

This from the woman who had dropped her towel. If he hadn't been so blasted tired, he'd have laughed out loud.

"You cannot sleep with me! I am a maid!"

"Good, then I won't have to worry about another man's bastard, now will I?"

She was quiet. Too quiet. He could almost hear the cranking of her brain.

"Are you going to..." Her voice trailed off.

He punched his pillow a few times, then plopped his head back down, facing away from her. He closed his eyes. "I'm going to sleep. Not ravish you."

She was quiet, blessedly so. He was drifting off to sleep and almost there...

"Then I was right that day in the bailey when I said I do not appeal to you." Her voice was annoyed.

Damn her. "Do not start with me."

"What? All I said was that I was right."

He turned to her and pinned her with his hardest look. "I suggest that you do not question my manhood, woman, when I am in the same bed with you. It would not be a wise choice."

"Do you always threaten people when you do not get your own way?"

"Aye, the way you always change the subject when you have no good argument."

"I do not do that!" She paused. "I always know what subject I'm speaking about."

"Perhaps you do, Clio, but no one else does." He yawned, then added, "I think you know exactly what you do when you are doing it."

He had her then. She could say nothing because if she changed the subject again, she would prove him right. He closed his eyes again, knowing he'd won this battle.

She jerked hard on the coverlets. "You took all the covers."

He smiled to himself, then said, "Clio."

"Aye," she said in a snippy tone.

"You changed the subject."

Morning sunshine spilled into the chamber in bright golden light, the kind that made you see double. Clio waited for her vision to clear. She moaned a little, some part of her wishing it were still night so she could go back to sleep.

Sighing, she closed her eyes again.

A blast of hot breath hit her neck. Her eyes shot open and she slowly turned, wincing with a small groan as sheremembered just what was in her bed. A huge and hairy male arm was clamped around her body, and her back was pressed against his hot belly.

His hard knee poked her in the derriere. Still annoyed, she picked up his heavy arm and dropped it on his hip.

But before she could scoot out of the bed, his thick leg sprawled across her hip and waist and left her pinned to the mattress again.

She was stuck and had little to do but stare at his foot poking out from the coverlets. Bored, she wiggled until her own foot was sticking out below his.

She stared at their feet.

She turned hers this way and that, eyeing it. She had short feet and stubby toes and her second toe was longer than the biggest one. She barely even had a toenail on her smallest toe, which had a fat top and a skinny little bone. Her feet were uglier than a basket of eels.

What was the purpose of toes?

One did not pick things up with their toes as did the monkeys at the Michaelmas Fair. When she walked, 'twas on the balls of her feet. Did her toes help her keep balance? Birds used their toes to hang on to branches or a falconer's glove. What good were toes?

She looked at his toes, which were long and more even than hers; they were like gate guards lined up according to size. Regimented and in order. She should not have been surprised. Leave it to Merrick to have perfectly formed toes. Except for the black hair on them.

She had bald toes, yet hers looked like a row of jagged teeth, not unlike the old Roman walls that randomly dotted the countryside. And rather like her life, with ups and downs and filled with dips and wrinkles.

Perhaps toes were something that gave clues to what your life would be, the way Old Gladdys swore that you could read your future in the lines of wee brown sunspots across your nose, or the way your hair waved when it was damp from May dew.

Toes might be there solely to help you understand the direction your life would go. After all, she thought with great insight, you were born with toes. You didn't grow them, like you did hair and breasts. She decided she would have to remember to examine the toes of her babes when they were born.

Her babes.

She turned and looked at the man who would father them. In sleep he did not look like an infamous and ruthless knight. Nothing about him gave clue to the man who was known as the Red Lion, the man she herself had seen wield a battle sword.

He was a quiet sleeper. She was certain he had no idea that Cyclops was curled against his back, so close that it looked as if her cat were growing right from the small of Merrick's broad back.

His hair was slicked back and past his shoulders, and he had grown a thick black beard in so few days. But the thing she noticed again with a stunned fixation was the length of this man's eyelashes. In sleep she could see how thick and dark they were, and she understood why when his eyes were open they looked so very very blue.

He breathed evenly in sleep and did not snort through his nose as her father had. For years the whole castle would awaken to what sounded like wild boars in the keep.

It had only been her father snoring.

She missed him. Her father had been a good man, kind and loyal to his king, Henry, even when the other barons had risen and followed de Montfort against the king they had sworn fealty to.

Her father believed in oaths taken. The one single oath he had made her give him was that she would obey their king and marry the man chosen for her. She had given her father that promise about wedding the knight called the Red Lion.

She had not known that same knight would hurt her so fully by treating her as if she did not matter to him.

Those long days in the convent hurt her deeply. But like her father, she would not disregard her oath, even though he was dead; she took pride in the fact that she had his sense of honor.

She told herself with complete assurance that her oath to her father was why she agreed to freely marry Merrick.

It had nothing to do with the fact that he no longer ignored her. That he had saved her life and that his kisses made her want more, and forget about pride and oaths and honor. Surely her agreement to wed him had nothing to do with the fact that Merrick treated her as if she did matter to him.

She turned to look at him.

He stared back at her, wide awake and looking as if he could read her deepest and most private thoughts.

It took all of her will to not look startled.

She stared at his eyes, then looked at his mouth. She remembered those kisses.

"If you keeping looking at me like that, woman, you will not be a maiden for long."

"Get off me, you oaf!" She shoved at his legs, angry because he could read her mind.

He kissed her hard on the mouth and she stilled for a moment. His beard was not scratchy, as it looked, but soft, and it tickled her face as he kissed her more deeply.

He smelled of thyme soap and musky sleep.

She almost slid her arms around his neck, but the fool raised his big head and grinned down at her. "Is that what you wanted?"

She bucked against him. He laughed. She kicked her feet out and heard him grunt. "Let me go! You are all hammy hands and bony knees!"

He still laughed at her, then rolled away and threw back the covers in one graceful motion.

Except Cyclops was there.

The cat screeched like the banshees.

"Christ in heaven!" Merrick reached for his sword. But he was wearing only the breechclout. He looked dazed, then he scowled at the floor. Cyclops was safely under the bed.

He muttered a curse, then strode across the room.

There was something about Merrick in that loincloth that did strange things to her. Things she liked and hated. Her gaze followed him as if her eyes had a mind of their own, and she had to force herself to look away.

It did no good and she found herself watching

him again, the taste of him lingering on her lips. The clean soapy smell of him.

In one corner of the room was a studded chest that she could have sworn had not been there before. He opened it and shrugged on a linen work blouse and his leather jack and he then donned and tied a pair of softly sueded brown braies. He sat in a chair and pulled on his boots, then stood beside her.

"Do you plan to lie in that bed all day?"

"I had thought you intended to chain me to your side."

He gave her a long, hot look. "Perhaps I'll get back into bed with you and finish what we started."

She threw back the covers and strolled from the bed. "I have things to do."

"Such as?"

"I have ale to brew from the Trefriw water." She paused pointedly. "Bridal ale."

"Ah, only one night in bed together and you are already rushing toward the wedding with such enthusiasm."

She spun around. "Would you just leave so I can dress? I would like some privacy. Take your hammy hands, that irritating grin, and those bony knees of yours and leave!"

He made a mocking bow and strode toward the doorway.

She shrugged on a deep emerald robe, muttering, "That is, if your big head will fit through the door." She wanted the final word.

He said nothing, but opened the chamber doors and walked out near the stairs.

"De Clare!" He bellowed. "De Clare!"

A few minutes later Tobin and Thud came barreling up the stairs.

"Aye, my lord." Tobin stood before Merrick, and Thud mimicked him, sticking his small chest out, positioning his feet the exact way the squire did, and raising his chin so he looked as arrogant as Tobin de Clare.

Merrick looked around. "Where's Thump?"

"Who?" Tobin and Thud asked simultaneously.

"The other one."

"Here I am, my lord. I'm coming. Twenty-one...twenty-two..." Thwack was slowly trudging up the stairs.

With the slow passage of Thwack-time, all three lads eventually were lined up in front of the chamber door.

Merrick turned to look at Clio, then he turned back to the boys. "Your duty today is to guard your lady Clio. She is not to leave the castle and you are to protect her and watch over her every move." He turned back to her and pointedly said, "I want you safe, Clio. *Inside* the walls of Camrose."

She caught her breath and narrowed her eyes while she looked for something to throw at him.

He had given her keepers!

He started to leave, so she said with utter nonchalance, "I had no plans to leave the castle this day. I will be in my brewery." She paused, then added, "Where there are no bony knees."

He just gave her a look that said he knew

exactly what she was doing, and he disappeared out the chamber door.

She stood there, feeling everything from relief to anger to something that felt like desire, the desire to clout him a good one.

There was a quick rap at the door.

"Aye!" she called out.

Merrick stuck his big head back inside. "I forgot to tell you something."

She crossed her arms over her chest and tapped her foot impatiently. "What?"

He grinned. "That wasn't my knee." Then he closed the door just as her boot hit it.

Chalybeate Ale

Mix malted barley, Trefriw water,
*   and brewer's yeast,*
Ferment until ripened to pale ale.
Add a flacon of Cowslip flowers,
Three pinches of Sweet Marjoram,
Two stalks of crimson Bell Heather,
A handful each of:
Angelica, Eccony, and Sweet Mint.
Ferment for two more days,
Add Fennel, Juniper, Apples,
Pears, Figs, and Rose Buds to taste.

*   —Medieval Bride Ale*

CHAPTER 25

It was one of those rare and wonderful days when the air turned clover-sweet and blue as the sky. Snow white doves cooed in the castle eaves and geese honked as they flew overhead in flocks shaped like huge black arrows.

The hour had come when the villagers brought their baskets to the castle to barter with their freshly picked crops for tin, iron, tools, and cloth goods—things to which only the marcher lord had access.

The bailey was teeming with women, children skipping at their sides joined hand in hand. The mothers had baskets hitched on their hips and filled with pearly white turnips and sweet leafy collard, dark emerald spinach and crimson crab apples.

There were crude carts with studded wheels that rattled over the moat bridge and were piled with chopped wood and hard coal. Fish and hay wagons rumbled inside with freshly mown hay stacked high as a hut and huge wooden barrels of flounder, monkfish, and herring that made the air smell like the sea.

Local fishermen had their fat round fishing coracles tied to their backs like giant walnut shells, the long ash oars strapped to the boats and sticking out from behind them like the feelers of a water beetle.

Wide and finely tied fishing nets hung like

harem veils from the paddles and looped around the men's floppy broad-brimmed hats. They pushed along squeaky carts filled with willow baskets of slick eels, brown-speckled trout, and stacks of fresh salmon.

With gaming bows slung on their shoulders, the hunters, dressed in the colors of the forest and pointed hats, carried pikes speared with such game as hare and squirrel, or bigger baggage of buck and boar.

Near the laundry hut, a young wash maid was hanging out the clean linen. It flapped and snapped in the light warm breeze. The bake house had fresh rye bread and stone-milled wheat loaves cooling on the window shelves, while wide, hollowed bread trenchers and plump meat pies were lined up in the hundreds and stacked on metal baking trays.

As always there were the incessant sounds of building, the pounding of pegs and nails, the chipping away of stone work for the bridges and the walls, the hammering of iron for sturdy gates and drain piping, for weaponry or heavy locks and hinges, anything strong that would protect Camrose from an enemy siege.

Just before Sext, Clio's red wagon had lumbered through the gates loaded with the spa waters. So now, Clio sat on a wobbly stool next to the brewery window, where she could see the whole inner bailey. To pass the time, she watched the hubbub, resting her chin in her palm while she waited for the ale pots to begin to boil.

Old Gladdys had lined up her jars and jugs

next to Clio's herbs and lichens. For this batch of ale, the old Welshwoman arranged the ingredients in the order of the stars during the summer solstice, claiming that anyone with half the sense of a barn sparrow would know that the stars and moon held secrets and magic just waiting to be discovered.

Tobin and Thud had finished unloading the water barrels while Thwack stood guard on Clio. 'Twas rather silly, considering she could outrun him. Anything weighing under a hundred stone could outrun him.

The sound of raised voices made her turn away from the window. "What is the matter?"

"We're arguing over whether 'time' rhymes with 'fine,' " Thud said.

"Why?"

" 'Tis a game, my lady, between the squires and the pages." Thud paused, then added quickly. "Throughout the ages." He grinned proudly. "For all of today we must speak in rhyme." He paused again, frowning for a long moment.

Tobin took a menacing step toward him.

Thud's face lit up like one of Old Gladdys's bonfires. "Until tomorrow at Prime."

"Aye." Thwack nodded. "Through the day and night. We must keep speaking rhyme, for a small passage of time."

"Good lad!" Thud patted Thwack on the back. "I'm glad."

All Clio felt at that moment was faint-headed. "Seems a silly game to me."

"Nay, my lady." Tobin de Clare stepped forward and stood before her in his usual proud stance. " 'Tis the first thing a page must learn. When Sir Merrick taught me rhyming, 'twas a full fortnight of speaking such. These lads will do so every third day for a month."

"Why?"

"It might seem foolish to you, my lady, but the exercise teaches how to think quickly. Sir Merrick says a knight must be as quick with his head as he is with his sword. Sir Roger and many of the other knights use the same training."

Tobin looked from Clio to the table where Old Gladdys was working. He watched her for a long time, then walked over to her. Thud mimicked his strides and was following so close at his heels that he kept stepping on the backs of Tobin's boots.

Old Gladdys looked up and eyed Tobin, obviously dismissing him, since she did not wink at him or mutter in Welsh. She just looked at him. "You want something, boy?"

"I am ten and six. I am no boy," he told her with disgust.

Gladdys shook her fuzzy head, then pinned Tobin with those sharp black eyes. "I am three score and nine and after all those years, lad, I know a green boy when I look at one."

"Where is Sir Roger?" Tobin demanded.

Old Gladdys paused for just the inkling of a moment, then began to wipe her gnarled hands on her black cloak. "I do not know."

"But the earl sent him with you and he did not return with you."

Old Gladdys shrugged. "The last time I laid these old eyes on Sir Roger, he was running with some blond bitch." Dismissing Tobin, she looked at Clio. "Is Brother Dismas in the castle?"

"Aye," Thud answered eagerly, then realized Tobin was going to clout him, so he quickly added, "I spy. I saw him blessing the fish, for tonight's dish." Thud exhaled as if he was relieved, then grinned at Tobin.

"I wonder if that fat little monk has missed me," Gladdys said with a wicked gleam in her eyes. She gave Clio a glimmer of a smile, one jaunty wave, then she turned and casually strolled from the hut.

Clio spotted her working her way toward the fish wagons and shook her head. She hoped she had as much vinegar as Gladdys did when she was that age. 'Twould be fun, to play so with the men's brains.

"Something is not right. That does not sound like Sir Roger," Tobin muttered thoughtfully. "He would never disobey the earl."

"Perhaps the lady was exceptional," Clio said, leaving the window and moving toward her worktable.

Tobin just shook his head.

A moment later the ale pots began to boil over.

Clio lay in her bed listening for the Matins bell and the guard horn that signaled a guard change. She had little to cling to but those distant sounds. Because she did not hear what she wanted to hear—the sound of Merrick's footsteps on the stairs.

He had not been anywhere nearby that day. She hadn't seen hide nor hair of him since that morning when he left her.

But she had been busy for most of the day, a day where she got much accomplished. 'Twas true. Her bridal ale was half done.

All that ale in only one day! She shook her head in amazement. She had put Thud, Thwack, and Tobin to work, since they had nothing better to do but ogle her while they stood there being her keepers.

They each tried to do a better job than the other. She'd never before gotten so much done in so little time.

The bridal ale was sufficiently brewed. Tomorrow she would add the last of the special herbs and flowers, then fill the oaken casks.

She sighed, punching her pillow a few times, then she lay there. Time moved by about as swiftly as did Thwack.

She closed her eyes, but sleep would not come. She tossed and turned and shook out her fluffy pillow. She scratched Cy's furry ears and listened to him puff. Mentally she counted lambs in the meadow, then tried to daydream an image of her wedding, but nothing worked.

She could not sleep.

One night spent with Merrick in her bed and her peace was no more. Gone. She snapped her fingers. Just like that!

'Twas all his fault, she thought sourly, plopping back against the mattress.

She rubbed her head. That was his fault, too.

With a deep sigh, she crossed her arms and thought back. He said he would not leave her alone. Odd, then, wasn't it, that she felt alone?

She threw back the covers and grabbed a fluffy woolen robe and struggled into it as she pattered across the room.

The floor was no longer cold stones that could chill her bare feet late in the night. An intricately loomed carpet now covered the cold floors. She opened the door, just a wee crack, and imagining herself as a court spy, she pressed her eye to the opening and looked out.

"Aye, my lady." Sir Isambard looked right at her. He stood guard, his sword drawn and his stance alert. His stare continued seemingly forever, and for one brief moment she thought he might actually smile.

She straightened swiftly and opened the door, trying to look adequately haughty and regal, and as if she had not been peering through a crack in the door like the old village gossip. " 'Tis nothing, sir. I thought I heard something. The sound frightened me," she lied.

"All is well, my lady. The earl has seen to your complete safety."

No, the earl has seen to my complete imprisonment.

She locked her hands behind her back and rocked on her toes, just staring at him. There was nothing she could do, which annoyed her to no end. "Well, good night, then, sir."

"Good night, my lady."

"Oh." Clio held the door partially open. "You haven't seen the earl, have you?"

"Aye."

She waited. 'Twas all he said.

"Where?" she asked, not bothering this time to hide her annoyance.

"Shall I send someone to fetch him for you, my lady?"

"No!"she barked, then said more calmly, "No, that is not necessary. I was just curious. Good night, Sir Isambard."

"My lady?"

"Aye?"Clio paused, with the door half closed.

"Even if Lord Merrick were gone, he would make certain you were safe. You needn't worry that you shall ever be left alone again."

Clio nodded and closed the door, then made a face, and she leaned back against the door. "Safe," she muttered. She looked over at Cy perched atop the pillows on her bed. "We're safe. Isn't that just delightful? Safe and locked up with keepers and guards and watchmen."

She shoved away from the door and walked over to the arrow loop. She pulled up a small footstool and sat staring out at the dark sky. She heaved a huge bored and frustrated sigh and leaned her head against the cold stone. "Oh, hell and damnation ...I'm a prisoner in my own castle."

'Twas late and dark when there came a sudden and loud pounding on the castle gate.

Merrick paid little attention. He was walking in the outer bailey, thinking, pacing, and trying to forget that he must crawl into the same bed as Clio.

After giving it much thought, he had decided that if he waited until she was asleep, he could better ignore the fact that she would be only a kiss away.

This cool night air was good for him. It helped him focus and control his urges. Urges for Clio that made him want to seek her out. He purposely had not and busied himself with other things and tried to tell himself he did not think of her.

But he did. Her image haunted him.

Bam! Bam! Bam! Now the pounding was at the iron door of the gatehouse.

Merrick stopped and turned toward the gate guard.

The man was sprawled on a barrel, sound asleep.

Merrick knew the guard, a man named Fenwicke, whose wife had died in childbed the week before. Merrick grabbed a bucket and filled it with icy well water, then strode across the bailey and dumped it on the guard's head.

The man jumped up, choking and snorting and hollering. Then he saw it was Merrick who had doused him and he began to grovel. "My lord, I'm sorry. I, I just…"

Merrick stared down at the man with contempt and said in a hard voice, "Go get someone to relieve you. And do not take this duty so lightly again. If you cannot stay awake, ask Sir Isambard for different work."

The man nodded.

"Next time I will not be so lenient. You will wake up to the blade of my sword."

"Aye, my lord. Aye. 'Twill not happen again. I swear."

The doors shook with another hard pounding.

"See who the hell is trying to break the doors down."

The guard slid the peep slot back, stilled for a long moment, then stepped back and looked up at Merrick. " 'Tis someone who claims to be Sir Roger FitzAlan, my lord."

"You know Sir Roger, man. If it's him, open the gate."

"But he does not look like Sir Roger."

Merrick crossed to the peep and looked out.

A man stood there in the dark, wearing naught but his breechclout. He glared at Merrick from eyes that were all too familiar. "Open the bloody gate, Merrick, or I swear on my mother's eyes I will cut out your liver and feed it to the wolves!"

"What wolves, Roger? Lady Clio has not been singing."

"So help me God, if you do not open this door…"

"Let Sir Roger in," Merrick told the guard, fighting the urge to grin. He stood aside as his man unbolted the heavy door.

Roger barreled through the opening like a man half-crazed, darting a quick glance over his bare shoulder as if he expected the Devil himself to follow him.

Merrick held the torch above him for light. "I was beginning to wonder what had happened to you. I just heard this eve that the wagon and that old woman had returned."

Roger looked like a madman, with his wild red hair, tangled like briars, and his straggly and unkempt beard. He blinked in the bright torchlight, then faced Merrick. He was shaking.

Merrick wasn't certain if his friend quivered from the cold or from his anger. He stuck the torch in the wall and unhooked the clasps on his woolen cape. "Here." He tossed it to Roger. "You look as if you need this more than I."

Roger wrapped the cloak around himself and muttered something about hell and madwomen and a she-wolf.

Merrick pushed open the peep and scanned the outside. "I don't see any wolves."

"She is out there. Somewhere. Biggest and most vicious bloody wolf I've ever seen."

"Come. There's a fire and food inside." Merrick turned and walked toward the hall.

When they were walking up the outside steps, Roger turned to him and said, "This is your doing, damn you. That Druid witch you stuck me with sent that wolf after me."

"Old Gladdys?" Merrick opened the doors and walked into the hall. He paused and looked at Roger in the light of the wall torches. He looked as if he had run all the way from Cardigan to Camrose. Through the woods and marshes and bogs.

The perfect chivalrous knight Roger FitzAlan had half the women in England, Rome, and the East panting after him. He always had, for as long as Merrick had known him. And Roger had reveled in every moment, every liaison, every sly wink and clandestine affair.

For years when they would go to tourneys or courts or diplomats' homes, women looked at Merrick and would hide their daughters.

But a few moments with Roger and they would gladly have given him their children and themselves. As far as Merrick knew, there had never been a woman Roger could not charm and control.

This Roger was afraid of Old Gladdys. Truly afraid. He actually believed all that drivel about curses and magic and the evil eye.

Roger stood by the fire, warming himself and muttering while he chewed on a hunk of white bread.

Merrick watched him, having never seen Roger this agitated. Even after a battle Roger FitzAlan looked as if he'd been dancing at a wedding, not fighting with sword and mace. 'Twas something they jested about when they toasted their victories.

Merrick truly had a difficult time holding his laughter. "What did you do to her?"

"Me? I did nothing, but run."

"She's a harmless and crazed old woman."

"Harmless?" Roger spun around and faced him. "God's hair, Merrick! The old bitch tried to ravish me!"

"Ravish you?" Merrick tried not to laugh aloud. He truly did. 'Twas not a simple task, hiding his amusement. So he took a deep breath and mentally counted in Latin.

"Aye." Roger paused, then added under his breath, "She took my clothes."

Merrick laughed so hard the walls shook. 'Twas the silliest thing he'd ever heard. As if an old woman could ravish a brawny young man, especially an accomplished knight like Roger.

"How in the name of St. Peter did she manage to get your clothes?"

"The old hag tore them off me."

Merrick looked at Roger's perfectly serious expression and he couldn't help himself, he bent double and howled and howled.

A moment later he landed hard on his ass. He was still laughing, but also nursing a sore jaw where Roger had punched him.

Rubbing his chin, Merrick stared up at his friend. It seemed that Sir Roger FitzAlan had lost his sense of humor.

Old Welsh
Fairy Song

0'r glaswellt glan a'r rhedyn man
Gyfeillion dyddan dewch,
E ddarfu'r nawn-mae'r lloer yn llawn,
Y nos yn gyflawn gewch.

From grasses bright and bracken light,
Come, sweet companions, come.
The full moon shines, the sun declines,
We'll spend the night in fun.

CHAPTER 26

Merrick stood inside the bedchamber and stared at the empty bed. There was no light in the room except the weak tallow candle he'd set near the bed. It sent pale and flickering light across the twisted bed linen and coverlets that looked to have been tossed carelessly aside.

He turned and scanned the room, knowing that no one could get past Sir Isambard, who for years had proved himself to be Merrick's most trusted man.

The first thing he saw was her hair; it flowed over her small hunched shoulders and back and piled onto the stone floor near the western loop. Her cat, the useless one-eyed thing that snored like a lion, was curled next to the small footstool, its fat head resting on his lady's soft silver hair.

He envied that cat, and just stood there, knowing he was alone, but feeling a little self-conscious. 'Twas for the silliest of reasons that he stood there.

It made him feel good to do so.

To the darkness, she brought a little of her own glow, her own light, and he needed to savor it, touch it, and feel it, so his life wouldn't seem so dark and empty anymore, because now she was going to be a part of it.

Quietly he crossed the room and stood over her, watching her sleep in such an awkward and uncomfortable position. Her woolen robe had slipped off her shoulders. She was wearing a sheer linen shift underneath. Her shoulder was bare and soft and flawless, even in the gold flicker of candlelight.

'Twas obvious that she could not sleep in the bed and had come here to the window. He studied her position, her head slumped atop her arms, which were resting on the ledge. He wondered what she had been thinking and what she had been looking for as she sat there.

Deep in his heart, he wished she had been looking for him.

He nudged the cat away from her hair with his bare foot and scooped her up into his arms. That hair, that miracle of hair, fell like silken moonlight over his arm and tenderly brushed his thigh and calf.

'Twas was one of the most sensual moments of his life. His chest grew tight, his senses filled with the sunshine scent of her, the aroma of fresh herbs and flowers that always clung to her like some exotic perfume oil. He felt light-headed, as if he had drunk too much or fallen from his horse.

He could not have moved for the life of him, but just stood breathing deeply and feeling as if this one small woman was melting into his very soul. She sighed and turned toward him, the way she had when she was wounded.

He pressed his lips to her brow and kissed the top of her head, closing his eyes against the stab of intense need that splintered through him. Slowly, holding her so very close to him, he crossed to the bed and set her gently atop it, slipping the robe off and tossing it onto the floor.

He moved to the opposite side, blew out the candle, and crawled in behind her. He lay there waiting to see if she would awaken, but she did not, so he pulled the covers over them.

She gave a small moan.

His breath caught as she turned toward him and lay her palms flat against his chest, just next to his beating heart. He moved his hand and covered one of hers. He wanted her touch almost more than his own breath.

In no more time than it took his heart to beat, Merrick closed his eyes and slept as soundly as she did, because he was finally home.

Someone was staring at her. Clio opened her eyes.

Merrick was watching her, his look sleepy and lazy and tinged with something soft that she could not identify.

He had a bruise that darkened his jaw purple under his morning beard.

She reached out with her fingertips and touched the bruise. "You are hurt."

"Roger came back."

"He hit you?"

Merrick shook his head. " 'Twas only in fun. I was laughing at the time. 'Tis nothing."

She frowned and moved closer to examine the bruise and the small brown-scabbed cut near his chin that was alittle redder and more swollen than the rest.

"It looks like it hurts."

He laughed. "Being hit in the helm with a mace hurts. This is naught but a scratch." He paused, his gaze seeming to take her all in. "But I find, woman, that I like to see you worry over my fine features and high good looks."

Even she had to laugh then and raised her chin high. " 'Tis not your looks for which I fear. I was afraid the blow might have knocked some sense into you."

"You never give in, do you?"

She smiled and shook her head.

His eyes grew drowsy; his fingers drifted over her face, touching her with a tender gentleness, with almost a sense of awe that made her forget completely that he was a fearsome warrior.

He kissed her then, his lips as warm and lazy as his stare had been when she first awoke. His mouth barely touched hers, just a mere brushing of their dry lips.

Yet her eyes drifted closed and she slipped her arms over his wide and strong shoulders, running her hand over the taut snakelike muscles there and then clasping her hands behind his hard, thick warrior's neck.

He deepened their kiss, touched his tongue to hers, filled her mouth, stroking her and making her feel as if she were flying with the sweet songbirds that called out in the distance. They sounded so far away, as if the world itself had left them alone.

She held on to him, and he to her, shifting slightly together. She could feel the thick curls of coarse hair as his chest pressed closer against hers.

They rolled until there was nothing between the mattress and Merrick's hard body but her soft one.

It felt so good and so right. She shifted again, almost squirming, and moved her legs apart because somewhere deep in the midst of her most private places she needed something, needed to feel him against her.

'Twas the most splendid feeling, the most

intimate touch she had ever endured when he rubbed against her with his hips. Her blood flowed through her veins like spilt summer wine, hot and sweet and rapid. She felt like crying and calling out his name.

His warm palm cupped her breast and his tongue swelled in her mouth. His fingertips touched her beading nipple and played with it. She grew hotter and wet in places that should have made her flush, but her skin could not turn hotter than it already was.

Her hands slid down over his broad back and she slipped them under the thin breechcloth. Her palms stroked back and forth over the soft downy hairs that covered the top of his buttocks and felt as fine as marten fur.

He moaned something against her mouth, a plea, a desire. 'Twas only her name, she knew, but it sounded like so much more when the sound seemed to come from his very soul.

She opened her eyes, needing to see his face, to see if he felt what she did. He was looking at her as he kissed her and touched her and moaned her name.

His eyes were the same warm blue of a deep English sky, his pupils the dark blue of midnight. Those eyes were no longer cold, and she wondered how she could have ever thought them hard and icy.

The passion she saw there was like her own, intense and overwhelming, and it made her want him more and more, She needed to get closer to him, to crawl inside of him, to touch him somewhere deep inside, and to have him touch her in places that just thinking about would surely send her to hell.

"Touch me." She breathed her sinful thoughts, and he buried his face in her neck and slid his hand from her tender taut-tipped breasts to in between her legs where she needed to feel pressure and hardness and touches.

She did not care that she would burn for an eternity, that she would live through all the tortures of purgatory. She spread her thighs wider, and his fingers rubbed harder and harder against that warm wetness that should have humiliated her, but instead made her move with his motions, faster and faster, slicker, toward some higher place that had to be heaven. It had to be splendid heaven, for if this were hell, she wanted to go there.

She gasped and gripped his bottom so hard, her nails were digging into his flesh. "I'm dying," she called out. "I'm going to die." She felt she was going to explode, to burst, but she couldn't stop herself.

He rubbed faster and faster. "Come, my sweet, come." He whispered in warm breaths against her ear. "Let it go. Feel it, feel it."

The intensity of what was happening to her was so strong, so very powerful, that the moment she burst she saw nothing but flashes of stars and felt her blood all rush and pool in her nethers, throbbing as if her life's blood were spilling from her. It went on and on, forever, this warm wet feeling that was better than dying.

He stared down at her, his expression so

tender and so full of feeling that she had to blink to see if perhaps she were dreaming.

"Again," he whispered, and when she shook her head and tried to move, he slid his hands up her arms and pinned them above her, while his lips skimmed down over her thin linen shift that was twisted like a cloth belt between her breasts and around her waist.

He buried his face between her legs and kissed her there, where her life had gone. 'Twas more than she could bear and she cried out and tried to twist away again.

His mouth followed her and kissed her so intimately that she almost fainted. His tongue went deep, as if it were only delving inside her mouth, then he sucked and took all of her in his hungry mouth until she burst apart again and again.

Between Prime and Terce, the same sin happened more times than she could count, until she had no life left in her. She lay there limp and wilted, her lips bruised and her body flaccid as a flower swept away by the sheer power of the wind and rain.

Merrick, however, seemed to have an inordinate amount of life, as if he had slept all night. He got out of the bed with so very much vigor in his step that his motions almost made her dizzy. He washed and dressed with more enthusiasm than she'd have thought a king's earl was capable of.

Somehow she'd imagined him as a warrior, someone who was not human, just a being whose duty was war and guarding the borders and making Camrose into a stronghold so massive that no enemy could ever pierce its stone walls.

She propped her head on her hand and watched him. He confused her, this gentle man who touched her as if she were his world. Part of her wanted to sleep, to escape this confusion. But with him humming and whistling and preening she could not sleep.

He looked up after toweling off his face. "What has you scowling so?"

"You stole all my life," she said, plucking impatiently at the bed linen and pulling small down feathers from the bed.

"If you keep picking apart the mattress, we shall have to sleep on that old hay tick."

She swiped at the feathers, which curled up into the air and then floated to the floor. " 'Tis not fair, you know. I have no life left, not even enough to get up, and you are footslogging around this chamber as if you have fire under your..." She paused.

"My what?" He was grinning at her.

"Your big feet."

He laughed loud and heartily and tossed the towel aside. "You know what the old wives say about big feet."

Before either of them could speak, there was a horrendous pounding on the chamber door. "Merrick! Merrick!"

Seeming to ignore Sir Roger, Merrick slipped on his leather jack and crossed the room as he buckled on his sword belt.

He stood over her as the pounding went on.

He bent down and pressed his hands flat on the mattress, pinning her just inches from his face.

She looked up at him, her gaze drifting all on its own to his sensual mouth, then to his bristled cheeks and his warm blue eyes. His face was so very close that she could smell the sweet soap scent on his clean skin—thyme and heather and mint. It made her heart speed up and her wits go walking all at the same time.

"Roger is still angry with me for foisting Old Gladdys off on him."

The door rattled again, then came Roger's loud voice, "Are you going to lie abed all day, Merrick? Get up, you sloth, so I can whip your arse on the practice field!"

Merrick dropped a quick kiss on the top of her head instead of her mouth, where she wanted it.

By the time she opened her eyes to scowl at him again, he had crossed the room and jerked open the chamber doors. He stood there in all his tall glory. "Well, if it isn't Sir Roger the Ravished."

Even Sir Isambard choked back a laugh.

Roger leveled a vengeful look at Merrick. "Your wit astounds me."

'Twas then that Merrick clapped him on the shoulder and apologized. Merrick de Beaucourt, the Red Lion, told Roger he was sorry about the old Druid.

Clio was shocked. She could not have imagined him admitting he was wrong, let alone telling anyone he was truly sorry.

She felt strange and uncomfortable, as if she had just walked around a corner and seen someone important naked, like the pope or the king. Had she been that very wrong about him? About his hardness and character? Perhaps she was the one who had been too stubborn to give way.

"Come," Merrick said in a completely different tone from the one he used when he'd said that very word to her. He must have noticed, too, because he turned back and looked at her.

Something hot and intimate passed between them. A sweet and sinful memory.

Roger straightened and peered over Merrick's shoulder at Clio. "Tell me that is not Lady Clio, the sweet and innocent maiden, lying in your bed."

She gasped and pulled her covers over her head, curling into a ball of humiliation.

" 'Tis her bed now," was all Merrick said.

"What are you about?" Roger asked with some tone of censure.

"She is still a maiden." Merrick's voice was all too cocky.

Clio lay beneath the covers and gritted her teeth together until they ached. How very splendid of them to stand in the door to her chamber and discuss her virginity as if it were the day's weather.

"Good day to you, my lady," Merrick said pointedly and closed the door.

Merrick and Roger turned to leave, and

something hard thudded against the heavy bed-chamber door.

"The iron candleholder?" Roger guessed.

Merrick shook his head. "Too muted. I'd say her shoe."

Roger nodded in agreement as Merrick turned to Sir Isambard. "Have one of the men, no..." Merrick paused for a thoughtful instant. "Have three of the men watch over her today."

"Aye, my lord."

Merrick and Roger went down the stairs side by side.

"I came earlier," Roger said almost too casually.

"Oh?"

There was a glint in Roger's eye. "To get you up."

"I went to bed late."

"I heard the lady shouting," Roger said, then was pointedly quiet.

A tense moment passed, the kind when time seemed to stretch out before them.

Roger looked at Merrick and smothered his grin. "Then tell me, my friend, did she die?"

"Aye," Merrick said without missing a step. "She died the sweetest death I've ever seen."

CHAPTER 27

A piebald gelding charged toward the quintain with Thud bouncing atop his flat, training saddle in the same floundering way a puppet bounces on its string—arms flying out, legs loose, and ass rising a good foot in the air.

With every full stride of the horse, Thud's head flopped about his neck as if it were broken, his hair slapping his brow and face.

"God's teeth," Merrick muttered. "How the hell does he stay on?"

Sir Isambard stood there rubbing his chin thoughtfully. "Stubborn determination."

The lad hit the quintain at a full, yet somewhat flailing run. Thud grunted loudly; it sounded as if someone had belched up a north wind.

The wooden target spun round so fast that Merrick closed his eyes and winced.

There was a loud *thud!*

When Merrick opened his eyes, the boy was sprawled on the ground a good five feet from his mount. Thud's lance had slipped from his loose grip and shot backward like an arrow from an upside-down bow, then rolled uselessly to a stop at Merrick's feet.

Tobin and some of the other squires were doubled over, crowing with laughter.

Thud adjusted his helm and shoved the visor back. He stared at Merrick, his eyes looking dazed.

Merrick stood there watching him, then pointed toward the horse.

Thud understood him and awkwardly got to his feet, then half stumbled toward his horse. He stuck one foot in the stirrup and gripped the saddle, then tried to mount.

On the wrong side.

Confused, the horse danced around in a backward circle with Thud hopping on one foot and trying to pull himself up.

The squires were all but rolling on the ground they were laughing so hard.

Sir Isambard cupped his hands around his mouth and shouted, "Switch sides, lad."

Merrick groaned and shook his head. "Don't you think the lad should learn to ride before he tries the lance?"

"Aye. But the boy insisted."

Thud had managed to mount the horse, and he rode—using the term loosely—back toward the starting mark.

Merrick walked over and handed him the lance. "Here, lad."

Thud took the weapon.

"Tighten your knees on the horse and move your body with him. Will keep you from bouncing off. Grip the lance tightly under your arm and try to keep it straight."

Thud nodded, listening intently and wearing a face that was serious with concentration.

"Aim for the target's torso." Merrick pointed at the practice dummy. "Right there, where the heart would be. See the splintered marks?"

"Aye."

"The moment you hit the target, lie low over the mount's mane and urge him forward with your knees. The horse will do the rest."

Thud nodded. He slipped the lance under his arm and took off, still bouncing like the leather football the squires used to play melee games.

He charged again, more daylight showing between his butt and the saddle than shone in the morning sky. He hit the dummy. Hard. The lance flew back again and the boy crouched low over the horse...just as the quintain spun by and swept him off.

But he didn't fall.

Thud clung atop the spinning quintain, his legs clamped around it while he spun round and round like a traveling acrobat. His riderless horse trotted easily over to a clump of nearby grass and began to eat.

This time the squires were on the ground, holding their sides and rolling around with laughter.

"Keep at it, Thump!" Merrick shouted, figuring a little encouragement wouldn't hurt the lad.

"Thud," Sir Isambard said from the corner of his mouth. "His name is Thud."

"Thud!" Merrick corrected, then looked at his man. "Where is the other one." He paused and frowned for a moment. What was the other lad's name? "Thwart? Where's Thwart?"

"Thwack."

"Aye." Merrick nodded. "Thwart, Thump, Thwack. 'Tis enough to confuse a saint."

"The last I saw of him he was trying to pick his mount from horses in the stable yard."

"How long ago?"

The older knight shrugged. "An hour or so before None."

Merrick glanced up at the angle of the sun in the sky. 'Twas well past None. Shaking his head, he took off toward the stables.

Clio strolled across the inner bailey, her guards, three of Merrick's men-at-arms, trailing along behind her like overgrown ducklings. However they were not her concern at the moment.

She was secretly searching for the earl of Lips, wonderful, wonderful lips, and trying not to be too obvious. Should he discover how she felt, the man would not be able to get his great swollen head through the castle doors.

She moved toward the stables. The familiar scent of freshly mown hay, mixed with the sharp tinge of manure, filled the warm air. She paused, then poked her head inside, where it was dark and dank, and it took a few moments for her vision to adjust.

The horses shifted in their stalls. One of them neighed and threw up his massive head. 'Twas Merrick's warhorse. She scanned the inside but could not see Merrick, so she left.

Around back, more horses were in the stable yard, where new fences had been made to keep them safely penned inside. Merrick had explained during a meal conversation with Sir Roger that he had done so in case of an attack. The men could find and mount them quickly. As if she could not figure that one out on her own.

She strolled toward the fences, then stopped. Her keepers stopped a few feet behind her, as if they were actually attached by puppet strings to her slippers and had to move when she moved, stop when she stopped.

'Twas humiliating and made her feel a snatch of rebelliousness toward Merrick and his need to control her every motion. She scowled and kicked a rock away in frustration.

She kicked a few more rocks just for the pleasure of kicking something solid and thick and heavy. Rocks were after all not unlike a man's head.

She paused and eyed the pen. After a moment's thought, she climbed up on the lowest fence railing and rested her arms over the top, then just concentrated on watching the horses.

They played about the yard, nipping each other and trotting around the fencing with their tails up as if to say, "Yes, look at me, watch me prance." They were stallions, the lot of them, she thought with no little surprise.

She turned to hop down from the fence, but stopped when she heard the quiet, distant sound of voices coming from the rear of the stable.

She smiled. 'Twas in truth not the arrogant male horses that had her attention, but a different arrogant male. Yes, she knew the distinct tone of Merrick's voice, and felt something twitch inside her belly at the deep sound of it.

She did not get down and go into the back of the stable. She had her keepers with her and they would surely tell Merrick if she were to eavesdrop. Besides which, if she concentrated, she heard fine right here.

"Remember, lad. Move with him," Merrick was saying. "Give him his head. Let the horse do the work."

Before Clio had a chance to discover whom Merrick was instructing, the rear stable doors blasted open. Her keepers moved into a protective circle around her, their weapons raised. As if the doors were going to harm her.

But before she could speak, a rider shot out of the darkness into the clear sunshine, and Clio clung to the fence railing, unable to believe what she saw.

Thwack was atop a huge black horse, its mane flying as they rode past. The lad, who to the best of her knowledge had never been atop anything other than one of the miller's oxen, was bent low, his hands on the reins. His knees were high and gripping the mount the same way she remembered Merrick's were when he'd charged those outlaws in the forest.

Thwack, sweet and simple Thwack, moved with the horse as if he were born there.

"That's the way, boy!" Merrick stepped from inside the stable. He was laughing. He cupped his hands to his mouth. "Lean low, lad, and ride!"

She jumped down from the fence and elbowed her way through her keepers, her skirts in her fists as she ran after the boy, half in awe and half afraid he was riding toward his death.

She did not care that his men ran behind her; she was afraid for Thwack. Her eyes had to be deceiving her. As she rounded the corner of the armory, with Thwack just ahead, someone ran past her, someone large, someone wearing a familiar brown leather jack. Someone with long muscled legs.

She gripped her skirts even tighter and higher, ran faster, trying feebly to match his long strides.

Her breath grew tight in her chest. Her throat burned. She could feel the sweat, the heat of exertion color her face.

He turned at the smithy's, the same direction Thwack had gone. She churned her hands and feet faster and faster and whipped around the stone corner of the smithy's and ran right into Merrick's open arms.

He lifted her as if she weighed no more than a feather. "I thought you'd never get here."

She stared up at him, unable to speak because she was trying to catch her breath. He was grinning down at her. He was not even winded.

She felt as if her chest were on fire. Her mouth was open and panting.

One hand slid into her tangle of hair and held her head close to his. He kissed her then, before she could speak or gasp or breathe. His tongue filled her hot mouth and made it hotter.

He kissed her hard and possessively, as if he were branding her his own, as he had during the early morning when he drove her mad with his mouth and hands and gave a taste of what passion was.

Oh, she had wanted this, his mouth on her again. She could live her life like this, tasting him and having him taste her. She went limp in his arms and he groaned into her mouth. The kiss was over too quickly, almost as if someone had pulled them apart. He tilted her head back so he could look down at her, and he whispered, "Later, woman."

She blinked up at him, but by the time she could think clearly, he was carrying her toward the practice field, where she could hear jeers and laughter from the pages and squires.

She wanted to curse him for the power his kisses had over her. She wanted to curse herself because it was something she could not control and at the same time wanted and yearned for so badly.

"You will want to see this." He set her down and gripped her hand, pulling her along with him as he strode toward the field.

"What are you about, Merrick? Why is Thwack on the horse?" She tugged on her hand, but he gripped it even tighter. "Let me go. Who taught him to ride? How did he do that?"

"For someone who was speechless a few moments ago, you found your tongue quick enough."

"What are you about?"

"You repeat yourself."

261

"Only because you did not answer me."

"Watch this." He pointed toward the practice field.

She wanted to tell him to go soak his head in the water trough. She glared up at him.

"God, woman, but you are stubborn." He gripped her shoulders and spun her so she was facing the field. "Now watch, damnit."

Thwack rode toward the quintain, where the squires were taking turns trying to pluck a jeweled dagger from the head of the practice dummy without being unseated.

"He will kill himself," she muttered, even though he looked as if he knew what he was doing. She just could not believe what she saw.

At that same moment, Tobin de Claire was riding hellbent toward the prized dagger. Thwack flew down the field from the opposite direction. The ground shook with the sound of the pounding hooves of those two horses.

Soon all those on the field noticed there were two riders. She saw Sir Isambard raise his fist high, as if in encouragement, and she could hear Thud shouting and whistling, yelling Thwack's name.

Tobin saw Thwack and kicked his horse harder.

Thwack leaned lower.

Tobin was closer. He reached out, grinning cockily and ready to grab the dagger.

Thwack's mount burst forward. Thwack snatched up the dagger just a heartbeat before the proud Tobin.

Clio stood there stunned, knowing she was

wearing a half smile. Sweet and slow Thwack on horseback was faster than the wind. To the sound of cheers, he rode around the field, the dagger held high above his head. He had one hand on the reins, but when you watched him ride, you knew he could do as well with no hands at all.

They all cheered and hollered, except Tobin, who looked as if he had taken a hard clout in the head.

Merrick turned back and looked at her, his face so arrogant and proud even she couldn't fault him.

"You taught him to ride like that."

He shook his head. "You cannot teach someone to ride like he does. And not in an hour. 'Tis a natural thing, between the boy and the horse."

"But he could not do that alone. He could not even saddle a mount."

"Aye, I did teach him that. Took forever, too." He grinned.

She smiled up at Merrick, then, wanting so badly to tell him thank you. But the words seemed too weak for what she truly felt and for exactly what she wanted to say. He was a kind man and a different man from what she had imagined he could be. 'Twas almost too much for her, all the contrary things she had discovered about him in only the last day.

He seemed to know that she was confused by her feelings. She could tell because the softness in his eyes said so. For just a moment she thought he might pull her into his arms again.

263

His gaze had shifted to her mouth. His look said he wanted to kiss her.

Then Thwack thundered past them. "My lord!" he called out.

Merrick spun around.

Thwack was riding back down the field away from them. Actually, he was riding in a wide circle. He came thundering back toward them, and Merrick stood in front of her as if to protect her from being run down.

"Stop, boy!" Merrick shouted. "Stop now!"

"I can't stop! You forgot to show me how!" Thwack sped past them heading in the opposite direction.

Merrick cursed, then he ran after him.

CHAPTER 28

It was an old Druid custom to stuff herbs in a keyhole for good luck. Had Clio been blessed with second sight, like Old Gladdys, she might have stuffed an entire thyme bush into her door that night before the moon ever rose.

As it was, she sat by the fire, her foolish heart merry and her mind anxious and filled with thoughts of Merrick's kisses and touches.

She sighed. That wonderful man she was fortunate enough to wed. 'Twas as if her youthful dreams had really come true. Here she was betrothed to a man who was sensitive to others. The kind of man sung about by troubadours. She had seen that gentle side of him, the kind lover and the fatherlike mentor who had cared about Thwack and given the lad back his pride.

Aye, Merrick de Beaucourt, the Red Lion, of late, the earl of Glamorgan, was a true gallant, a chivalrous knight.

An hour or so past Compline, he finally opened the door to her bedchamber. 'Twas all she could do not to shout out a thank-you. He was finally here. Her beloved.

She sat very still by the fire. She was glad for the strong flames of an oak fire instead of the weak warmth of a brazier. Although, for some odd reason, she was not cold when he was in the room.

Her hair was damp from washing with a special soap concocted of daisies that Old Gladdys had made during the last of the winter's new moon and swore would make her hair shine brighter than the sunlight and moonlight combined.

Clio carefully pulled an ivory comb through her long, damp hair and tried to get out the rest of the tangles. Her hair was still knotted. She had been so nervous about waiting for Merrick that she had dismissed Dulcie. So now she was stuck with her wet, knotted hair and its tangled mass of ends.

She tried to ignore the sounds he made as he moved about the room. She tried and failed.

She could hear him remove clothing. The soft swish of cloth against skin. His footsteps on the carpet, then the gentle tap on the stone floor.

From the corner of her eye she saw him cross the room and hang his leather jack and linen shirt on a peg nearby.

She could see his skin, bronzed, slick skin.

The comb slipped and flew from her hand. She muttered something vicious.

Merrick crossed to her in a few long strides. He bent down and picked up the comb.

She stared at his bare back, the broad and tight muscles and gleaming skin. She forgot to breathe.

"Turn around." His look was indulgent and it might have irritated her if it weren't for the fact that she wanted him to comb her hair. She wanted him to touch her.

She faced the fire and waited, trying not to look smug.

His hands were gentle. He drew the comb through her hair in long, sure strokes. When the comb hit the tangled ends, he just lifted it and slowly worked the comb through with a gentleness she wished Dulcie had.

The girl always pulled out huge clumps of Clio's hair, so that once in a while she accused the maid of trying to snatch her as bald as Walter the Miller.

But Merrick again showed to Clio his gentle side, by the care with which he combed her hair, as if he thought it of great value. He was completely silent. The entire time, as if this

266

were the most serious of tasks. The only sound in the room was that of Cy's snoring on the bed. And the loud thumping of her nervous and foolish heart.

She closed her eyes and leaned her head back a little. He rubbed his hands through her hair, massaging her scalp and temples. She moaned because it felt so good.

He stopped abruptly, his hands threaded through her damp hair.

She opened her eyes, looking at him with her head tilted back so his face was upside-down to her. Even in this position, she could see his features clearly.

His look was pained, as if she had hit him with her fist.

She straightened and turned around. 'Twas then she saw the desire on his face. He was trying to hide it, to control his passion the same way she did. And it looked as if he was no more successful at hiding his feeling than she was.

She studied him more closely, and found she liked what she saw. His face and features, the ones she had once thought were too hard to be handsome, now appealed to her in a way that made her weak when she looked at him.

His dark brows and clear, light eyes. The jaw that could clench so tightly in anger framed the dark whiskered cheeks that showed deep slashes when he grinned or smiled.

His mouth was wide and thinned because of his tenseness. But she knew it could be soft and could make her feel things she had not believed existed.

He looked away from her as if forced to do so by something stronger than both of them. He blindly handed her the comb, then crossed over to a chair opposite her with no explanation.

He sprawled in the chair as if he had no bones left. He looked ill at ease and continued to stare at the fire, saying nothing to her. 'Twas almost as if he were a thousand miles away.

"What is wrong?"

He gave a sharp and brittle bark of laughter that she had not expected. "Wrong?" He shook his head. "Nothing, except that tomorrow cannot come too soon for me."

"Tomorrow?"

"Aye. Tomorrow."

"Are you leaving?" She hated the weakness she heard in her voice. It was as if she were saying, "Don't go."

He turned toward her, really looked at her then, plainly surprised and puzzled by her words. "No, I'm not leaving. The king is coming here tomorrow."

"The king is coming here?" she repeated, her voice sounding squeaky and as if it belonged to a village fishwife, not to her.

"Aye."

She forgot to breathe. He was mad of course. He had to be. Completely insane. The king at Camrose, surely not. How could such a thing be hidden from her? She waited for him to explain.

He did not, but just sat there.

Finally she asked, "What do you mean the king is coming here?"

"The king. Edward," Merrick said, still sprawled back in his chair.

"Edward?" she repeated stupidly.

"Surely you have heard of Edward. The son of Henry and Eleanor, the man who wears a crown, sits on a throne, and rules England." He straightened and added in a mocking whisper, "He's married to the queen."

The look she gave him should have cooked him. "You did not tell me the king was coming."

"Did I not?"

"No." She stood and looked down at him. "You did not."

"I was certain I told you the king was coming."

She planted her hands on her hips. "You did *not* tell me the king was coming."

"I remember telling you there would be only one more delay until we would marry. That day on the battlements. I remember it distinctly."

"Aye, you did say that, but you failed to mention that the 'one thing' was the king of England."

"Well, now you know," he said casually, as if he were speaking of the time of day or the color of the sky and not something as important as a royal visit. "He is coming tomorrow," he added. "For our wedding."

"Our wedding?"

"Aye." He gave her a long and confused look. "Why are you so upset?"

"You did not think to tell me that we would wed tomorrow. I *am* the bride."

"No. Because we will not wed tomorrow. It will be in few days. So what?"

"Why did you not tell me?"

"I thought I had."

"How could you think you told me something and yet did not?"

He shook his head, plainly confused. "I'm not certain how to answer that. I do not understand you."

"Would you have me shamed before my king?"

"How could you be shamed, woman? There is no shame on you. Besides, 'tis not only the king. The queen is coming, too. She will keep you fine company, as will many of the courtiers who will come along."

At that, she lost the ability to speak. He could not be that stupid. Could he?

"We are to have a proper wedding," he continued as if the most important ceremony of her life were nothing to concern her. "I am the king's earl and you are his ward. The archbishop himself will marry us," he told her proudly.

"The whole court? The archbishop?"

"Aye. 'Tis nothing to send you into a dither. They are human like us."

"Are you mad?" she began to pace the room, waving her hands in the air. She could not believe this. "I have nothing ready for them. Where will they sleep?" She stopped pacing suddenly. "Dear God in heaven, what about the food? Where will we get the food to feed so many?"

"There will be a hunting party the first thing tomorrow. No one will starve."

"You oaf. Do you not understand anything?"

He leaned forward in his chair, suddenly tense, his look dark. "I understand that this morning you could not get enough of me."

She flushed.

"And I understand that if you call me an oaf again, I shall not remain in this chair for long."

She couldn't help herself. She began to cry.

"Are you crying?" He sat there as if he did not know what to do. "You are crying."

She sobbed and sobbed. "How could you do this?"

He stood up, yelling, "What the bloody hell have I done? I do not understand you. Any woman would be proud to have the king at her wedding. 'Tis a great honor."

"I know," she wailed. "But I will be shamed. Camrose is not ready for a royal visit."

"Of course, it is. They finished the stone bridge over the new and wider moat yesterday. The towers are stronger. There are now both an inner and outer barbican and two iron portcullises. I have the walls manned with the best of my men-at-arms—archers, the very best. Longbowmen, trained to protect. No harm could come to the king, the queen, or the court while they are at Camrose. You should be proud, woman. Instead you are standing here blithering."

"I am not blithering," she said through her tears. "How could you not tell me the king and queen were coming?"

"I thought I did tell you!" He bellowed.

"Out!" she pointed toward the door.

"What did you say?"

"I said get out!"

"And if I refuse?"

She threw her head back and marched toward the door.

"Do not touch that door," he warned.

She glared right at him and grabbed the door handles.

He did not move. He looked as if he could not believe she was defying him.

The insensitive and heartless oaf. She turned around and grabbed his sword belt with both hands. The thing felt as if it weighed more than she did. How did a man wield such a thing?

He watched her then, clearly amused. "And what are you going to do with that? Cut out my black heart?"

"After tonight, my lord, I am certain that you have no heart."

"Put it down, Clio."

"You cannot tell me what to do."

"You are mine, woman."

"Not yet, I'm not. You forget we are not married." She jerked open the doors. He did not move but stood there, looking amused.

She dragged his sword out the doors with her.

His laughter followed her. "After you figure

out how to lift that weapon, what do you intend to do with it? I have a plan," he bellowed after her. "You can kill the king with it so he won't notice your poor housekeeping."

She slammed the doors on his laughter as hard as she could, pulled the sword from its sheath, and wedged the strong, forged blade through both the door handles.

She stood there, waiting a moment.

It did not take long for him to push on the doors. With his battle sword tightly wedged in the iron handles, the doors did not budge.

"What the hell...?"

There was a long pause.

"Open this door, Clio!"

She blithely plucked a torch off the wall. Humming, she turned and walked merrily down the stairs.

"Woman!"

She paused on the steps, her face level with the bottom of the doors. She could see the shadow of his big feet under the crack between the floor stones and the bottom of the wooden doors.

"Aye, my lord?" she asked sweetly.

"Open this door."

"I have much too much to do. After all, Merrick, the king is coming." Then she left.

The Maid
of the Green Forest
(Second Stanza)

Oh, take me to thy fair palace,
Oh, take me for thy queen,
And racy wine shall then be thine
As never a man has seen.

—from "The Legend of King
Alaric's Wife,"
ancient Welsh folktale, first put
into written verse by
John F.M. Dovaston, 1825

CHAPTER 29

Edward the First, king of England, and his queen, the younger Eleanor, rode through the gates of Camrose Castle the following day. Golden bells rang from the gold braided halters on their matched white mounts. Those perfect horses were almost as richly dressed as the king and queen.

Heralds had ridden ahead and were mounted

atop the wall walks. Their horns were hung with the banner of Edward Plantagenet, and they played their horns to announce the arrival of the king of England and his beloved queen.

Behind the royal guard came the pennants of the church, the cross upon a field of red to stand for the blood of Christ. Clad in gold and white was the archbishop, his cloak lined with white fur and his guard dressed in gold armor with surcoats enblazoned with the cross. Behind them followed cardinals in crimson red and bishops in white and silver.

Then came a bright and bejeweled train of nobles, their fine ladies riding at their sides. All were clad in richly colored garments of crimson, amber, emerald, and sapphire blue, and decorated with the heavy raw jewels favored in the Plantagenet court.

The royal train ran as far back as the eye could see, a gay and impressive ribbon on the horizon. With them came wagons and oxen carrying gifts to Camrose and to Sir Merrick. These were presents from the king to the honored man who would wed Lady Clio of Camrose, the king's own ward.

At that very moment, said ward stood beside her betrothed in all her glorious and golden beauty. In looking at her, few would know what was going through her busy head.

Clio stifled the first of two sudden urges: to yawn, for she had been awake all night seeing to the readiness of the castle and servants. She supposed the king would feel justified in ordering her beheaded if she were to look upon all this pomp and honor with the least amount of boredom.

She knew she was supposed to look suitably impressed. 'Twas hard to be impressed when she was overcome with another even stronger urge: to kick the earl as hard as she could.

She wondered what would happen if she were to just draw back her foot and...

"Do not even think about it." Merrick warned without looking at her.

She stiffened. Could the man read her mind?

"You are wearing that look, Clio."

"What look?"

"The one that signals trouble as surely as if you bellowed a battle cry."

"I do not know what you could possibly be yammering about, *my lord*."

"Look impressed, *my lady*, or you will offend our monarch and my friend."

She plastered a weak smile on her face and did her duty. Not because Merrick ordered her to, but because she had her own pride.

She would not let anyone know how she felt. No one. She would not show that she was hurt and ashamed that Merrick would treat her so callously.

It bothered her as much as his abandonment had, though perhaps this time she felt more betrayed, because she had thought he was different. She would hold her head proud and pretend she was happy.

She looked at the king, who was riding

through the gates. She had not met the man before. Only his father, Henry, and his fearsome and manipulative queen, the older Eleanor. 'Twas that woman who had so quickly banished her from court.

She knew some of Edward, a man who had proved himself to be a doer instead of a dreamer. Some said he was a framer of just laws and a man of sharp intelligence.

He had learned battle tactics and mechanics of war under the tutelage of the great Simon de Montfort, a man whom he later defeated in a treasonous rebellion against Henry. It was said Edward won his victory over the barons with a master tactician's skills, and he defeated de Montfort at his own game.

But as Clio looked at her king, riding closer to her with each step of his white mount, she was surprised to see he was as blondly handsome as Richard Coeur de Lion and tall and strong as an English oak.

Edward rode into Camrose with all the height and majesty of a true king. His expression was full of fire, and she had no doubt that Merrick was right when he had said this was the man to make England strong, undivided.

But there was something else in Edward's expression, a kind of aura that made him more human. 'Twas almost like a strength and odd human sweetness that gave credence to man's belief in the godlike origins of kings.

His surcoat was emblazoned with three rampant leopards and was laced to his metal skull cap. He wore chausses of steel that covered his long-shanked thighs. His beard was light and golden, his lips full.

He had creases in his cheeks and near his eyes that showed a man who saw humor in the world. His skin wasa reddish sun-tinted color that gave him the healthy look of a man who could rule forever.

He rode into the courtyard, and Merrick took her hand tightly in his, as if he thought she might do something foolish like snatch it away.

She held her head high as they walked down the few steps to greet the king.

Edward raised one immense hand in the air and the procession stopped. He swept down off his horse with a warrior's ease, the golden bells on his saddle were the only sounds in air.

The king grabbed Merrick in the friendly embrace of a long-lost brother, hugging him tightly while they laughed and greeted each other with loud slaps on the shoulders.

She did not understand men. Any moment she expected them to grunt together or bump heads like the wild boars in the forest.

Was this jolly bear of a man her king? Wasn't he all too human? The man laughed and joked with Merrick.

The moment the king shifted his merry gaze toward her, she sank into a curtsy, her head bowed low. Her knees were knocking together, and she took deep breaths so she wouldn't do something truly humiliating like faint at his feet.

"Ah, so this is the Lady Clio." His voice was kind and filled with amusement. The king took her hand, and she looked up as she straightened. "I think my mother, God rest her bitter soul, must have been mistaken, my lady. For you do not look like 'that horrid devil's changeling' to me."

She flushed bright red, felt the heat flood her cheeks. She could still hear the queen's angry words.

Edward gave her a warm smile. "Whatever possessed you to put monk's ink in her oil bottle?"

Clio sighed. "My own youthful exuberance, your majesty." She would not admit that the queen had been complaining of gray hairs and was desperately seeking a cure. Clio had thought it a bottle of hair oil, not the oil the queen used to rub on her eyes at night.

"Mother looked like a badger for almost two months." Edward said with another laugh.

" 'Tis good to know the years have not changed your propensity for jests, *my love*," Merrick said, placing an arm affectionately around her shoulder. "Why, just last evening she played a foolish prank on me."

His love? She gave Merrick a cool look that promised revenge.

He reached up and tweaked her nose.

It happened so fast she almost could not believe it, but the innocent look he gave her told her he knew exactly what he was doing. They both knew, too, that she could do nothing about it. 'Twas like a raw youth given license to sport in any way he wished.

Within minutes they were greeting the

queen and the others. Clio had to stand there, smiling, while Merrick joked and laughed with each visitor; it was the longest morning of Clio's life.

He patted her head like a trusted dog, tweaked her nose too many times to count. He pinched her cheeks and gave her slobbery kisses, and pinched her bottom so many times she would not be able to sit for a week.

And all this in the name of a playful lover's affection.

When they finally turned to follow the others inside, Clio stopped him with a firm hand on his forearm. "If you pat me on the head once more, I will bark. King or no king."

Merrick just laughed and gave her a swift pat on the cheek.

"I will not get angry, my lord," she promised, her head high and her steps determined as she walked beside him into the keep. "I will get even."

But neither of them knew her revenge would come in a matter of hours.

That day, the tables in the great hall at Camrose were laden with huge, golden-brown hunks of roasted venison and spiced rabbit. Wild boar stuffed with green winter apples and hams the size of a knight's chest were served on platters of pewter and garnished with braised spinach greens and leeks cooked in golden honey sauce.

There was flounder with rosemary stuffing,

280

salmon steamed in dill weed, and pickled eel decorated with bright red crab apples. The bakers had spent the entire night baking meat pies, saffron girdle breads, and chicken pasties.

Custard tarts were covered with fruit and figs and precious raisins, and before the king and queen was a raised silver bowl filled with red Sicilian oranges and shiny ripe nectarines.

Bacon pudding and cherry pottage sat in large serving bowls next to the salt sellers and locked pepper caskets with their small silver spoons and shaker holes. Rare capons were set aflame and crowned with eggs that were cooked right inside their brown speckled shells.

Placed before the archbishop and other clergy were roasted peacocks stuffed with honeyed figs and apple mash. The proud bird's plumy feathers had been reapplied after cooking and fanned to show their bright jeweled colors. Then they were placed on platters so large it took two servants to carry them.

Merrick looked about him and decided Clio was being foolish. This feast was one of the finest he'd ever seen.

He was suitably proud. He cast a glance at his betrothed, who sat at the head table looking as stiff as an old corpse.

"The feast does Camrose well," Merrick said quietly, hoping to placate her some. "There is no shame in this. You worried for naught, woman."

She did not look at him, but leaned close and

whispered, "But for how many days can our larders supply this much fare? As of today, there is no white flour left."

"We will hunt again tomorrow. The men will want meat." Merrick gave a wave of his hand. "White flour is not important."

She gave a long and unreadable look. "It is to me," she said under her breath.

"Why just to you?" He had trouble keeping the scorn from his voice.

"There is no white flour for a bridal cake," she said softly, her head bent as if she thought she might cry.

He eyed her head for a moment, surprised that she would be upset about something as silly as a bride cake. He did not understand women very well. They made the smallest things into such huge events. 'Twas like turning a childhood spat over a toy into a full-fledged war.

He turned and raised a hand to signal one of the nearest servants—the master of the butlery—who then clapped his hands and five brawny men rolled in huge casks of Clio's latest batch of ale.

Merrick supposed they needed some levity in the room. Sitting there watching Clio's unhappiness was doing little for his mood. The king was here and it was time to celebrate. He figured the ale would loosen their spirits.

When the servants unplugged the casks and poured the beer into pewter serving ewers, all in the room saw Clio's ale for the pure brew it was. The clarity was as clear as spring rain-water, while the color of the ale was rich and golden, like summer honey.

Edward eyed the ale with great appreciation, and when he was told that Lady Clio had brewed it, he nodded and gave her a golden ring encrusted with emeralds as a reward.

"A toast to the bride!" Someone from one of the lower tables cried out.

"Aye!"

The servants moved through the crowd, filling goblets and cups with Lady Clio's ale.

Edward stood and held his chalice high. "To Lady Clio of Camrose!" He took a deep drink of ale. He swallowed and his eyes became bright blue.

All held their breath while the king looked down at his chalice, staring at the beer. He raised his head and smiled, then took another even bigger draft.

"Lady Clio of Camrose!" all the guests shouted, raising their cups and goblets and drinking as deeply as had the king.

"Aye, to Lady Clio of Camrose," Edward repeated. "Whom Sir Merrick tweaks on the nose." He drank more ale.

Queen Eleanor blinked twice, then turned and looked at her husband as if he had grown a second head. Frowning, she took a small sip as she watched her husband closely.

Clio and Merrick also exchanged puzzled glances.

Merrick shrugged and took a deep drink of

the ale, which was the best beer he had ever tasted. He leaned toward Clio. " 'Tis fine." He paused, then felt this intense need to add, "Better than French wine."

Merrick swilled down the rest of his ale. A strange heat traveled from his belly to loins to his head. 'Twas like his blood came alive. He signaled a servant to refill his cup, then took the ewer from the servant's hand and set it before him. "Leave it. You twit."

He stood, raising the cup high. "To my bride, who has too much pride!" He drank deeply.

The archbishop was on his third chalice of ale. He shot to his feet and shouted, "Tan her hide!"

The room erupted in laughter at this bright new game that the king himself had started. Each person tried to have a wittier rhyme than the next.

And so it went for the whole meal.

Since Clio was the bride, they toasted her lips, and her hips. They drank to her eyes, and her thighs. Her luscious meal fare and her glorious hair. Her small nose and her bare toes.

But even Merrick was surprised when he himself stood and bellowed, "Here's to Lady Clio with her mouth full of sass."

He paused and looked down at her, enjoying her flush. He took a deep drink and looked out at the tables, all of them waiting...

He grinned, then raised his cup high. "And her small, tight ass."

Don't undertake to drink
a whole pitch of beer.
Because if you then talk,
from your mouth comes nonsense.

—Papyrus Anastasi IV

"Whatever possessed you to toast your bride's ass?" Roger asked Merrick.

" 'Twas the thing that was on my mind at the time," Merrick grumbled.

Roger began to laugh all over again.

"Silence!" Merrick groaned. He sat on the battlements, where the cool wind blew, holding his pounding head in his hands while he asked himself the same bloody question. Why? What the hell had possessed him. "Just cut out my tongue and be done with it."

"I believe the fair Lady Clio would prefer that task, my friend." King Edward clapped Merrick on the shoulder and sat down next to him.

" 'Tis your fault," Merrick muttered. "Who ever heard of such a stupid game."

The king rubbed his chin thoughtfully. "I do not know why. I did not plan the thing. It just happened. However, once I said that first rhyme, I thought it rather amusing, myself. And one of the advantages of being king, Merrick, is that you can do all the stupid things you want and no one thinks it odd."

"Then Merrick should be king," Roger

said. "He has done more stupid things of late than we have in both of our lifetimes combined."

"You two can quit speaking of me as if I'm not here."

"Are you here? We thought you were off somewhere dreaming about your lady's sweet tight ass."

"Go to hell, Roger."

"I will. I am certain of it. And I hope the road to purgatory is lined with naked and wicked women. I care not if their asses are tight."

Merrick looked up at his friend. "I hope that road is lined with their husbands."

"Cease this," Edward said, standing up. He began to pace in front of Merrick.

It made Merrick dizzy and his head light, so he stared at his feet. "You both are giving me a headache."

"We must think," the king said, still pacing. "You need to do something to placate the fair Lady Clio."

"Falling on my sword would not do it?"

Roger and the king laughed.

But Merrick did not find this amusing. He knew he could not have humiliated his betrothed any worse than he had.

Yet she had said nothing. But just sat there while the room laughed at her. He knew her pride well, and knew it had taken a hard blow, one struck by him alone.

He was ashamed.

She had been right about him. He was an oaf.

A stupid oaf.

He took a deep breath and stood for a moment while his mind drifted toward some way he could show her the respect she deserved, the same respect his words had stolen from her that very night. He looked down at his feet for a moment and thought back over all of their conversations. Then he stilled.

"I'll be back," was all he said to his friends, and he strode away from the battlements without another word, leaving Roger and the king of England staring at his stiff back.

CHAPTER 30

Two days later, in the late afternoon, while the men were off hunting again, Lady Clio had her small tight ass situated on top of a straw pallet in a windowless alcove off the solar. She pushed a needle through the tambour in her hand, not paying one bit of attention to the size and quality of her stitches. All she wished for right then was solitude and a blessed moment's peace and quiet.

As any good chatelaine would have, she had given her bedchamber to the king and queen, while she and many of the court ladies spent their few hours of sleep crammed together like orphans in the small and airless stone room that was usually kept for visiting nuns or noble pilgrims.

The problem was they spent their waking hours together, too. But Clio did not know these women well, not like they knew each other. She did not fit in with them. When she was with them, she felt like a heathen in a room full of Christians.

"God's red blood! I am bored." Lady Sofia, a young cousin of the king's, a girl barely twelve years of age, tossed down her needle and plopped atop a pile of thin woolen blankets with her skinny arms crossed stubbornly over her chest.

"Do not swear, child," Queen Eleanor scolded her. "You know Edward would not approve of such language from you."

"Why not?" Sofia said petulantly. "Besides teaching me to swagger and spit, I've learnt my most masterful and inventive swear words from him."

"He is a man. Great men are expected to swear."

"I wish I were a man," Sofia said. "Men can hunt and swim naked and bask for hours in the sunlight. I want sun-bronzed skin," she said, pinching the pale skin on her forearms and frowning. "I look dead."

Another lady with long red hair and milky skin looked up and said, "Last eve, when I was out walking with Sir Roger FitzAlan, he told me that the Roman Church has disallowed women to stay in the sunlight for any length of time."

"Aye," a black-haired lady added. "Sir Roger, who took me for a ride atop his warhorse yesterday, claimed that the pope himself said the sun bleaches the hair and since hair grows from the brain, it can damage our minds."

"How stupid," young Sofia said with disgust. "Surely you do not believe that drivel? If hair truly grew from the brain, all men would be bald."

Every woman in the small room laughed at that bit of youthful candor.

"From the mouths of babes," muttered the queen with a sweet smile that showed she, Eleanor of Castile, had a fine and charming sense of humor, unlike the other Eleanor, her ferocious mother-in-law.

"I wish I were a king," Clio said wistfully, staring at the flickering flames of the candles next to her.

"So do I," Sofia said. "Then I could do as I wished. If I were king, no one would *dare* tell me what to do."

Eleanor laughed. "If you were king, my child, everyone would tell you what to do."

"I do not care." Sofia's chin shot up proudly. "I would not listen and do as I pleased."

"Ah, I see. Just as you do now," Eleanor said.

They all laughed, for it was well known that Lady Sofia was a spirited girl who drove the king mad with her defiance.

Even Sofia had to bite back a small smile.

It was not lost on Clio that this Queen Eleanor did not banish the exuberant Sofia from court for her youthful follies.

Her own court visit had seemed so very long ago. Time seemed to have taken forever to pass, and yet she could not say exactly where all the time had gone. Clio felt as if she had been waiting forever for something important to happen in her life.

She grew quiet and just plied her needle without care to the size of the stitches or the pattern. 'Twas something for her to do so she wouldn't feel as if she were a rock in a room full of jewels.

The queen turned and cast a quick glance at Clio, then took a few stitches in the cloth she was working.

While the other women chattered freely about men and freedom, riches and weddings, and the latest scandals, the queen stood calmly and moved over to stand near a bright branch of tallow candles, where Clio was silently working on her stitchery.

Clio looked up and gave the queen a weak smile.

Eleanor straightened and clapped her hands. "Leave us be, ladies. Go out to the solar and do your gossiping there. I long for some quiet time with the bride."

The women left, all but Lady Sofia, who was watching both Clio and the queen from eyes too bright for a young girl of only twelve. "Can I stay?"

"No," the queen said sharply.

"Why not?"

"I have to speak to Lady Clio about her marriage."

"Why?"

" 'Tis none of your concern."

"Oh. I understand. You are going to talk about the bedding." Sofia stood then and gave them a wicked smile.

"Out!" Eleanor pointed toward the door.

"I do not know why it must a secret." Sofia marched toward the doors. "I have heard all about it from John and Henry."

"I must speak to my sons," Eleanor muttered.

"I have decided to take the veil." With that pronouncement, Sofia gave a sharp nod of her head. "I would rather wed God and live in a nunnery than let a man do that to me."

Eleanor laughed then. "Edward will have to wed you to someone other than the Lord, my child. Although I suspect there are times when my husband would feel that God does deserve you. However, I suggest you forget any nonsense you have concocted about locking yourself away in a nunnery. It will not happen."

"You would not like it, Sofia. I've been in a convent," Clio admitted. " 'Twas more boring than being in a ladies' solar and doing stitchery."

"Nothing could be more boring than stitchery," Sofia grumbled and skulked across the room. She paused in the doorway. "If my cousin Edward is to choose a husband for me, then he had better choose well. A man who is my equal, for I'll not take just any man. He must be gallant and brave and chivalrous. He must adore me." Sofia disappeared, then poked her head back around the corner. "And I still say not even a husband hand-picked by the king of England will stick me with his privy member."

"Sofia!"

The girl disappeared again.

Eleanor just stood there, shaking her head.

Clio was laughing. She could not help it. She could remember thinking those same thoughts.

Eleanor sat down next to her. "She is young and headstrong. Edward swears she will drive him insane with her romantic ideas and independent ways."

"I remember feeling that way," Clio admitted. "All that youthful belief in chivalry and honor and gallantry."

Those thoughts did not seem so important to her now. There were other things she wanted from her husband. Things that were important, like love and respect.

"You are unhappy." Eleanor stared down at her.

Clio shrugged. She did not know what to say. She was unhappy. In fact she was scared and confused and miserable.

"Do you not care for the earl?"

She shrugged again.

"You may forget I am queen and tell me the truth. Please. This is important."

Clio tried to think of some positive things to say. "He is brave and rich and he can be handsome when he is not shouting orders."

"I see." Eleanor looked as if she wanted to smile, but she did not. "What else?"

"He rides well."

"I see."

"He saved me from some Welsh outlaws and he nursed me back to health."

Eleanor nodded, appearing to listen intently. "Do you think you could love him?"

"He kisses well," Clio admitted, flushing at the thought of his lips on her...everywhere.

"What do you not like about him?"

"He is a stubborn, arrogant, pigheaded, unfeeling lout."

Eleanor nodded thoughtfully. "I see. So you do not wish to wed him."

"Aye," Clio agreed, then paused. "No. That is not the truth." She sighed. "Oh, I don't know what I want. Aye, I do. I want to wed his lips."

Eleanor threw back her head and laughed out loud. Then she took her hand. "I think I understand."

"Do you?"

She nodded. "Edward and I were wed when I was ten and he was fifteen. We had not met before. It was an alliance between Henry and my brother Alfonso."

"You had no say in your marriage either."

"My brother loves me. He is an educated man and a contemporary thinker. Our home had a library that was full of Arabic papers charting the stars. He supported poets and musicians and physicians. The castle was filled with the latest of inventions—astrolabes, sun clocks, water clocks, even a mercury clock. So many fascinating things to see. Anyway, he told Henry he would not agree to the marriage until he inspected Edward."

"Inspected him? The prince?" Clio giggled.

Eleanor was laughing, too; then she leaned closer to Clio and said quietly, "The truth is, he wanted me to get a look at him and to agree to wed him freely. He did not want to see me given to a man he could not respect. My husband's family..." she paused, searching for difficult words.

"I understand," Clio said. "John was a bad king and a horrid man, too."

"Aye, and Edward's father, Henry, had trouble keeping his word. He broke an alliance with my mother in favor of Eleanor of Provence. My brother was concerned for my happiness."

"You agreed to marry the prince."

"Aye. I thought him the most handsome young man I had ever seen. He rode into Burgos on a Spanish charger, looking so tall and long-legged, with his flaxen hair clipped close below his ears and those clear blue eyes. He rode tall in the saddle. I think he was the tallest man I had ever seen. His back was straight from a stiffened tabard and he wore long boots of the finest leather. He spoke with such emotion and fire." She sighed. "I agreed. Oh, I agreed so quickly. And I have never regretted that decision."

"It is well known that the king adores you."

"It was not always so." She watched Clio closely. "You look surprised."

"But I thought it was always a great love match."

Eleanor shook her head. "What does a ten-year-old girl know of love, or for that matter, a fifteen-year-old prince? While he waited for me to grow into a wifely age, he was a roistering leader of bachelor knights. I bore him two children before he fell in love with me. I was twenty and I knew the day it happened. I arrived in Dover and as soon as I stepped ashore, I could see it in his face."

She grew quiet with her memory, and Clio stayed silent, waiting to hear what she would tell her next. This story fascinated her.

"That is what I wanted to tell you. Love does not always come the moment you meet someone. In fact, many times it is just the opposite. Life is not like those childhood dreams we have of knights and gallantry and courtly love. Those are just stories we are told, but that is not what love is. It is so much more."

"I don't think I understand," Clio told her.

"Love grows from something else. It is hard for me to explain. But I know it in here." She placed her hand over her heart. "It is not a simple thing for a man to love a woman. It is easier for us, I think, because we do not have to understand a man to love him. We can love him for who and what he is, even if we do not like it. Women are capable of loving men with all their faults."

"And men are not?" Clio asked.

"It is different for a man. Someday I think you will understand." She stood up. "But I have said enough. By now Lady Sofia is probably telling the world about her plans of chastity. I'd best go find her before Henry gets wind of her foolish chatter. He'll betroth the girl to his next enemy."

Clio stood and reached out her hand to the queen. She sank into her deepest curtsy and bowed her head in respect. "Thank you."

Eleanor stopped, then looked at their joined hands and nodded. She pulled Clio to her feet and took both of her hands. "I would like a friend, Lady Clio. Even at court when it is full of women, I have few I can speak freely to and even fewer I can trust."

Clio smiled, and a lifelong friendship was born.

The Maid
of the Green Forest
Fourth Stanza)

But ere I become thy wedded wife
Thou a solemn oath must make,
And let hap whate'er thou must not dare
That solemn oath to break.

—from "The Legend of King
Alaric's Wife,"
ancient Welsh folktale, first put
into written verse by
John F.M. Dovastson, 1825

CHAPTER 31

Clio stood before the polished brass piece, a small but precious part of her huge bride-price. It felt strange to see her reflection in something hanging on the wall, rather than looking down into a stream of silvery water.

Only that morn, Dulcie had washed her hair with dew gathered before sunrise the day before. Afterward, when Clio's hair was still wet, Dulcie had rubbed sweet almond oil into it, claiming that Old Gladdys promised it would shine even more than all the stars in the summer sky and surely capture the heart of her husband.

Her maid was becoming more romantic, especially since a certain handsome young red-haired troubadour with a voice like a nightingale's had come to Camrose to entertain for the earl's fine wedding.

Just last eve, Clio had seen Dulcie and the young man disappear behind the dark corner of the buttery. She had heard Dulcie giggle.

She looked away from her maid with her dreamy eyes and stared at her own reflection. Was this how she looked to others?

To Merrick?

She did not know exactly how she felt about the young and serious-looking face that stared back at her. She had not thought of herself looking this way.

Her hair was wonderful, even she could not deny it. The color was so pale and different. She had always thought her hair was the color of yellow flax, not uncommon.

But it was not flaxen, but so pale it was almost the color of that precious white flour she wished she had for a proper bride cake.

She stood there studying her features, her small, thin nose and the deep dimple in her chin. Had someone hit her when she was a babe?

Her father had had a small hole like this in his chin. She remembered back to a time her memory had lost for a while, when she was a small child sitting in his lap. She had asked him why he had a hole in his chin. He laughed and told her that was where the Viking had stabbed him, then hugged her tightly when she touched it and began to cry for him.

What an odd face she had...Each feature a part of her heritage. Her father's chin. Her mother's nose. Her grandmother's hair and eyes. Her grandfather's stubbornness. It all came back to her, casual comments made in jest over the years when her parents had been alive.

For the briefest of moments she felt lonely, and a weak, vulnerable part of her longed for her father to be here on this day, as she had longed for her mother the day before.

A loud knock at the door made her start. "Aye?"

Dulcie came inside. She took one look at Clio

still sitting there with her hair down and still a little damp and clad in only her linen shift, and she crossed the room clucking like one of the chickens in the bailey.

In less time than you could blink, Dulcie was pulling an ivory comb through her hair with such force it was as if she were trying to use that comb to exorcise the Devil himself.

"Ouch! Dulcie, have pity on me. I doubt Merrick would wish for a bald bride."

"But there is so little time, my lady. You should be down there, ready to mount your bridal horse. I heard the earl is already at the chapel."

"Do not fret so. The earl will expect me to be late." She yawned and stretched.

"If I were marrying the earl, I would not be late."

"If you were marrying the earl, I could have gotten a good sleep last night."

"You did not sleep well?"

Clio just shrugged.

"Are you afraid, my lady?"

Her insides were quivering and she felt as if her head were empty. Aye, something was happening to her.

"Do you need...advice?"

"Advice?" Clio frowned.

"About this night." Dulcie was not looking her in the eye. "About the bedding."

Clio studied Dulcie's serious pink face and burst out laughing. Dulcie continued to drag the comb though Clio's hair as if it were the most important duty in the world.

"Dulcie." Clio grabbed the hand with the comb and made her stop.

The girl looked at her then.

Clio tried to make her face look stern and shocked, like Sister Agnes's. "You are unmarried. Perchance is there something you should tell me?"

Dulcie blushed so bright a red that her face looked like a shiny fall apple. "I hear things that people would not say to a lady such as yourself."

"What have you heard?"

"Many things. Things that will shock you, my lady."

"I see." Clio paused, somewhat curious, but not certain Dulcie knew any more about bedding a man than she did. "Have you slept with a man?"

Dulcie looked horrified and quickly made the sign of the cross. "No, my lady. I swear I am a maiden."

What could one maiden tell another? Wasn't that like trying to ask an angel about sin?

Clio decided to test her. "Have you heard that men kiss with their tongues?"

Her maid grew redder and stared at her toes. "Aye. David the Sheepwasher stuck his tongue in my mouth at the last May fair."

"What about the troubadour?"

Dulcie's head shot up, then she smiled a little. "Him too."

There was a long, drawn-out moment of tense silence between them. Then Clio plucked at some loose threads on the hem of her shift. "Did you hear that a man can kiss you like that, with his lips and tongue in other places?"

The maid frowned. "What places?"

"Your breasts."

Dulcie shook her head vehemently. "Those are for your babes, my lady, not for your husband. Someone has been telling you fool's tales."

Clio bit back a smile and decided not to tell Dulcie about the other places Merrick liked to kiss. The maid would never believe it. In truth, Clio would not have believed it if someone had told her.

A simple kind of peaceful feeling came over her, the kind where you realize that you are not truly as frightened as you thought you were.

She felt better. She wasn't as light-headed and fluttery, especially when she remembered that when she married Merrick, they would have the freedom to kiss whenever she wanted.

She smiled a secret little smile while Dulcie braided her long hair at the sides, then twisted those thin braids back away from her face and secured them low on the back of her head with a thin slip of silver ribbon.

She stood up then, and Dulcie slipped a white samite gown trimmed with silver threads and pale gray miniver over her head. They both pulled out her hair so it hung long and straight and past the back of her knees.

There was a tap at the door and Dulcie opened it. Queen Eleanor came inside.

"Ah, I am just in time, I see." She held out

a lovely and intricately wrought silver-link belt with a pearl clasp. "This is a gift from Edward."

"It's lovely," Clio said in awe, for it was the most beautiful belt she had ever seen.

"And this is from me." Eleanor clipped a small silver dagger with a filigree sheath onto a link in the side of the belt. The jeweled dagger hung from the chain, looking a little brazen and suggestive.

Clio glanced up and caught the glimmer in her friend's eyes. "How delightfully wicked." And they laughed together.

On her head, her maid placed the circlet adorned with those tiny pearl drops, the ones that looked just like fairy tears. Long silver ribbons fell like Maypole streamers from the back of the circlet and twisted down and through her loose hair.

"You are so lovely, my lady."

"She is right, Clio." Eleanor smiled. "Every man there, wed or no, will wish he were Sir Merrick this day."

Clio was embarrassed by her praise and tried to jest. "Only this day? Will they not envy my lord any other day?"

"That is not what I meant, and you know that."

"Aye, I am jesting. For I feel no different. I am still me, Clio. Fine cloth and wicked jeweled daggers and huge pearl drops do not change who or what I am."

Eleanor nodded. "You are a bride. Today is special if for no other reason than that. 'Tis something a woman lives for, waits for, dreams of."

"Then should I not be more happy? Should I not want to shout from the tower that today is special?"

"I think perhaps you have more..."—the queen paused to search for a word—"more will than most women. The female masses would be pleased just to have the earl look at them, much less wed them."

Clio thought about how she would feel if Merrick were to wed someone else. Her fists formed strong knots and she frowned.

'Twas not something she had thought about, nor something she liked to think about. She had come to think of Merrick as hers alone.

"I thought that might make you appreciate him." Eleanor laughed. "You look like you have murder on your mind."

"Do I?"

"You know you do."

It felt good to laugh. It felt better to have this woman as a friend.

"Clio?"

"Aye?"

"You will be happy. I am certain."

Clio wasn't certain and wished she could feel as confident as Eleanor did.

" 'Tis only that you like to know that you can do as you please. I can imagine that the thought of binding yourself to a man like Merrick is difficult. He is a strong man used to having his way."

"Aye. He is. But I am used to having my own way, too."

"I did not say that." Eleanor grinned then,

giving away the notion that she was thinking it.

"That I am stubborn?"

"I did not say that either." She was still grinning.

"No, but Merrick did. And he was not pleased with me at the time."

"Come." The queen threaded her arm through Clio's and guided her toward the doors. "Trust me. He will be pleased with you now."

The king's heralds blew their trumpets. There was a sudden stillness, a silence that filled the warm air with anticipation.

Merrick stood tall and tense in front of the chapel doors. With sudden clarity he felt the raw spectacle of this ceremony, the ritual of the sacrament of marriage, the importance of it, and for the first time in his memory, he was uncomfortable being at the center of such pomp.

For the briefest of moments he had a new and different sense of respect and camaraderie for Edward, who had endured so well his coronation.

Merrick sought to relax, but he could not.

Not even after he had taken deep breaths of clean air through his nose instead of his mouth so no one would notice. He felt winded and sweat was dripping down the back of his neck and through his hair. His pride made him fight to look cool and calm.

'Twas a vulnerability that almost frightened him, his reaction to this day; his reaction to this one woman. Because he could not control this weak feeling. It frustrated him and made him feel as if he were going into battle without his armor.

He was a warrior, a knight, his king's man. He was an earl, for godsakes. He felt like a coward, one that wants to turn and run at the first sign of conflict.

He took another deep breath, yet all he wanted to do was throw back his head and give forth his loudest battle cry. Anything that would crack through the awkward quiet that seemed to him as if it went on and on forever.

But then, in less time than it took for his heart to beat, it came—the sound he had unknowingly been waiting for. The distant, clear song of silver bells.

A gasp went through the crowd and his breath stopped in his chest as if he had taken a blow.

She rode toward him on a snow white palfrey, a gift from the king and a symbol of her purity.

Yes, he thought, she was still a maiden...barely. He almost smiled to himself and felt a kind of peace when he stared at her. Suddenly he did not feel so very alone in this.

The palfrey's mane and tail were braided with silver ribbons and bells, and sheer silver fabric decorated a bridal saddle tanned and bleached until the leather was the same color of the clouds in the sky.

The crowd, the same one that had milled

around the courtyard only moments before, parted, forming a road in the middle of the inner bailey that led right to him, standing on the steps of the chapel with the huge arched doors just beyond.

Those silver bells rang and jingled and brought a sense of joy to the air, the way songbirds woke you on a clear summer day when the country was at peace and all was right with the world.

Around him the people began to sing:

Bring my love to me.
Lady-o, lady-o,
A bride she will be.

White horse, white horse,
My heart I give to thee
Lady-o, lady-o
For all eternity.

He listened to the song, a chant really. Its words and their meaning soaked into his head for the first time. He had been to other weddings, had chanted those same words himself since he was a mere youth.

But it had always been no different from the way he recited Hail Marys and Paternosters as penance. Just so many words he repeated again and again, so that after a while he only spoke by rote.

The words had never meant anything to him. Until today.

He stood there a little dumbfounded and confused, feeling emotions he did not want to feel. The horse brought her closer. The ringing of the bells grew louder and sweeter. He could see her face clearly now.

God, but she was beautiful.

And he thought with some humor and a little selfish relief that she looked more frightened than he was.

Her hair was smoothed back away from her face and she wore the jeweled circlet he had had made for her in Rome; the tiny pearl drops on the headpiece enhanced the green of her eyes. Those wide and smiling eyes that haunted his dreams and his days in the way no other woman ever had, or ever could have.

Her gown was white samite, the color of the clouds hovering on the high hills of Brecon, and threaded with pure silver threads that made it look as if she were wearing the streaks made by falling stars.

His mind flashed to that night long ago in the desert, when he and the other soldiers had witnessed all those stars shooting across the sky. A night, one hauntingly miraculous night, that had stayed in his memory for so long 'twas almost as if it were yesterday.

At that instant a low breeze caught her long silver hair and blew it forward so that curling strands of it covered her breasts and hung down past the white saddle. The thought that she was to be his wife, his alone, almost paralyzed him.

Then she was there, before him, looking down at him and waiting for their life together to begin.

He stepped forward and put his hands around her waist. Her look softened, and she did not look so frightened. He smiled then, for the notion that she felt safer with him made him proud.

As he lifted her off the horse, she placed her hands on his shoulders. For just a moment, their eyes met and all the emotion, this massive depth of something unnamed, passed between them with a sharp pang that was almost painful in its intensity. 'Twas so strong and real and seemed to pierce into some part of him that Merrick never knew existed.

Still reeling a little, he concentrated hard so that he could set her gently on the steps to the chapel. He waited, taking two deep breaths, then he looked down at her and held out his hand. Together they walked toward the chapel, where the archbishop waited to perform the sacraments of marriage.

Sunlight caught in a window and blinded him for a moment with its brightness, but it did not matter if he were blind, for all that was in his head was the image of his bride.

And years from now, when his sight was weak and his limbs not so strong, when his black hair was gray and his grandchildren were almost grown, Merrick would still remember this moment as clearly as if it were etched upon his mind by the very hand of God.

The look in her eyes, the smile on her lips, the secret bond that passed between them, for it was then, at this brief instant in his lifetime, that he understood God's gift to Adam, and the Lord's love of the man He created, for He gave him something more precious than gold or wealth or power, that most wonderful of all things.

He gave him a woman.

CHAPTER 32

Clio learned an important lesson that day about being a bride. She was kissed, fed, danced, pinched, or fondled by everyone. Everyone except her husband.

But she learned something else. For the two days prior to their wedding, her husband had ridden out, scouring the countryside for white flour.

There had been a special look in his eye when the servants rolled in a huge cake, a cake made with sweetened white flour and fresh wild strawberries. Atop the cake was a gilt bird cage with white doves, an exceptional symbol of romantic love.

Merrick had been watching her face when the cake came in, when the guests cheered and oohed and ahhed. She could see in his eyes, he had done this for her. It was the most romantic thing and it confused her, made her feel strange and uneasy, yet made her want to be closer to him, to thank him.

She knew it was a rare man who truly cared about his wife's pride. She thought she might do something foolish, like cry.

'Twas fortunate indeed that at just the right moment twelve acrobats formed a tower of balancing men shaped like a peacock's tail, and drew attention away from her.

She slipped out the side doors and walked swiftly down a narrow flagged courtway toward the castle kitchens. Just a few quick steps and she was outside the keep in the fresh air.

In the distance, the moon was the color of amber and looked so huge and close she wanted to reach out and touch it.

She could hear the revelry, the cheers and the music. She had enough of dancing and laughing and being thrown from man to man for a kiss, a pinch, or to stomp on her poor toes.

Though she knew he stood there and could feel him watching her, she chose to keep her eyes closed, even when she could feel the heat from his body as it moved closer.

Something soft touched her cheek. She caught the sweet scent of a rose. "Hmmmm. I adore the scent of roses, Merrick."

He said nothing, but she could almost see his smile when she said his name.

"You gave me a cake."

"Aye," he whispered. "You like it."

"Aye," she whispered back. "Thank you. 'Twas the kindest and most precious of wedding gifts."

He laughed softly. "You are the only woman I can think of who would consider a cake made of white flour the most precious of wedding gifts."

She just smiled, deciding not to tell him that it was his thoughtfulness and the gift to her pride that meant so much to her.

He slowly drew the rose over her lips, then down her jawline and across her eyelids.

Feather touches. A lover's stroke.

"Don't stop," she whispered.

He replaced the rosebud with his lips.

She loved his lips, his mouth, his taste. He kissed her as softly, the same way he had touched her with the rose. She could taste the sweet potent cider flavor on his lips.

The moment he had sat down at the high table, he had made it plain to all that he refused to have any strong drink. Wedding or no. She supposed it had something to do with the night he made such bawdy rhymes about her.

"At this moment, sweet wife of mine," he whispered in that low tone of his. "There cannot be another woman anywhere in the world as beautiful as you."

It was odd that this time his voice sounded hoarse with an emotion she had never heard from him before. A deep sense of awe mixed with earthy desire that sounded as if it were slowly killing him.

Still she did not open her eyes, but let his lips love her slowly and tenderly, like the touches of a butterfly.

She ached to touch him and to open her mouth, but she wanted to prolong this tenderness, cherish it as a sweet memory of the day they wed.

He moaned her name and pulled her away from the wall, and against him. His mouth closed hot and open over hers.

She slid her arms around his strong neck and just hung on, dragging her hands through his thick black hair, gripping him and making him kiss her even harder.

Her tongue flicked into his mouth and stroked his teeth, tongue, and lips the way he stroked hers. His hands slid to her bottom and he lifted her and pressed her hard against his groin.

His mouth moved to her ear, where his tongue dove inside, wetting her ear. Then he sucked in a cool breath that sent gooseflesh and chills down her arms, legs, and spine.

She moaned his name, thinking he should stop licking her ears, but secretly begging him not to.

He stepped back and she felt the hard stones of the wall press into her shoulders and hips. He pinned her there with his body, pressing and shifting and moving in low slow rhythmic circles that made her want to crawl inside of him.

His hands slid down her legs, jerked up her gown, and pulled her thighs around his hips so he could press that hard knot of him against her.

It felt so good that she rocked against it, wanting more and more.

He touched her everywhere. His thumbs circled and teased the tips of her breasts through the thin samite cloth, then moved down to stroke the backs of her bare thighs and buttocks.

He groaned her name over and over, then reached between them and drew his fingers across her nether lips, rubbing as she felt herself melting there, where her flesh was wet and raw with the need for his touch.

There where she felt as if she was about to shatter apart. Where she wanted his fingers, his mouth, and, oh, God, she wanted his tongue.

His hand left her feeling lost and empty. He jerked at the ties on his braies. Then he stopped suddenly, cursing under his breath. He took a deep breath and leaned his forehead on the wall next to hers, his breath harsh and panting.

"God's blood," he mumbled after a lifetime of breathing, "I cannot take you against the wall."

"I don't care," she whispered, the need in her so strong that she had no pride and could not wait any longer. "Just do it. Now, Merrick, take me now."

He moaned her name.

"Do it," she snapped.

"Clio..."

She gripped his hair in her hands and made him look at her. "Damn you. Take me now."

The next thing she knew he swung her up away from the wall. She almost shrieked aloud as he flung her over his broad, hard shoulder and strode across the bailey.

"Merrick," she said in a harsh whisper, "put me down." She bounced along, her only view was his lower spine and bottom.

"Hush."

"Merrick!"

He kicked the stable door closed and walked back to the rear of the stable. He climbed up a short ladder to the loft.

"What are you doing? Where are you taking me?"

He tossed her down into the soft fragrant hay and began to strip off his clothes as he stood over her. "I'm taking you in the hay."

She burst out laughing and pulled off her shoes, pretending to fling them at him.

He was bare now except for his braies and he turned and untied them, then pulled them off.

She did so love him in that loincloth.

She fumbled with the silver belt, but he bent down and had it off of her before she could blink. He pulled her gown over her head, then knelt back on his heels and looked at her for the longest time.

It made her hot and dewy when he looked at her like that, as if he ate every inch of her with his eyes. He grabbed the hem of her shift and ripped it in two so quickly she gasped and instinctively grabbed at it.

"No," he told her in the deep husky voice.

Then he leaned down over her and kissed her long and deeply. Her hands stroked down his back and pulled him on top of her. She tugged at the strings of his loincloth, then pulled one side free.

He laughed and twisted so he was bare and naked and ready for her. "Touch me," he breathed into her ear before he tongued inside of it again.

Her hand touched him then, feeling his

strange steely length, stroking the tip of him.

It's too big, she thought, not realizing she had spoken the words aloud until Merrick froze. Then he began to laugh. "Just the words a man wants to hear, woman."

"I don't think this is amusing." She shoved on his shoulders. "Let me see it."

"Let you see it?" He laughed even harder.

She raised her chin, not liking that he was laughing at her. " 'Tis my right. I am your wife."

He held up a hand while he appeared to be trying very hard to control his stupid male hoots of laughter. Then, biting his lips, he rolled off her and onto his back next to her, giving her a full frontal view of him.

She studied his privy member for the longest time. Finally she looked down between her legs and frowned. "I don't think so..."

And shaking her head, she began to scoot away.

CHAPTER 33

"No, you don't, woman." Merrick shot across the hay loft and grabbed her by the ankles.

"I've changed my mind." She gave him a serious and direct look.

Her absurd sense of dignity made him want to laugh. "You cannot change your mind."

"I shall take the veil," she said with more arrogance than sense.

"Clio," he said simply, trying not to laugh at her. "You are wed to me."

"We can have the marriage annulled."

His first instinct was to bellow that no one, not even the bloody pope, would dare annul his marriage. But he could see that she was truly frightened and not being just female and contrary. There was honest fear in her eyes.

It had been his experience that goading her a little, creating a challenge of some sort, would make her react, usually without thought to fear or sense. He let her stew, then asked her, "Is this the same person speaking who was begging me to take her against the wall of the keep less than half and hour ago?"

Her chin went up and she said, "I never beg."

"You begged."

"Never." She shook her head back and forth, her hair swinging with her. She kept denying it as if she were trying to convince herself of the lie.

And he knew then he must handle her easily and gently to gain her trust in this. He softened his tone. "I promise I will be gentle with you."

The look she gave him said she did not believe him.

"I give you my word."

She didn't believe him, but he could see that for just a moment, she wanted to.

"We will make a pact," he suggested.

"What kind of pact?"

"If I do anything that you do not like, you say stop and I will stop."

She chewed that one over for a moment. "You will?"

"Aye."

"You give me your word as a knight?"

"You have my solemn oath."

She studied him as if she were searching for the truth, ever the skeptic. Then, every so often, she would cast a tentative glance down at his nethers. If she had known what her eyes told him, she would have died of embarrassment. His proud and absurd wife.

"All you need to say is stop. That is all, and I will cease what I am doing." He leaned forward, still holding her ankles. "I swear to you."

She did not try to pull away as he moved closer, so he kissed her softly on the lips.

He applied no pressure and did not use his tongue. He just gave her the softest and sweetest kiss he could.

She blinked at him when he pulled back and studied her expression. She was still worried. He could see it plainly.

He brushed his mouth tenderly over her brow and her cheeks, then his mouth drifted to her ear. "I give you my word," he whispered.

"Oh, Merrick," she said on a deep and resigned sigh, "I want to believe you."

"I promise...I promise..." He flicked his tongue over her lips, wetting them, then pressing his mouth over hers and rubbing softly over her slick lips.

That seemed to do it.

She moaned and slid her hands up into his hair again, pulling his head closer to hers and kissing him as if she could not stop herself.

Their mouths ate at each other hungrily and fully and deeply. He slid his hand under her slight body and pressed her back down in the hay, supporting his full upper weight on his forearms.

Their passion came stronger and more furiously, as it had before. 'Twas a consuming kind of thing he had not experienced with any other female, and was curious and new and humbling all at the same time.

Soon they were rolling together, each fighting for control of the kisses, the embraces, the touches, and the passion.

She was atop him, her mouth and tongue moving with him. He grabbed her waist and pulled her up his body, then took a breast deep into his mouth and suckled her.

With a deep moan of pleasure she threw her head back. Her hair slid down on his arms and sides, brushing his ribs like ribbons of silk.

It drove him mad, that hair, and he played the other breast with his lips and tongue and heard her earthy groan of pleasure.

He flipped her onto her back and kissed his way down her belly, then back up to her breasts, and down again. He loved her like that for long moments when time seemed to stop, and there was nothing but skin and kisses and moans of sheer and absolute pleasure.

He dragged his open mouth over the bones at her hips, the plush white skin at her navel, and the tops of her soft, warm thighs. Then he lifted her to his mouth and loved the center of her, tasting all of her womanhood. Her flavor and scent drove him mad, made his tongue react in frantic licking and swirling motions.

She grabbed his hair in her knotted fists and cried out, "Don't stop."

He felt her legs stiffen and tasted the salty start of her release against his tongue, which was inside of her as deep as he could go, giving her the most intimate of all kisses.

She came, again and again, until with every panting breath that passed her lips she moaned his name.

When her passion had begun to pass, he lay his head on her belly and tried to control himself. He felt tears rise in eyes and could not believe it.

She was his wife, tender and untried, passionate and everything he could have ever wanted. He moved up her body and hid his face in her fragrant neck, ashamed of his tears and afraid to let her see them.

She stroked his neck and back. They lay there like that, the two of them, naked as the day they had come into the world, free to love each other without restraint.

And there passed between them a feeling, a tenderness, something that created a bond stronger than any mere bedding. Something more than mere love.

He shifted and kissed her with his eyes

closed, then moved his hips between her thighs. He arched up, then shifted so he touched her with only the hard quivering tip of him. "Look at me."

She opened her eyes.

He saw her surprise and a frown of confusion. He did not understand, until she whispered his name and reached up, one finger trailing a damp path that still streaked down his cheek.

He did not know the tears were still there and took a deep breath so he would not show her how unsure and shaken he was by her. "Shall I stop?"

She shook her head.

He pressed inside slowly, evenly, and halted when he felt her maidenhead and saw her eyes grow suddenly wide.

"This will hurt."

"So they tell me," she mumbled in a hoarse voice.

"You tell me when I can move. Or what you want. I will not do anything without your consent."

She seemed to think about her answer forever.

He thought he might die waiting. But God in heaven, what a sweet way to die.

She searched his face for the longest time, as if she were looking for answers. She lifted her hands and rubbed her thumbs in small gentle strokes under his eyes.

That damn wetness was still there, spilling over onto her thumbs.

She gave him the sweetest smile he had ever seen; it said without words, "I trust you."

She raised her mouth to his and touched his lips, then moved her hands down to cup and stroke his jaw. She rubbed the very tips of her soft fingers very gently along his tense neck, moved her palms over his bunched shoulders and down his back.

She combed her short nails through the fine hairs on his low back and buttocks. On her next deep breath, she closed her eyes and thrust her hips upward. His hard shaft went right through her virgin's wall.

He was the one who gasped in surprise.

She made no sound, but her breath came in short rasps.

He did not move, could not. She was so hot, so very soft and hot, it was all he could do not to spill his seed like some green lad inside his first woman.

At that moment, when she gave herself to him so fully and bravely, he knew that he was the luckiest man alive to have her. This was a woman whom he loved more than he had thought it possible to love anyone or anything. And Merrick knew he could never ask for more from life than this.

"I love you, my wife. I love you. I love this. I love the feel of you around me so warm and hot. God, but being inside you is more splendid than my dreams," he admitted quietly.

She smiled at him then, wistfully and with

a misty, faraway look in her deep green eyes, as if her dreams had been weaker than reality, too. She kissed him, as he had kissed her, with all the feeling one human being could put into a kiss.

After deep and wanton minutes, she pulled back, looking up at him with eyes that showed no pain. "You did not keep your promise."

"What?" He froze. God, how had he broken his word?

Finally her eyes began to sparkle with something he could only describe as wickedness. 'Twas then she wiggled her hips and gave him one of those challenging and impish smiles. "I never said stop."

CHAPTER 34

The next morning, just past Terce, Clio stood on the steps of the keep, her new husband standing a few paces away while he spoke quietly with Roger and the king, Edward, who was returning to London.

Every few minutes, she cast furtive glances at Merrick, because she just had to. 'Twas almost as if she expected to blink once and find out this all was a dream.

But this time Merrick caught her look, and the corner of his mouth curved up slightly into a private and crooked smile. Her stomach flipped, and she felt herself flush.

She ducked her head for a second, because ever since they had come back to the great hall the night before, they had been teased by all. Most of the comments had to do with the hay that was poking out of Merrick's surcoat and layered through her long hair.

Luckily at that very moment the doors to the hall opened and the queen came out, directing her maids and ladies. When she was through, she turned, then pulled Clio from her curtsy and smiled. Eleanor looked so very regal and lovely with her dark features against the rich red damask of her gown and her vair-lined cloak.

Her black Spanish eyes made a mock examination of Clio's head; then she leaned down and whispered, "I see all the hay is gone."

At that they both laughed. Clio found that she truly liked Eleanor, who was sincere and not the least bit haughty or cruel. Clio felt this foreign-born queen was the first female friend she had truly ever had.

And she realized something then, something very dear to her. She'd wedded a man she loved, a strong man, who also gave her riches that one could not place a value upon, riches like love and pleasure and companionship.

She was fortunate, most fortunate. In Eleanor, he had given her a woman friend, and a truly fine gift indeed.

"I shall miss you," Eleanor told her, her words echoing Clio's thoughts.

They embraced, then Eleanor pulled away,

still holding her hands. "Promise you will come to Canterbury. I want you to see Leeds, the place that is our true home. 'Tis not a huge and drafty place like the one in London, but glorious." She leaned closer and whispered, "Edward does not know it yet, but I have plans for a lovely Moorish garden like the ones in Castile."

"Nell?" Edward called out in his loud and booming voice. "I see you whispering to our new countess. What are you about?"

The queen looked at her husband, a vision of innocence. "Me? Why nothing."

'Twas obvious to all he did not believe her, so she smiled at him and added something low in Castilian.

The king burst out laughing. He walked over and looked down at Clio.

Merrick moved with him and now stood at her side. She felt his hand glide across her back, then stroke lower and lower until it rested low and possessively.

She was almost afraid to look into her husband's handsome face, never knowing exactly what emotion she would see there. But she could not stop herself and did chance a quick look at him.

His eyes said he wanted her.

She adored that look.

"Hear this, countess," the king was saying in a stern and regal tone. "If you do not take care of my best man, Lord Merrick, I shall have to send my mother here to instruct you in your proper wifely duty."

The other Eleanor. Saints above! 'Twas a horrid thought. Clio felt suddenly ill.

"Edward!" Eleanor scolded. "Look at her. Poor girl. At just the mention of your mother, the color has sapped away from her face."

"Aye," the king agreed. "Mother seems to have the effect on too many."

"The countess is a new bride and should have no worries. Stop your jesting."

"I will not sic my mother upon you. Do not fret." Edward slipped an arm around the queen's shoulders. "Instead I shall have mother visit us at Leeds."

Eleanor quietly cursed in Spanish, which made the king laugh loud and long. "Does no one want my dear mother?"

There was absolute silence, which said more strongly than any words, that indeed, no one wanted to tangle with Eleanor of Provence.

Just then Old Gladdys came out the doors of the keep. She stood there and looked down her long, hooked nose at all who were gathered together on the steps or mounted in the courtyard—king, queen, nobleman, and clergyman.

Now, there was someone who could handle Henry's Eleanor.

She stood there, her back and hands pressed against the doors in the come-hither stance of one of the amorous dairymaids; then her gaze lit on Roger. Her smile turned wicked, and she began to wink at him.

The king leaned over toward Merrick. "What is wrong with her eye?"

Merrick looked at Clio with a bit of amusement in his I gaze. "Nothing. Except she has turned it upon Roger."

The king turned to look at Roger FitzAlan, one of the most brave and strong of his knights.

But Roger was gone.

Merrick stood next to his wife and watched the royal procession riding over the distant hills, a colorful caravan of hungover wedding guests that formed a slow and plodding line behind the royal guard.

In the rear was the troop of traveling entertainers: the mummers and musicians, the tired bards and hoarse troubadours, the acrobats with their tall stilts and the wily fortune-tellers, their pockets filled from the antics of the night before. They were off to attend the huge Mayfair set to take place in a broad meadow in Yorkshire.

"Come," Merrick said, grabbing Clio by the shoulders and turning her back toward the keep. "We have much to do."

She looked stunned, then a little downhearted, as if the only joy between them was last night, and now duty was the only thing important in their lives.

"Do you meet with the master builder again?" Her voice was clipped and she walked toward the doors with stiff steps.

He almost laughed at her. But he wasn't daft. Instead, he closed the doors behind them and stood there for a long and drawn-out moment. Then he saw they were alone in the entrance to the hall.

He leaned down close to her ear and said, "God, but I thought they'd never leave."

She looked up at him so fast it almost made him lightheaded.

He grinned down at her and grabbed her hand, pulling her up the stairs.

She laughed joyously, running along to keep up with him. "That is no way to speak about your liege lord and the most powerful man in all of Britain."

"There are certain times for the company of friends and kings, and times to be alone." He was headed for their bedchamber. "This is not a time for guests."

"I adore the queen."

"She is a kind woman and Edward dotes on her," he said. "And I am glad they are gone."

They reached the top of the stairs and stopped suddenly.

The way was blocked by a maze of wedding gifts that had been stacked in the solar.

"Good God..." He took it all in. "Look at all this."

There were plates of gold and handwrought chalices. There were maser bowls and trunks of cloth, jewels, and furs. Tapestries and precious silks, eastern cottons and finely woven linen. It looked as though they had pillaged a palace.

"There is so much," Clio said, sounding as overwhelmed as he felt when he stared at all of it.

They were mostly gifts from the court and

the king, who had insisted that he dower Clio additionally with a huge amount of gold and silver.

Merrick had almost laughed aloud. Years ago he had been a man who had to fight tourneys to pay his men's wages. There had been times when he could not pay, but his men had stayed with him. Now he was one of the wealthiest men in all of the kingdom.

But the irony was, he no longer cared about riches and dower gifts. He did not need them to bribe him to wed his wife. Not even for Camrose, which had been the prize he had first coveted.

He knew with surety that he would have gladly fought every knight of the realm for the privilege of wedding her, even if she'd come to him in nothing but sackcloth and ashes.

A moment later, he scooped her up into his arms and turned toward the bedchamber, striding through the doors and kicking them closed behind him.

Clio's plump maid spun around and gasped when she saw them.

"Leave us!" He ordered, nodding at the doors. "Now!"

"Merrick!" Clio said, half scolding and half amused.

"Wait!" He looked down at his wife. "Did I mistake your desire, wife? Do you wish her to watch? Or perhaps join us?"

His words hung there.

In a flash the doors flew open and slammed shut.

He laughed loud and hard. "Your maid moves faster than Roger."

Clio slapped his shoulder. "You are terrible."

"Aye, but I wager she'll not bother us if she thinks I have the kind of appetite that desires a threesome."

"Three people?" She snorted. "Stop jesting."

He just smiled at the stubborn, yet innocent disbelief in her expression.

"Do you truly think me to be that gullible?"

"I suppose not," he said, trying to look serious and chagrined for her sake.

"It makes no sense. There is naught for the other person to do."

He dropped Clio on the mattress and pinned her there with his body, deciding to end the conversation, since it would not matter. She was all he could ever want.

He lowered his head and kissed her the way he had wanted to all morning, long and leisurely and with all of the feeling that was in his heart.

For the longest time he had thought a woman could never be important to him. His life was war and battle and pride.

There had been no softness in his life. No woman who was a part of it, not since he was a lad of six, when he was fostered away from his mother, the only woman he could say he was ever close to knowing

Though she had given birth to him, she was naught but a memory. A cipher in his past life with black hair and a soft voice, but nothing more.

Later, as he was loving his wife, sharing a miracle that humbled him it was so intense, he struggled to see how very deeply he could be inside of her. He sought to touch her soul with the essence of who and what he was, to bind them together forever, because he knew then he had not lived, not truly, until her.

The Tale
of the Alewife

My wife she was a brewer,
I brought her barley malt,
She turned it into magic ale,
Instead of what she ought.
But no one yet did realize,
The power of the brew,
For they gulped it down
Without a frown,
Or even one small clue.

—13th-Century Welsh
Folklore

CHAPTER 35

Time moved by swiftly. Soon the scarlet poppies that had bloomed in the stubble of early spring turned into summer nightshade, then into first glimpses of Michaelmas daisies with their bright yellow centers.

Only the day before Clio had noticed that the leaves on the cherrywood trees by the eastern road had begun to turn brown at the tips. On the last market day, the villagers had seen a flock of wild swans flying overhead. So once again, the season was beginning to change, much as life at Camrose had changed.

The wide moat and stone bridge were completed. There were two walls between the keep and the moat, each with two huge iron portcullis gates and plenty of missile holes. Merrick had been pleased.

All the old stone and wood walls had been reinforced, and the parapets were revamped to protect archers and the oilmen, as well as the guard lookouts.

Most of Merrick's major protective changes were done or close to being done. The masons and carpenters had started enlarging the keep, adding another wing off the eastern side, with drawings sketched for bedchambers with chimneys and other comfort rooms to house the family and provide quarters for the frequent visitors who came to Camrose.

The borders themselves had been quiet, but word came of trouble in the north, near Rhuddlan, and a few random incidences as far south as Radnor. Merrick changed the construction of garrison quarters to areas over both barbicans, then had to go to the coast to oversee the shipments of badly needed building supplies: mortar and stone, iron and oak timber, that came by ship from England and was unloaded at Cardiff.

Now, there were times when Clio walked through the castle and could not believe this was the same place she had come home to, the castle the Welsh had ransacked.

Once again, as in her youth and the heyday of Camrose, the whitewashed and freshly plastered walls were hung with rich imported tapestries, and every stone floor was warm with an exquisite Turkish or Moorish loomed rug.

Their wedding gifts had been dispersed to special places throughout the castle, a brass birdcage with turtledoves in a niche in the solar, an urn with a base of blown Venetian glass sat near a new window with precious diamond-shaped glass panes that when you gazed out of them, made the late August sky look wavy.

The old rough furniture, beds, tables, and benches, and old cooking pieces were given to the servants and villagers. Copper pots and huge kettles lined the kitchen boards, where new ovens crafted of cast iron lined the bakery walls, and seven open spits had mechanical wheels that were run by water weights and could each easily turn a side of beef.

Brother Dismas had returned from a pilgrimage to Rome; he was a whole new martyr, full of the latest in superstitions and papal pronouncements.

He refused to eat anything with walnuts, because of course everyone knew that witches and spirits gathered under the black walnut trees. Two weeks before, he had taken to wearing blue because witches didn't like blue, it being the color of heaven.

While the monk was gone, poor Sir Roger had become Old Gladdys's target for her trickery, and not a week passed that someone about the place didn't have a new tale or jest to tell about her hot pursuit and tormenting of Sir Roger FitzAlan.

He showed up at supper one eve just before he left with Merrick wearing a rich, new royal blue surcoat. A few moments later, Old Gladdys, with her winking eye and dandelion hair, walked into the great hall dressed in a robe of vivid sky blue. She sat down right next to Roger.

But this day, Clio awoke to the long rays of late sunshine slipping through the new west window that Merrick had ordered for their bedchamber. She sat up suddenly, flinging back her long hair and frowning.

What hour was it?

She glanced toward the mercury clock, a saint's day gift from Queen Eleanor, that sat across the chamber on a small burlwood table with an onyx top. She squinted at the hour, still seeing double from waking up to that amber sunlight.

'Twas late, well past Sext. She wiped her eyes with a hand. Over half the day was gone.

What is wrong with me?

For the last fortnight she kept sleeping later and later, no matter if she went to bed well before Compline.

She started to rise, but the room swam before her eyes. She sat back down quickly, shaking her head, then fell back on the bed until the light-headedness passed.

The chamber door opened, then clicked closed, but she didn't look up, just lay there instead with her arm slung over her eyes.

The steps that pattered across the room were light, not manly like Merrick's.

'Twas Dulcie, she thought, then heard the light sound of pouring water.

She lifted her arm and peered across the room.

It was her maid.

She took a deep breath and pushed herself up, her arms still propping her up.

Dulcie stared at her with a sharp and disapproving frown, as if sleeping so late were a cardinal sin.

Ignoring her, Clio arched her back and stretched her fists high in the air, yawning again.

After twisting this way, then that, she admitted, "I am so very tired."

"I do not know why when you slept for most of the night and day." Her maid sounded snippy. It seemed she truly missed that troubadour who had sung at the wedding.

"I know." Clio sighed wearily. "Perhaps it is because Merrick has been gone. I sleep better when he is here."

"You sleep less when he is here," Dulcie pointed out.

Her maid was right. They never slept for more than two hours between loving.

So she sat there, hopeful, but uncertain, afraid to get too excited. Perhaps her wish for a child could be coming true. In her heart, though, she did not want to be let down again. She was almost afraid to want it too much.

After a long stretch of silence, she asked, "Do you think I might be carrying a child. Finally?" She wanted so badly

to give Merrick a child. A babe that was part of both of them, a symbol of their love.

For the past six months, since the day they had wed, she'd hoped and prayed, only to have her hopes dashed when the new moon came and with it, her body's signs that she was not breeding.

"You cannot be with child. You just had your woman's flow."

"Aye." She did not know what was wrong with her then. This lazy, listless feeling. With another wistful sigh like so many over the last few months, she washed and dressed, deciding she needed to do something to take her mind off her woes.

By the time the sun was setting, Clio had
finished a fresh batch of ale. It had taken
longer this time, for it was only she and old
Gladdys working in the brewery. Ever since
that early spring, Thud and Thwack spent most
of their days training under the tutelage of the
squires and the other knights.

She still sought the secret Pict ale, but had
had little success. She thought she had hit upon
something special when everyone who drank
the brew began to sneeze.

Even Merrick. But then she found out one
of the cook's lads had spilt precious pepper
in the ale ewers and was afraid to tell anyone.

For this day's brew, Old Gladdys had arranged
the water pots in a ring, like the fairy rings and
sacred stones in the western hills. Then she had
staggered the latest herbs and other ingredients
according to their cures and whether they bloomed
with the sun or the moon.

The supper bells rang loudly, and Clio's head
popped up. She had dozed off again. Frowning,
she scanned the room.

Old Gladdys was sitting in a willow chair,
braiding marsh reeds into herb baskets.

"How long did I sleep?"

Gladdys shrugged. "As long as your body
needed."

'Twas the third time that day she'd dozed
off. "I wish I knew what was wrong with me."

"You don't know?" Old Gladdys threw

back her head and laughed. "Married to a bull like your dark lord and you cannot think of what is wrong?" She shook her fuzzy white head. "Foolish girl."

"I just had my woman's flow. I cannot be breeding."

"Some women have their flow every moon until the babe is born."

"They do?"

She nodded.

"Then how can I know if I am breeding?"

The old woman studied her for a long time. "Stand up."

Clio stood. Old Gladdys got up and walked around her three times, rubbing her chin and eyeing her belly.

She stuck out a bony finger and poked her in the tip of her breast.

"Ouch!" Clio grabbed herself "Why did you do that?"

"Your breast is tender?"

Clio nodded.

"And you sleep all the time?"

"Aye."

"Here, spit in my hand."

"Why?"

"Just do it."

Clio did.

The old woman rubbed her hands together then wiped them on a cloth she took from a leather pouch that hung from her robe. She walked over to the cooling ale pots and waved the cloth over the coals while she chanted some Welsh song.

The cloth caught fire and she swirled around and threw it across the room.

"Hurry!" She waved her hands at Clio. "Stomp out the fire with your left foot."

Clio ran over and stamped the fire out.

Gladdys hunkered down and stared at the ashes for the longest time, then she looked up at Clio. "Press on your other breast."

Clio did and flinched.

"Is it sore, too?"

"Aye."

Gladdys straightened. "You have a babe in your flat belly that should be born about the time of the Easter bonfires."

Clio prayed she was truly hearing those words and that she wasn't dreaming. "Truly?"

"Aye."

Clio stood there, afraid to believe it and afraid not to.

"What made you think you were not breeding?" Gladdys asked.

Clio search the old woman's crinkled face. "Perhaps the fact that I had not put out any fires with my left foot?"

The old woman cackled and cackled. "You are not so gullible as some of the others."

"Please tell me the truth. I have to know the truth."

Gladdys gave her a direct and honest look. "You are breeding."

"Dulcie said I could not be with child," Clio mumbled.

"Did she now? She should know, a maiden

who swears to all that your ears will fall off if you kiss under a full moon."

Even Clio had to laugh then. Dulcie had been spending too much time with Brother Dismas of late.

"I gave birth to seven sons and three daughters." Gladdys said with much pride. "Not once did my woman's flow stop."

"You have children?"

Old Gladdys just smiled wickedly and gave her a sly wink "Sir Roger does not know what he is missing." Then she laughed.

Merrick and his troops and wagons moved up the steep road that cut across the Taff Valley. "Twas late and there was no moon this night. He was tired and frustrated, and instead of riding through these dark hills, he wanted to be home in bed with his wife, whom he had not seen in too many days for his liking.

Roger came riding up from the rear.

"Is the wheel fixed?"

"Aye. Was only that the load shifted."

Merrick reined in and scowled. "Who was the bloody fool who oversaw the loading of that mortar? I'll have his neck for not paying attention to his work."

Roger gave him a long look. "The fool?"

"Aye," Merrick barked.

"I'm riding next to him."

"What are you blathering?"

"You supervised the loading. As I recall, your

exact words were, 'It will not be done properly unless I stand over the bloody fools.' "

Merrick did not say a word. He couldn't. He remembered the moment clearly. After a few brooding moments he said, "I'm tired."

"Tomorrow even you'll be home, and hopefully by the next day you will have stopped barking orders at one and all and biting off the heads of those who chance to ask you a question."

"I need to get back to Camrose."

"Believe me, Merrick, we *all* want to see you back at Camrose." Roger rode alongside of him for a few minutes more.

Neither spoke. There was nothing to say. They just needed to ride. Another day and they would be home.

From the rear came the sudden sound of a horse's hooves. Both Merrick and Roger reined and turned back.

Sir Isambard rode toward them hard and fast. His sword was drawn. He called out Merrick's name.

A second later an arrow flew through the air. It hit the old knight squarely in the neck. He grunted. His horse reared and he fell.

"Scatter!" Merrick shouted, and suddenly Welshmen swarmed out from the rocks.

It was a trap.

CHAPTER 36

The ale casks ran dry late the next afternoon. At Clio's order, the bottler brought the fresh ale up from storage in the buttery and served it with the evening meal. With Merrick and many of his men gone, the meals in the hall were much quieter than when the castle was full.

Because the men seemed intimidated by her presence, Clio ate her late meal in her chamber. She saw that they had a good meal, then left them to their man talk of battles and hunting and "the truly big one that got away," whether it be salmon, deer, or a ferocious enemy.

She was still tired and her appetite was waning. She got ill, light-headed and queasy, as soon as the sun set, so she went to bed and lay there, staring at her belly as if she expected it to swell with her child right before her very eyes.

She could hear Cyclops snoring and she leaned down and peered under the bed. "Cy?"

He opened one eye and stared at her. "Merrick is gone. 'Tis safe. Come up?" She thumped on the mattress and he moseyed out, leapt up onto the bed, and curled next to her shoulder. She settled back against those silken pillows.

As she stroked him, he purred in her ear. The

sound soothed her, drowned out the men's laughter from belowstairs.

She stared at her belly for the longest time. It was so hard to believe that inside her was a life. A living being. A child. A little person who was half Merrick and half of her.

Would it be a boy or girl? Would he or she have blue eyes or green? Fair hair or hair as sleek and black as midnight?

"What do you look like?" she asked her belly. "Halloo in there. This is your mother."

She began to rub her stomach, gently, the way she would someday rub this babe's back.

"I shall talk to you every night, my child. Let me tell you about your father. He is, oh, so very handsome, with black hair and blue eyes and the most wonderful mouth, at least when it isn't bellowing orders."

She smiled. "You will be very proud of him, for he is the bravest knight in all the land. The king made him an earl. The earl of Glamorgan. But he is better known as the Red Lion, and all fear him. But me, and perhaps Sir Roger and King Edward. You will like them and they will be your godfathers.

"But back to your father. I know him in the way you shall know him. He is a kind man and gentle, but firm, and he will not let you be anything except the best you can be. He will not be easy; however the truly wonderful thing is that he will love you with all that ferocity in his warrior's heart."

She began to cry a little, tears choked her throat and burned in her eyes. She placed her palm flat on her belly, hoping to feel something, anything, a flutter, a heartbeat, a kick, and she wished Merrick were here, so she could tell him what they had done and see his face.

She finally had a gift to give him. "Well, my child," she said. "Sleep well. Oh, I almost forgot. I give you my forgot. I give you my word that I will not sing you any lullabies. I realize that would be cruel for you because you would have to stay there and listen, a captive audience. You could not run away, now could you?

"I sing so poorly that I suspect you would think twice about whether or not you wanted to come into a world filled with such noise. Oh, dear Saint Swithun! I just had a horrible thought." She tapped a finger against her chin. "I hope you do not inherit my voice. Poor wee babe."

She sighed. "Good night, my child. Good night." She closed her eyes, then said, "Know that you are loved."

And before the men had even finished the first cask of ale, Clio was sound asleep.

Merrick knew something was afoot the moment he rode over the rise. He could see the silhouette of Camrose in the distance, but there was no light of any kind.

Surely even from this distance he should be able to see the torches for the watch guard. He rubbed his eyes. They burned from lack of sleep. He was weary and sore from the fight they'd had in the valley, a bloody battle. Besides Sir Isambard, he had other wounded in the wagons.

And like himself, he knew his men were tired and hungry and needing the succor of Camrose.

"What is it?" Roger moved to his side.

"Look there."

Roger followed his gaze. "Oh, God..."

A second later Merrick put his spurs to his tired mount and rode like hell toward the dark castle.

Merrick pounded on the gate, but the porter did not answer. He shouted up to the parapet but got no response.

"How the hell are we going to get inside?" Roger asked.

Merrick paced back and forth, thinking. What the hell was going on inside? He stopped and stared up at the barbican, rubbing his whiskered chin.

Then he walked over and kicked at the door as hard as he could. When there was still no response, he turned to his men. "Make as much noise as you can. Shout, yell, clash your swords." He turned to Roger. "Come, help me pound the bloody hell out of this door."

It did not take long for the peep to slide open, showing the glimmer from a weak candle and one black eye.

'Twas Old Gladdys.

"Unbolt the door, old woman. 'Tis I, Sir Merrick."

"I can see that," she said. "Do you think me blind as well as daft?"

"Hurry. I have wounded men."

"Is Sir Roger harmed?"

"No," Merrick said.

At Roger's quiet groan, Merrick reached out and grabbed him. "Move a pace," he gritted, "and I'll tie you up and hand you over to her. Now answer her."

" 'Tis I, Sir Roger FitzAlan."

A moment later the bolt slid and the chains were released. Then the door opened wide.

Merrick angrily strode through the doors. "What is going on? Where are the guards? The watchmen? Why are no torches lit?" He jerked a dead torch from its iron base, dipped it into a jug of oil kept beneath, and lit it.

"Roger. See to the gates and get those men inside. Take the wounded to the hall." He stood there for only a heartbeat, looking around him. 'Twas as if the place were abandoned.

"There's one of your guards." Old Gladdys pointed at a dark corner.

Merrick moved the light closer.

It was the porter. He sat on the ground a few paces away.

Searching for blood, Merrick moved closer, thinking the man dead. His back was propped against the stone wall as if he had been standing there and just slid down. His head was cocked to one side.

He was not dead. He was snoring.

Merrick shouted, "Wake up!"

'Twas as if he had not spoken, let alone bellowed, an order.

"Wake, you!" Merrick gave him a hard nudge with his foot. The man still slept.

Roger had opened the portcullis and his weary men were filing inside, the wagons lumbering behind with the five wounded men.

Merrick turned and ran through the next set of gates, pausing at each post, where every man, every guard, was sound sleep. He pushed open the doors of the great hall so hard they slammed into the walls and rattled on their hinges.

He lit the wall torches from the one he carried and light filled the keep.

At the tables, where some had been supping, his men and the guards and even the servants were all sound asleep. Some had their heads on their arms, while others were sprawled out on the benches.

'Twas as if they were all poisoned.

He ran up the stairs toward their bedchamber. He was almost afraid to open the bedchamber doors. Afraid he'd find her harmed or kidnapped by whoever had drugged his men.

But as he crossed the room to the bed, he could see her form. She was asleep, as the others had been. A sweet and peaceful look on her face. He touched her shoulder just to make certain she was alive and his eyes were not tricking him.

The Welsh could have attacked and taken all. His men, there to protect his wife, would have been sound asleep. Someone had done this. The Welsh could be mounting an attack now.

He ran down the stairs and out into the bailey, shouting orders to the tired men who rode inside. None of the guards would awaken, so he sent his exhausted men to take their posts, while he and Roger set about trying to find out how this happened.

CHAPTER 7

'Twas still dark when Clio sat up in bed, startled, beacuse she was awakened by a loud cough. She blinked, and her blurred vision sharpened.

She stared at her husband.

Beneath the weak light of a waning torch, he was slumped in a chair, directly across from the foot of the bed. His long legs were out in front of him, crossed at the ankles. His fingers were steepled and tapping against his thinned mouth, and his eyes were cold and clear and held no greeting, no softened look for her.

She had seen him like this only once before— in the clearing when the Welsh attacked her.

"Merrick?" She tossed the coverlet aside and slipped out of bed.

He did not speak. He did not move. He was filthy and scratched and looked as if he had fought his way across Wales.

"Are you hurt? What has happened?" She stood by the chair and looked down at him. He was still staring at the empty bed.

"The Welsh attacked us at Taff." He dropped his hands, then turned his head slowly. He looked at her. Just looked at her. Coldly.

She placed a hand on his forearm. "What is it?"

His silence and his tension became a live thing; it filled the room the way fear can, giving you that overwhelming feeling of futility and weakness. She hugged herself, because it was obvious that he would not.

"What was in the ale you made?" He did not move.

She frowned. "Just malted barley, water, yeast, and different herbs and flavorings. Nothing that could cause harm to anyone."

"No harm?" His laugh was hard and filled with acidlike cynicism. "Aye, my lady. No one was harmed." He pushed himself up and stood above her, making her feel small and insignificant. "Instead, every single guard, man, and servant, all slept so long and hard that I rode home to a dark and unguarded castle."

He looked as if he wanted to hit something. She stepped back. "You are angry with me."

"I am afraid to touch you, woman, for fear

348

I will shake you until your teeth are loose."
He pinned her with an angry look. "Do you
have any idea what could have happened? At
first I thought the Welsh had poisoned the whole
castle. Anyone could have scaled the walls and
taken over the place. They could have killed
every single person inside. Do you even understand this?"

"I am sorry." Even to her own ears the
words sounded flat and empty. She meant
them. They were spoken with true sincerity.
But the reality was, the words were nothing.
Just sounds spoken that could not change
what had happened.

She could hear shouts from the bailey below.
A burst of light came through the windows.
She spun around.

"I ordered them to burn down the brewery."

"You did what?"

"You will no longer brew ale."

"But, Merrick, please—"

He raised a hand. "Do not say anything
more. I cannot stay here." There was such a
hardness to his voice, as if he had nothing to
give her. "I have men who are wounded. Sir
Isambard is the worst. He lost so much blood
that he hovers on the brink of death."

Tears streamed down her cheeks. "Let me
help them," she cried. "Please, let me help you."
She reached out a hand.

He turned his back on her and walked to the
door. "I think you have done enough." Then
he left.

She stood there, unable to move, only able to cry. Her chest heaved and sobs came from deep in her belly.

Her breath caught and she looked down at her flat stomach. She placed her palm on it.

A moment later she was lying across the bed, her head buried in the pillows. She never had a chance to tell him about their babe.

Clio spent the next few days treating the wounded. She had not seen Merrick since he walked from her room.

Word had come that Welsh raiding parties had also attacked Ruthin, near Clwyd, and the earl of Chester was arming his men against rumors of aborted attacks in the north.

Merrick had taken a few hours to arm fresh troops and then split them into separate groups of patrols, some whose duty it was to guard and patrol the southern borders, while others sought to locate the Welsh camp.

Clio swiped a hank of damp hair from her face while she sat on the edge of a cot and changed the bandage on Sir Isambard's neck wound. He was weak and pale from blood loss, but the worst had passed the night before, and they knew now that he would not die.

Old Gladdys had helped her treat the wounded men with special herbs and medicinal teas that gave them strength and built up the blood. Some were already back at their duties. Sir Isambard was the only one too weak to move.

The old knight watched her motions from his sharp, but kind eyes. "You have gentle hands, my lady."

She gave him a wan smile, because that was all the smile she had left for anyone. "I never would hurt someone." She paused, thinking about the ale and how angry Merrick had been at her. "Not intentionally."

"He was angry about your ale."

She nodded.

"I have known my lord for years, since he was a young knight traveling from tourney to tourney in France. He has a sharp temper, but he is just. He does not long hold a grudge, especially I think with you, my lady. He was angry because he was worried about you. He drove all of us mad trying to get everything loaded in Cardiff so he could rush back here."

"How I wish that were true."

"It is true. Camrose was not the reason he wanted to return. Give him time. His anger will fade."

She thought about that, then asked, "But can I ever win his trust back?"

"I don't believe you have lost his trust."

She just shook her head. "I hope that's true. Now, here. Drink this." She lifted a cup filled with warm nasturtium leaf tea to his mouth.

He drank it with his old eyes squeezed tightly shut. Like a small boy rather than a knight who was the size of a Roman column. "Saint Peter's eyes! But that vile stuff tastes like dirt."

"Aye, but it has made you better and will continue to help you heal. Now get some rest." She stood, placing her hand low on her aching back. She felt so drained and weak.

She walked slowly across the hall and out of doors. The sun was high and the watch trumpet sounded. Her heart picked up a beat in the hopes that Merrick had returned.

She picked up her gown and moved across the inner bailey. The gate guard was raising the outer gate. She strained her head to see.

'Twas only hay wagons delivering feed for the castle livestock. She sighed with disappointment and wondered when Merrick would return.

Would it be days? Weeks? No one knew.

She turned and moved slowly across the bailey. There were some herbs still stored in the buttery, and she needed to make another poultice to apply with the changing of Sir Isambard's next bandage.

A shout sent her spinning around.

One of the hay wagons caught fire. A team of horses reared up. The bailey was chaos. Wagons overturned. Men shouted.

Fiery hay flew through the air. She grabbed a maid whose clothes had caught fire.

They rolled on the ground and into a corner near the stable.

Hay flew like rain from more of the wagons. Suddenly, the bailey was filled with

Welshmen, raiders, with their daggers drawn and longbows arched, shooting and stabbing at anything that moved. Others ran through the bailey with lit torches, setting things afire.

Smoke filled the air. She lay on the ground, her arms wrapped around the crying woman.

Rebel Welshmen were inside Camrose.

He hid in the brittle branches of the cherry-wood trees outside Camrose castle, staring at the flames and smoke that curled up into the sky. He was waiting for nightfall.

Just a few minutes before, Thud had been inside, hiding in the garderobe. When the raiders tore apart the castle, he had shimmied down the hole into the latrine pit and stayed there.

From there he had watched them drag a few of the squires and some of the other pages away. Thwack was among them, his feet and hands chained together so that when he walked, he stumbled and the Welshmen kicked him.

Thud had waited until they passed, waited until no

one was about, then he had shimmied up over the lower wall and jumped into the moat.

He had stayed there, at the edge of the waters until he could scurry through the grasses and into the trees.

When nightfall finally came, he slid down the tree trunk and ran toward the northeast.

CHAPTER 38

'Twas dark as pitch along the lower rim of the Black Mountains, where Merrick had set up camp. This all had been for naught. Other than a few wild-goose chases, they had found no sign of the rebels.

They had patrolled as far north as the Wye. Tomorrow they would move back south, toward Camrose.

Merrick checked the men on watch, then crossed over to his tent and went inside. Tobin was asleep on a cot, his hands holding Merrick's heavy mail over him like a blanket.

Merrick stood there, stripped off his jack and linen blouse, then sat on his own cot and pulled off his own boots. He leaned over and blew out the single candle and lay down, threading his hands behind his head and staring up at nothing.

When he closed his eyes, he saw his wife, crying and begging him.

I never beg.

He remembered those boastful and pride-filled words of hers. The way she threw up her chin as if to say she was not afraid of him.

He hated that she had begged him, that he had pushed her that far. While justified, he supposed he had been harsh with her over the ale.

He knew why. He had been so frantic to get

back to her, like some green lad in the throes of his first lust. He was angry with himself because of that, this need he had for her and the way it made him act. He'd found fault and blamed her, because *he* was so worried about her safety.

He was a fool sometimes. A fool who loved his wife.

Clio moved as furtively as she could. Crawling alongside the battlements on the eastern side of the castle wall, careful to keep quiet so she would not be caught.

All of Merrick's men, even the servants and mason workers. Every man, woman, and child at Camrose had been chained or tied together, then locked inside the chapel, even the wounded.

She had seen them moving Sir Isambard; it had taken all of her will not to call out, afraid that with the rough way they dragged him down the steps he would begin to bleed again.

Welshmen had swarmed like ants all over the castle, looking for her, ferreting out others, shouting and running in
a frantic search. They did not know she could understand their words.

The leader was David ap Gruffydd, a man who had made agreements with King Edward, then recently recanted his oath and gave his allegiance back to his brother, Llewelyn ap Gruffydd, the grandson of the Great Llewelyn.

The Welshry had plans to recapture the

strongholds at certain key positions in the borderlands. Ap Gruffydd told the men he wanted her alive. As Merrick's wife and countess, she would serve as a hostage and a means with which they would lay another trap for the Red Lion and his troops.

Like a bad omen, chills ran down her spine when she heard the Welsh leader claim, in the name of all of Wales, he would never relinquish this castle, even under siege.

Now, as she sat huddled against the stone parapets, she raised herself up and peered out into the distance. She could see the dark fields around Camrose and she prayed that Merrick would be safe. That she would be able to hide and stay free long enough to signal him or to somehow sneak past the guards and open a gate.

He was her world, her life, and she had to make him see that she loved him. She had to win back his trust. She would do whatever she had to do so that he and his men would not ride into another trap.

If she could just stay here, hidden until they returned, she might be able to signal them, then open the gates before the Welsh could catch her.

Camrose was truly as strong as Merrick had wanted. He would never get inside without help from within. He was a man who would fight to his death before he allowed the Welshman to defeat him.

So as the wind picked up and blew in some

clouds of rain, she hid as the drops began to fall, knowing she had no choice, for she was his only chance.

It rained all night and was still drizzling when Merrick's camp was getting ready to pack up and leave. The sun was just coming over the misty eastern hills when he heard the shout of a watch guard.

Merrick stepped out of his tent, his sword drawn. A horse loped into the camp, a small drenched lad hanging on to the horse's neck. Someone grabbed the loose reins and stopped the mount.

Merrick caught Thud just as he fell off, soaked, smelling like a swill pit.

The lad fought for breath and blinked, looking up at him as if he could not see him. "Sir Merrick?"

"Aye. 'Tis I, lad. What is wrong?"

"The Welsh have taken Camrose."

Merrick cursed. "Lady Clio? Is she safe?"

"I do not know. They have everyone, I think. I escaped, then stole a horse and rode here."

"Someone see to the lad. And pack up. We must leave!" Merrick looked off toward the southwest, the direction of Camrose. And Clio. He stood there, his head pounding and his fists shaking. He took a deep breath, then gave a loud cry, like an angry wolf caught in a trap.

With both his hands he jammed his sword into the muddy ground, then knelt there, his head bowed. He swore with his life he would save her.

Clio moved as quietly as she could. She was near the chapel and the spiral stairs that led from the lower parapet to the chaplain's room, where Brother Dismas had his quarters. It had been quiet here, and other than the guard that was watching over the chapel doors, she had seen no one.

She took it one step at a time, slowly, so no one would ear. She just made the middle turn when she heard the shout. Behind her.

"There she is!" She spun around. Three Welshmen came flying toward her. She turned and ran. She slipped and suddenly she was falling.

Her head smashed into the hard stone. Pain shot through her and she tumbled, down and down and down...

She heard a scream. So terrifying.

God in heaven, it sounded like her.

That was her last thought.

CHAPTER 39

For over a week they had tried to break into Camrose. They could not. No attack could breach the walls. Men were killed and they had no word from inside. Nothing.

David ap Gruffydd would not negotiate.

It only took two days for the other patrols to join Merrick's, and messengers had been sent to Edward and to the neighboring marcher lords for aid. It seemed that more than one castle was under siege.

Merrick had spent most of the last few hours going over strategies. Nothing looked promising. It was late, about an hour before Matins.

His squire brought him his meal, then left him alone as he'd asked. Merrick turned and looked at the platter. There was a pewter cup next to a trencher of stew. He ignored the food and picked up the cup.

A sense of dread came over him.

It was filled with ale.

Bile clogged his throat and he leaned over and spilled his stomach, heaving over and over and again.

He wiped his mouth, then straightened and stood frozen. His hands hung limply at his sides. What good were they? He could wield a sword and mace and an ax, but he could do nothing to get to his wife.

He felt as if the life were sucked from him.

The breath he tried to take hurt. The air began to quiver in his chest. He could feel his emotions rising inside of him so furiously and with such power that it was all he could do not to cry out.

Almost overcome by desperation, he walked outside his tent, needing the taste of air. He stood there and stared up at Camrose, the fortress he'd built to be strong and solid, impenetrable.

His king's pride.

His heart's destruction.

The irony of it hit him hard and sharp and like a sword through his heart. The awful truth was that he could not break inside Camrose to save his wife. The place he'd built to keep her safe, now kept him out and kept her away from him.

He caught sight of a flicker of light in the distant tower and was drawn toward it like a moth to flame. He walked across the field, past sleeping men, through the mud and over the shimmering red embers that were left from the campfires.

His hungry gaze never left the strange distant tower light that no matter how far he walked, did not seem any closer.

He thought he saw a shadow cross the window. A flicker of darkness against the golden light.

His imagination? He did not know.

He wished it were her, hoped it was her,

walking there, as he was walking, pacing in front of the window, waiting for him.

Just a sign, all he needed was a sign, so he would know if she was safe.

It twisted inside of him, this doubt and feeling of helplessness, this eerie sense of loss and the pain of not truly knowing.

The mind was a cruel thing; it played tricks on you. One moment you dreamed of holding your love. You could taste her, smell her, hear her voice, feel her touch. You awoke in a cold sweat because you wanted so badly for it not to be a dream, but to be real.

Then you saw the reality.

She was there, far away, yet so close. Helpless.

And you were here. Impotent.

He stood there for the longest time, remembering that his last words to her had been in anger.

Finally the distant light dimmed, then flickered out, making the tower look like a huge black shadow of something that wasn't really there.

He closed his eyes against the emotions that swelled in him again. He hung his head in defeat.

With nothing left to him, he fell to his knees in the mud and bowed his head over his tightly knotted hands, praying to God for another chance with her.

For Clio, his Clio. Praying for the woman who meant more to him than his very breath, more than even his salvation.

The next night they brought the monk to him. Brother Dismas was crying and wailing. He saw Merrick and stumbled across the ground, falling to his knees and sobbing.

He babbled that they had sent him to the Red Lion. He was supposed to give him a gift from David ap Gruffydd.

In his hands, he held a blood-soaked gown. Merrick stared at it.

He knew the gown. 'Twas that ugly yellow thing Clio had worn on that first day at the castle. He stared at it for the longest time, feeling as if he were in the throes of a nightmare, not wanting to see what he saw.

The blood. Red and soaked on his own wife's clothing. Part of him, the so hope-filled part of him that still believed life was not the hell it seemed, hoped that she had given the gown to her maid...to someone. Anyone.

"She is dead, my lord," Brother Dismas wailed. "She is dead."

"Who?"

"I saw her fall down the stairs. She tumbled and tumbled like a straw doll. But then it was so bad. She lay there in all this blood." He raised the gown before them and shook it. "She lost the babe. In all that blood, she lost a babe."

"A babe?" Merrick grabbed him by the cowl and dragged him up from the ground. "Who? Damn you man! Who is dead?" He

shook him so hard the man finally stopped
bawling.

Brother Dismas just stared at him as if he
didn't see him.

"Who?" Merrick repeated.

"I'm sorry, my lord, but your wife. I swear
on the holy Cross it was Lady Clio."

CHAPTER 40

Old Gladdys moved around the room where
Clio was kept prisoner.

She had lost the child. She did not remember
it, not exactly. She remembered screaming with
pain, as if she were in some torturous nightmare,
and she remembered Old Gladdys slapping her
and telling her to shut up while she had straddled
her and kneaded her belly again and again.

She had not been beating Clio, but had
been fighting to save her from bleeding to
death. 'Twas a battle the old woman won.

For Clio the days had passed too swiftly when
she slept them away, and too slowly when
she was awake. Once she had gotten out of bed
and climbed up on a bench so she could look
out through a high arrow loop.

She could see the campfires of Merrick's men
in the fields around Camrose. She could see
the shadow of a tent. She knew it was his.

He was out there. So close. Yet so far out of her reach. She garnered what little peace she could from the knowledge he was there, and lay in bed, doing as she was told.

She looked up at Old Gladdys. "I have failed him, haven't I?"

"Your husband?"

She nodded. "I could not help him. I failed in my plan to help, but more than that, I have failed him as a wife." She stared at her hand clasped over the belly where her babe had been. The child she'd promised she would never sing lullabies to. She felt the sting of tears again, then raised her head and said, "There is no longer a child."

"You have not failed him. It matters naught. Your lord does not love you for the babes you could give him."

Clio rose to her knees and leaned toward the old woman. "Gladdys. Tell me. Please. There will be other babes?" She began to cry. "Please? You must know. I beg of you. Tell me like you told Gerdie the goose girl. Please tell me I can give my lord another son or daughter."

" 'Twas a baby girl you lost," Gladdys said. Before she turned away, Clio saw the pity in her old eyes.

The look was almost more than Clio could take at that moment. "Oh, God in heaven, please tell me I will give him another daughter."

The silence and the meaning behind it hung there, a horrid thing, like a dead body that hangs from an executioner's noose.

The old Welshwoman gave her a direct and honest look. "I cannot. I wish I could, but I cannot tell you that." She turned and knocked on the locked door. The guard let her out.

A second later Clio heard the lock click and she was alone again.

Clio wrapped her arms around her small body and began to rock, rock back and forth, back and forth, the way she would have rocked her child to sleep.

A huge wailing cry threatened to explode from her chest. She gritted her back teeth together and her whole body shook. She continued to rock harder and faster and more frantically, as if she could rock away all of this horrible reality.

It went on for the longest time, the deep black anguish, grief so overpowering that thoughts of any kind ceased to exist. 'Twas the same way her mind ceased to exist when it was on a plane where there was nothing but this unbearable empty ache.

Finally her body, which was already weak and tired and sapped of everything, sagged back on the bed. She curled into a tight and pro- tective ball.

'Twas nothing but a motion of pure futility when she pressed her knees to her chest and held on, almost as if she could keep safe the babe she had already lost.

She buried her face in a pillow and cried and cried, until a blessed dose of sleep finally numbed her pain.

It was dawn when they found him asleep in the dirt.

"Merrick! Get up."

Merrick groaned and turned over, his arm flung over his eyes. He cursed viciously.

"Damn you!" Roger said. "Look at me!"

"Can you not leave me be, Roger?"

"To wallow in your self-pity? I think not. Get up. Your wife needs you."

"My wife is dead."

"Your wife is locked in the tower."

He raised his arm and squinted at Roger. "How do you know?"

"I know because that ugly old witch told me. She just escaped and came to us. She claims she has seen Clio, alive, and nursed her herself."

"She escaped and did not bring my wife?"

"She could not get her out alone, not without causing suspicion. They have guards around her."

Merrick rolled over and buried his head in his arms. He took deep shuddering breaths.

She's alive. Thank you, God. Thank you. She's alive.

"Merrick?"

He felt Roger touch his shoulder and turned his wet face toward his friend.

"Aye?" His voice was muffled and scratchy with emotion.

"Come, friend. All will be well. She is alive."

Merrick nodded, swallowing hard and trying to catch his quivering breath.

Roger sank down on one knee and placed his arm around Merrick's shoulder. He gave him a look of reassurance. "We have found a way inside."

Merrick moved through the tunnel slowly and quietly. His muscles were taut as bow strings. At certain moments he had to force himself to remember to breathe. He knew it would only take one wrong step, one small noise and they could give themselves away.

Mining underneath the castle was dangerous, especially now that the moat was so massive. Collapse was almost certain, even in this weak spot where the eastern wall had not been completely finished.

One small spot. A place that the old Druid had found and used to sneak out.

When he saw her and heard that Clio was alive, truly alive, he had wanted to kiss the hag.

Now, as he moved through the narrow maze of tunnels, some not reinforced with wood, he held the torch in front of him and hunkered down in the narrow sections that were barely wide enough to crawl through on hands and knees.

Overhead he could hear the shouts of the battle going on above him. They were the shouts of his men, mounting a false attack meant to throw the Welsh off so he and Roger could use the tunnel to get inside.

They did not speak, neither one of them wanting to make any noise that would give them away or perhaps even make the tunnel collapse. The timber they used to reinforce some sections was slim and old and not the best, but it was all they had to use with so little time left to them.

They needed to strike swiftly.

For years he and Roger had fought side by side and knew each others' motions and thoughts so well. That experience served them well this time. They did not need to speak, but followed their plan and moved to the end of the tunnel.

This was the moment with the most risk, when Merrick slowly used a small pick to cut away the last of the dirt. It was dry and dusty from the heat of the day and fell into his face and eyes in a fine dust.

The cloud choked him and made him want to cough, but he could not, for there were Welsh guards just a few strides away, talking quietly as they patrolled the inner yard.

He turned to Roger and raised a finger to his lips, pointed in the direction of the guards. He drew his dagger and put it in his teeth, then pushed himself up through the hole, scrambling over the edge and bellycrawling along the rim of the east wall and past the two guards.

When they were out of hearing distance, he turned to Roger. "Free the men in the chapel. I'll get Clio. I will signal you once she is safe. Then try to get the gates open from the inside."

Roger nodded and they separated.

He made his way up the side stairs, dodging guards and hiding in dark corners. He moved to the area of the new section of the keep, then to the small room meant for housing weaponry.

He got rid of the two guards swiftly, then used the keys to unlock the door.

When he opened it, he stood there, looking at his wife. She sat on the bed braiding her hair and looked up, her face as shocked and frozen as he was.

'Twould have been easier to cut off his sword arm than to pull his eyes away from her.

"Merrick!" Her voice was but a whisper and she struggled to get down from the small bed.

He did not know who ran first, but she was in his arms, finally in his arms. He spun with her and ran, his dagger ready, with her clinging to his neck as he moved down the stairs faster than he had ever run in his whole life.

They sped across the bailey and he pulled her with him to the tunnel. "Jump down," he whispered, then followed her inside.

He grabbed a torch that was farther inside the tunnel. Moved back and waved it to signal Roger and his men. Then he came back to Clio. "Can you run? Walk? What?"

She looked into his eyes and nodded. She was crying silent tears. Neither spoke of the child.

He grabbed her and they moved through the tunnel, crawling in some places. He dragged her with him in others.

She cried out once and the ceiling spilled

dirt and rocks. Water from the moat began to drip on them.

He pulled her tightly to him, still on his knees from crawling through a short space. " 'Tis not much farther."

He pushed her in front of him as they moved. He could see the other end. "Look. There." He pointed and she turned toward the end.

She looked back. "We made it!" Then her eyes flashed upward. She gasped.

He felt the dirt above him rumble.

The ceiling begin to fall.

"Run, Clio! Run!"

"Merrick!" she screamed.

He reached through the mud tumbling down on him. He could feel her body. She was turning toward him.

"No!" he shouted just before water and mud filled his mouth.

He shoved her as hard as he could toward the tunnel's end. Then a blast of moat water hit him so hard all he saw was blackness.

CHAPTER 41

Clio sat in a hard wooden chair at Merrick's bedside, her head resting in the crook of her arms and her hands still threaded together in prayer.

She did not know how much time had passed.

Hours? Days? She seemed to remember the sunlight of the day and the coolness of the night, but that was all.

She had just sat there, waiting and praying, as time lost any meaning for her.

But Merrick did not awaken. He lay there, not dead but not really alive. His face still bore the bruises of the tunnel collapse.

They claimed it had taken too long to dig him out. He should have been dead. She could remember someone saying he was as good as dead, for his mind was gone.

She refused to give up. And she threatened to claw the eyes out of anyone who said otherwise.

He had a cut on his jaw and dark bluish stains on his head, temple, jawline, and neck. His face was swollen. His lips were pale and chalky, almost as if they were frosted with ice. His hair was matted with dried blood and sweat.

But he had no fever. If he had, she would have at least felt that he was closer to this earth than to heaven.

She tore a piece of cloth from those stacked by the bed and dipped it into a small ewer of water on the bedside table. She wet his lips, then carefully wiped the blood and dirt from his face and neck, his body, his hands. Then his feet.

Her mind drifted back to that night when he had first slept with her, claiming he was her new keeper. She remembered comparing their toes.

She looked at them now. And her breath wouldn't come.

It took her long moments to control her shaking hands. Then she slowly dipped the cloth in the water and gently cleaned his face and his neck again.

She wrung out the cloth, then turned back; leaning down, she touched her lips to his. Lightly.

He was breathing. She could taste his breath. Merrick's breath. His chest rose and fell evenly, with breaths so shallow they were hardly there.

'Twas as if he were in so deep a sleep that he might never awaken. She sat there watching him breathe, almost afraid not to watch him. Because she was so terribly afraid that he would stop breathing if she dared to look away.

His life was slipping away. Slowly.

She reached out and took his hand in hers. She held it, stroked it, then threaded her fingers in between his. She clung to him that way for a long, long time, trying to keep him with her.

In her mind it made precious sense to her that as long as they were touching, as long as she held his hand, he was still with her, still alive.

"Merrick," she whispered, needing to say his name aloud "I love you. I love you. Don't leave me. Fight, my warrior. Please. Don't give up on the most important battle you've ever had. For me. For us. My Merrick, please fight."

She held his hand to her own heart, pressed his palm flat against her chest, hoping to give him strength. It was an idea born of desperation.

The longer she sat there the closer she came to believing what all the others had told her: she could not bring him back.

She squeezed his hand and watched his face, looking for a sign. No matter how hard she squeezed his hand. He did not move. No matter what she said to him. He did not respond.

She began to cry. Tears spilled onto her cheeks and made streaks; the sobs came from somewhere so deep inside of her.

These were the tears she couldn't find earlier. When he was trapped. When they all dug like madmen to find him, to pull him from the mud and water of the moat.

The tears that wouldn't come because she was so terribly scared for him that she didn't dare cry. Until now.

I hear you, my love. I hear you crying. You sound so far away—a maiden locked away in a tower by cruel fate and I cannot find any way to reach you. For some reason I cannot move.

A knight who cannot move. Why? I fight battles. But I cannot fight if I cannot move. My body will not answer my commands. I cannot feel it. I do not know where my legs are. I cannot speak. It is as if my head were not part of my body, as if my mind were all that is left of me.

But it is not. I am still here. My Clio. Do not cry. I am still here.

The servants talked about her as if she were the one who was mad. She didn't care; all this because she wanted to wash his hair. The blood and the dirt. It was still there. Reminders of what he had suffered.

She refused to leave him that way. She set a ewer of warm water on the table and bent down to pick up a cloth she had dropped.

There was tapping at the door.

"Come," she said, sitting back up and pushing her hair from her face.

Roger came inside.

"Is anything wrong?" she asked.

He gave her a smile, then moved to the bed. He stood looking at Merrick for a long time, his face not showing what he was thinking. "Someone said you wished to wash his hair." He did not laugh at her.

"Aye." She poured warm water into a wooden washbowl.

"I thought you could use some help."

She looked up at him. "Thank you. I can. Will you lift his shoulders for me. Here, like that."

While Roger held him, she poured water over his hair and rubbed it with soap until it shone as black as a raven's back. When she was finished, she set the bowl aside and turned back.

Roger was toweling his hair. He saw her look and flushed, as if he was embarrassed. He handed her the cloth. "Here. You should probably do this."

She smiled. "Thank you."

He shrugged, still staring at Merrick. " 'Twas naught." He turned to leave.

"Roger?"

He looked back.

"My words, my gratitude, 'tis not just because of this." She waved her hand over Merrick's damp head "Washing his hair. What I meant was to thank you for caring about him."

Roger nodded and left without a word.

She closed her eyes; tired from fighting this, she lay her head on the bed.

So she did not see his eyes open until she awoke.

CHAPTER 42

After that they brought in the London physicians. Merrick was awake. Or looked as if he were. Sometimes he would open eyes.

He could move if you got him up. He could swallow liquids like soup and water and wine. He could relieve himself and did so often.

But he did not speak. There was no life in his eyes.

Clio stood by the bed and stared at the physicians.

They wanted to trepan him.

Trepanning. They casually explained to her that it was boring holes in his head to relieve his brain.

She could not believe what she was hearing. "Are you mad?"

"You are a woman, my lady, and as such you cannot understand what we know to be true." The physician, sent by a well-meaning Edward, was a pompous idiot.

"And what is it that that I am incapable of understanding?"

The man laughed at her. "I would be wasting my words."

"Explain anyway. That was what the king wanted. Am I correct?"

He flushed, not liking being reminded of who had sent him. He gave a sigh and she wanted to trepan him.

"The earl has damaged his brain." One of the assistants, one of the five with him, held out a measuring stick and pointed to a mark on it.

"What is that?"

"I measured his hair, my lady."

"It is common knowledge that hair grows from the brain." One of them explained to her as if she herself had no brain.

The other one held up the stick, for her to see. "Look here, this is where I marked it and this is where it is now. You can see his hair barely grows. This is proof that his brain is harmed."

She crossed her arms over her chest. "I cut his hair. I found it easier to wash that way."

The men huddled together and were whispering.

"This is not necessary. Believe me when I tell you the earl's hair is growing just fine."

The looks the physician and his men exchanged were condescending, to say the least. They did not believe her and thought her a liar and incapable of thinking, much less of understanding their proof of Merrick's problems.

For just one insecure lapse of sense, she asked herself, what if they were right? God help her, what if these foolish men were right?

Then she looked long and hard at those men who were standing there and telling her that they wanted to bore holes in her husband's head.

No, her sense cried out to her. No.

She looked at them and pointed to the door. "Get out."

"But, my lady, the king himself sent us. He is Sir Merrick's liege and friend and wants him to have the best care."

"I do not think Edward wishes you to bore holes in his friend's head. Now, I said get out."

A week later another man came, another physician. He seemed to her to be understanding until the next morning, when she walked in and found Merrick covered in leeches.

Clio crossed the room like a raging bull and pulled the disgusting slugs from Merrick's arms. "I said you will not touch him!" She heaved the leeches at him one by one.

"You will not poke holes in his head or put vermin on his skin. You will not touch him.

377

Do you understand?" She grabbed at the man, but he was quick enough to duck.

She wrapped her arms around herself, and she screamed, "Get out! Get out now!"

Time took on a curious quality, as if winter had set in and frozen it in place. She did the daily things, the routine.

She bathed him every morning before she fed him and dressed him. She spent time with him and had Roger and Sir Isambard carry him into the sunlight when the days were warm enough.

At one point she even had them sit him on his warhorse. She would do anything she could to try to get him to come back to her. She felt so close. So very close.

When it became too much, she thought of everyday things: The tapestries that needed shaking. The hungry hounds that needed food. The soiled linen that should be washed.

The meat that had to be killed, dressed, and salted for winter. She concentrated on the mundane. Because if she didn't have to think, she wouldn't have to feel.

So she walked through the days like a cipher, mindlessly doing what had to be done, but beyond feeling, beyond pain, beyond anything, because the whole thing was just too horrendous for her to even acknowledge.

She had to fight this her own way. And she had to fight, daily, hourly, because if she gave up, she would just curl into a ball and let the enormousness of it all swallow her.

She took to sleeping with him at night. She wanted to be near him. So she lay her head against his chest because she had to hear his heartbeat. It gave her hope and something to cling to when it seemed as if her whole world was slipping away.

Sometimes she would remember back to that time when she didn't know Merrick, when he was only a knight who had forgotten her for all those years.

She was ashamed and humbled. All those worries she'd had about their life together. Never once had she thought about something like this happening.

For him to be here in body and breath, but not in his mind or spirit. She lay next to him one night and sighed his name as she did every night. "Your heartbeat is still here, my love. I know it. I can feel it."

She waited for the sound of his voice, as she always did, but heard nothing. She rested her head on his chest and murmured, "He is here. He is here. But Lord in heaven why, oh, why doesn't he know it?"

I hear you. I can hear you. One day I smelled the rose you rubbed along my lips and nose. And I remembered doing the same to you, the night of our wedding.

Sometimes I can feel your touch, like now,

379

when you rest your head on my chest. I can feel your tears. Always I can feel your pain. I carry you here, in my heart.

I do not want to leave you. I want to stay. I want to love you again. I do, but I cannot reach that place. I try, but it is so very far away from me.

Clio, please. Do not give up.

The first snow came, but no routines at the castle had changed. Camrose went on as it had before, because Merrick's men knew him well. They knew how he commanded them and without him there, they grew to command themselves the same way.

Even Tobin had grown. He treated Thud and Thwack with respect. He demanded that the other squires do the same. He taught the lads with patience, the way Merrick would have.

That fall, Tobin de Clare had grown, not just in height and breadth, but in spirit, in humanity. He had lost that adolescent arrogance and become a man.

The squire had spent time with Merrick, crying at first, then sitting and talking to him as Clio did. She grew to like de Clare and the others.

All of Merrick's men came to see him. They claimed they could do no less when his wife, one small woman, would not give in. What cowards would they be if they did not believe?

She grew to tolerate Brother Dismas and his cures and holy oils, his prayers and masses on Merrick's behalf.

She talked to Merrick every night, every day. She talked of her dreams or her childhood. She told him all the things she had done that drove her father to pray to save her soul.

She tried to remember her mother and tell him about that. She made up stories about what his childhood must have been like, from her view of course.

But nothing changed with Merrick. Each day passed until winter had come and gone and spring was there. Nothing changed in Clio's existence except the weather.

Then, it was a bright spring day, the sun was shining and the birds sat on the windowsills and sang. Cyclops was curled next to Merrick and the world outside looked lovely.

But ever since she had gotten up, she had been feeling as if something was wrong. There was this sharp pang inside of her and she had snapped at the servants and grumbled at anyone who would listen.

Late in the day she grew quiet and moody. She had no appetite. Finally she locked herself inside the room with no one but Merrick and herself She sat on the bed and combed the knots from her hair as if she were punishing herself.

The comb caught and she grew frustrated. She stood up and cursed, then flung the ivory comb across the room.

It cracked against the stone wall and broke in two.

She stood there, staring at it. Then she remembered how Merrick had combed her hair with it that night so long ago. She ran over and picked up the pieces of broken ivory, clutching them to her, and she began to cry. She sat there sobbing and rocking on the floor.

A light flashed in the distance, just after the sun had set. She stood and went to the window, pushed the glass panel open, and stared at the eastern hills.

There were bonfires. Great bonfires. It was Easter.

She closed her eyes. Easter.

Their babe was to have been born on Easter. The daughter she would never have.

She stared down at the broken comb.

It seemed to stand for everything in her life that had broken. Her parents, her babe, and her husband. Her life seemed to be breaking apart before her eyes.

She walked over to the bed. Merrick lay there, his eyes open, his look blank.

"Wake up!"

He did not move.

"Damn you, wake up!" She grabbed his shoulders and shook him, hard. "Wake up! I will not do this alone! Our babe! We lost our babe. You will not do this. You will not stay like this. I will not let you. Wake up. You are my husband. I want to have your children. You owe me a baby. You owe me one. One with black hair and blue eyes and a temper! Merrick! Stop this!"

She was sobbing for her baby, for her husband, for her mother and father and everyone she had lost.

She screamed until she was hoarse.

She threw things. She ripped the tapestries off the walls and broke anything she could get her hands on.

For long minutes she tore the room apart, breaking furniture and urns, and just killing things.

She stopped finally, stood in the center of the room, her chest heaving, her hands shaking, sobbing because she could not stop even should she try. She stared down at her empty hands and flung herself onto the bed, her arms around Merrick.

She huddled against him. "Merrick, my Merrick. Please...I need you."

Then she fell into a deep sleep.

"What is the damn cat doing on the bed?"

Clio lay there for a moment, her mind still half in sleep. She could feel the warmth of Merrick's chest, the way she always did. She sighed and moved her hand up to feel his heartbeat.

"Woman! Stop trying to distract me. I asked you a question."

My God, she was hearing things. The earl of Grumps.

There was a horrid cat shriek and a dull thud.

Clio whipped up. "Cyclops, what are you about?"

The cat was on the floor, his paws out and his tail up. He was hissing at something over her shoulder.

"I told you to keep him off *my* bed."

"Merrick?" She turned and stared at her husband. She frowned. "Merrick?" She moved close to his eyes. They were anything but blank.

"Aye?" His voice was disgruntled.

"You are angry."

He crossed his arms over his chest. "I told you to keep that cat off the bed. Damn thing bit me." He scowled down at his shoulder. Then he looked up. His scowling expression softened. He reached out a hand and touched her cheek with a fingertip. "You are crying."

She nodded, unable to speak.

"Come here." He held his arms open and she fell into them. "Stop crying." He patted her shoulder.

"You're back. Oh, God, you are back."

He tilted her head up and looked into her eyes. "I was never gone. I could not leave you, woman. You said it yourself. You need me." Then he kissed her.

I kiss her.
Her lips are open
And I am drunk
Without a beer.

—*Song of Harper*, ancient Egypt

EPILOGUE

'Twas over three years before the birth of their first child—three long years, considering Clio's impatient nature. But on a bright spring day when the scarlet poppies bloomed in the stubble of spring brush, Edward Arthur Julius de Beaucourt came into the world.

His mother insisted on examining his toes. Merrick had never heard of such a thing... looking at the babe's toes. She pronounced them perfect, just like his father, which only confused Merrick more, since Clio had never, to his knowledge, called him "perfect."

But he knew what they had was as close to a perfect love as heaven allowed.

Over the next ten years, five more sons were born, all with what their mother called "gate guard toes."

There was Roger John, a lad with black hair and green eyes, just like his oldest brother. Both were brawny boys, with quick minds and brave spirits. They would become two of the greatest knights in the history of England.

Next came William August and Gerald Phillip, both fair-haired with Merrick's blue eyes and their mother's glib tongue. They were the scholars, more into experiments and inventions than horses and the practice field.

The last of the sons were Thomas Mark

and Griffin David. Or as they were affectionately known at Camrose: Trouble and More Trouble.

They were as different as night from day, but their minds were filled with wonderfully similar ideas...mostly pranks.

Years later, when Merrick's sight was weak and his limbs not so strong, when his hair was gray—something he blamed on his two youngest sons—and when his grandchildren ran through the halls at Camrose, he still remembered that gift he had been given so long ago.

'Twas still fresh in his mind, as if it had been etched there by the very hand of God. He turned and looked at his wife and saw the look in her eyes, the smile on her lips, the secret bond that still passed between them, the way he could still kiss her and feel drunk without beer.

He was the most fortunate of men, for, just as before, he understood God's gift to him. God had given him something more precious than gold or wealth or power, that most wonderful of all things.

He had given him this woman.

Dear Reader,

One of the first questions people ask writers is "Where do you get your ideas?" The truth is that ideas come from the strangest places: lines of dialogue that just pop into your head when you're doing something mundane, like brushing your teeth; sights along a rural roadway; or, as in the case of this book, a beer commercial.

I want to acknowledge some special people whose contributions to *Wonderful* were invaluable. The great medical minds of the San Ramon Women's Medical Group and Eileen Dreyer, RN, author, and diva—who graciously and patiently shared their knowledge and did not hesitate when I said, "medieval coma."

A special thanks to my brother-in-law Gerry Stadler for having the foresight to take four years of Latin a long time ago. An enormous thanks to Beth Rowe for her conceptual input, to the Susans—Susan Wiggs and Susan Elizabeth Phillips—for their brainstorming. All helped trigger some truly magical ideas for me. There would be no book without them.

Thanks to my daughter, who gave me the best line in the book, the Pocket miracle team—Amy Pierpont, Kate Collins, and of course, my editor, Linda Marrow, whose patience, insight, and gift of creative license are so important to me.

Historical notes:

The powerful heather ale referred to in this book and its legend are true. As chronicled, "no beer throughout history has aroused so much speculation and curiosity as the lost Heather Ale of the Picts." The first ale brewed in the British Isles, Pict ale was famous for its hallucinogenic powers.

The secret recipe did die out sometime around the fourth century along with the Picts. However, as late as the nineteenth century, heather ale was rumored to have been brewed in some small isolated areas of Britain.

Interestingly, modern science has found a certain unusual type of red heather to have ingredients similar to LSD. This plant is believed to be the ale's "magical ingredient."

Our own thumbs-up sign comes straight from the practice of ale brewers who used this method to determine the readiness of their brew. Most medieval ale was brewed by women. This profession was one of the few ways a respectable woman could support herself and live a life of independence.

And finally, the superstitions mentioned in this book were those of the time, including all the references to hair color and the Church's philosophy on women. Amusing, isn't it, that blond jokes have been around as long as men have?

For those of you who hate to say good-bye to the characters in a book, you won't have to this time. Sometime in 1998, Pocket will publish *Wild*, a second medieval tale tied to *Wonderful*. Clio, Merrick, and some of the others will have cameo roles in Sir Roger FitzAlan's story, where we will all see if he ever finds that Arab horse again, and what happens when he finally meets the person who stole it.

So, until the next book, I wish you all the very best and hope your days are filled with laughter and love, and all those things that make our lives so very wonderful.

Sincerely,

P.O. Box 8166
Fremont, CA 94537